ELITE FORCES DIVISION
THE FIRST FACTOR

AN ILLUSTRATED NOVEL BY
EDWARD J. STINSON JR.

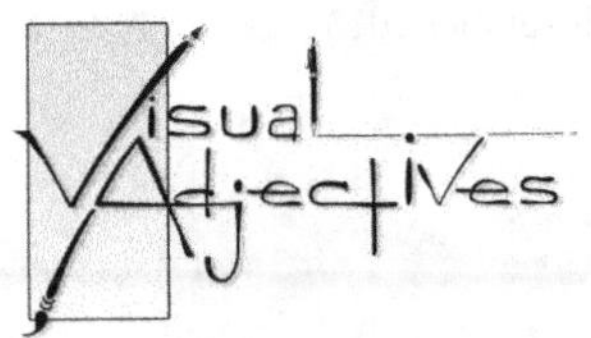

VISUAL ADJECTIVES
DELRAY BEACH, FLORIDA

ELITE FORCES DIVISION The First Factor
Book I
An illustrated novel

Pencil and ink by Edward J. Stinson Jr.
Layout and design by Michelle Lawrence
Cover color by John Mondelli

Published by Visual Adjectives, LLC, Delray Beach, Florida.

Visual Adjectives, LLC
14280 Military Trail, #7501

Delray Beach, FL 33482

Web: www.VisualAdjectives.com
E-mail: info@VisAdj.com

Library of Congress Control Number: 2013955424

ISBN-13: 978-0-9833329-1-6 (trade paperback)
ISBN-10: 0-9833329-1-6 (trade paperback)
ISBN-13: 978-0-9833329-0-9 (eBook)
ISBN-10: 0-9833329-0-8 (eBook)

First American Paperback Edition: November 2013

I do not strive to be the best writer or the most elaborate writer.
I strive to tell stories.
I strive to create a legacy that will outlive me
and give the future generations a story to tell.
Through that . . .
I know I will find my own form of immortality.

-Edward J. Stinson Jr.

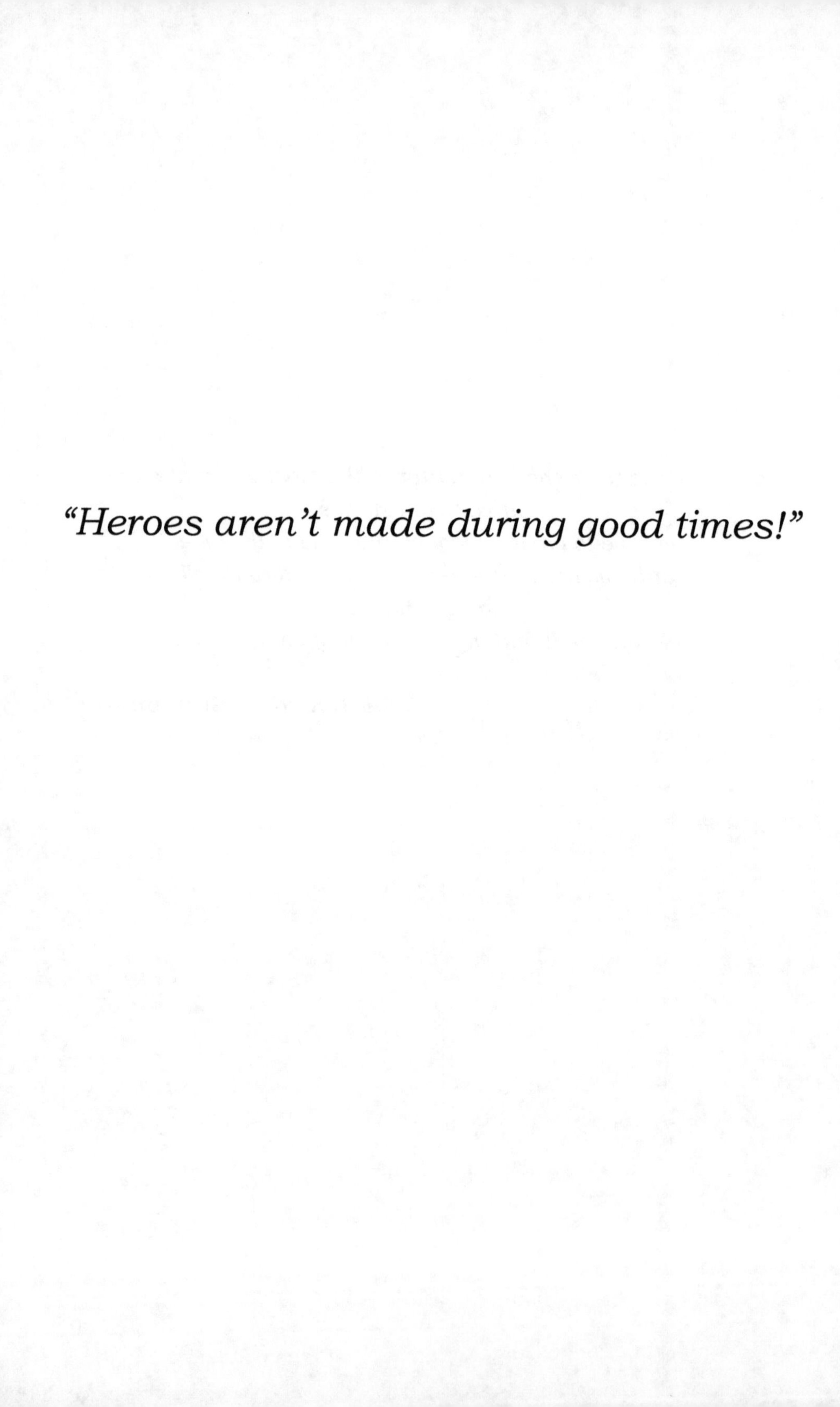

"Heroes aren't made during good times!"

ELITE FORCES DIVISION
The First Factor

AN ILLUSTRATED NOVEL BY
EDWARD J. STINSON JR.

GLOSSARY

EMD	Enemy of Mass Destruction
ETA	Estimated Time of Arrival
EXTRABILITY	Possession of abilities greater than that of the normal man.
Intel	Intelligence
Overwatch	One small unit or military vehicle supporting another unit, while they are executing fire and movement tactics.
PDA Unit	Personal Digital Assistant Unit
RA-Core	Retro N-ionic Amplification Core
SitRep	Situation Report
TOC	Tactical Operations Center
VidCom	Video Communication

PROLOGUE

Ring.
Ring.
Ring.

Beep.

"Hello?"
"We know about Nimlok."
"Who is this?"
"The public will know it exists."
"Who in the HELL do you think you are?"

Beep.

"Hello?"
"Hello..?"

"Damn."

LORD SYPHON

"I spit on you, Senator! I spit on your nation and I spit on your way of life! I do this as a gentleman offended by the etiquette of savages displayed at the same dinner table feasting on our like-food called liberty."

"W-What?!? Who are you?"

"Sovereignty is about freedom and choice!"

"Release me! How did you get in my home? Where's my family?"

"That was the purpose of your nation's birth. It aged into conflict because of her lies and secrets. America reached its rebellious adolescence as a bitch-in-heat released into a den of dogs!"

"W-Why are you doing this?"

"I have no pity for America's future, Senator. For - she is a whore."
WHACK!!

"AARRGH!! H-He broke my nose!! GODDAMMIT, your man broke my nose!!"

"America pushed this war unto us and we will not go into the darkness quietly. We will destroy the very roots of all that threatens us with no regard for sex, age, or mercy."

"Please, I-I'm bleeding. I need a doctor..."

"What your country has done to us will never be forgotten nor forgiven, Senator...and I expect the same, for what I am about to do to you."

"..."

"Bring his wife and daughter out."

"NO!! Please! T-Think about what you are doing!!! They have nothing to do with this."

"I will ask you this question one time, Senator. If you do not answer it, I will kill one of them and you will watch."

"PLEASE...God...Don't do this!"

"Where is the meteorite, Senator?"

"Oh, God...I-I don't know...Please, I d-don't know..."

"You disappoint me. The girl is chosen...remove the cover from her head."

"D-Daddy?!? DADDY!!! What's goi....yurck...gurgle...d-da-da...?"

"Her heart is slowing, Senator...for it is mine to control. The soft glow of light surrounding her is from my divinity as I welcome her into the clutches of darkness."

"JESUS...Stop it! STOP IT!! GOD, PLEASE...STOP!!!"

"He is not with you today, Senator. Watch how she shakes . . . struggling for one more breath. She doesn't want to die. Her eyes continue to fight for light as the inevitability of dusk befalls them. This is your fault, 'daddy'." The ghastly words are spoken near the feet of her rapidly cooling body.

"No...No...NO...NOOOO!!! WHY?!? Jesus, WHY?!? That was my daughter!! She was my daughter!!!!"

"I know. Now, where is the meteorite?"

"You bastard! You FU...."

"Bring his wife in."

"PLEASE, NO – NO –NO!!!! God forgive me!!! I'll talk!! I'll TALK, DAMMIT!!! Just d-don't kill my wife!!"

"Where is the meteorite, Senator?"

"U-Udosion Labs. The Goddamn rock is in New York at the Udosion Labs."

"Thank you, Senator."

"Please free my wife...please."

"You will both be freed."

"Free us now! Please, free us now."

"Shrine, bind them to the body of the girl and burn the place to the ground."

"Yes, Lord Syphon."

"Noooooooo!!!!"

CHAPTER 1

GENESIS

"So God created man in his own image,
in the image of God he created him;
male and female he created them…
What about the deranged and those born with physical defects?!?
Its man's responsibility to fix what God has forgotten,
evolution should always be ours to control;
especially at the right price!"

– Alexander Demonestri, CEO of Blankadyne, Inc.

0500 Eastern Standard Time

The Udosion Labs Complex gives the deceptive appearance of a small elementary school; it does not want to be noticed. It sits at the base of a small still-grassed hill in plain sight, secretly eager in purpose. It seeks to aid in man's evolution of man, but education of the youth is not its agenda. Within the small elementary school facade however, lays a vast technological hub hidden from the eyes of curious locals. Operations within its belly are tucked away as an undisclosed secret, more than ten miles away from the closest working class civilians. This is the strength that makes it so forgettable.

There is an illustrious indigo meteorite stone of more power than promise contained within which comprises the content of this location's deepest secret. It is a source with the potential to make men into gods and the few that know of this are endangered.

The woods have been cleared around the building for half a mile. This is to provide a buffer zone that discourages 'inquisitive' people from coming too close. The highway, which is a little over a mile away, has a single poorly marked exit sign, labeled 'Udosion Labs, Inc.' for just the lab. The scratched off blue lettering is just as uninviting as the rusted, bent post that stands as its weary support; barely erect but refusing to fall. The road leading to the lab is a narrow, winding split lane street with the fading traffic paint worn in the center and crumbling edges. The course of the cobbled path prevents any vehicle from being able to gather much speed on the approach to the security gate.

~~~

Today is Daniel Emma's 57th birthday and he has chosen to spend it at work. He maneuvers his 1972 Ford primer-painted pickup to smoothly leave the highway at the narrow exit. This has been his route five out of every seven mornings for the last 17 years. He goes through his common routine of dressing haphazardly while driving, slightly late for his mundane security post at the front gate. With a meager swerve on the road as he gives the last pull on his tie, he catches a glimpse of a steel-gray van parked on the side with a short slightly overweight man changing a tire. Daniel sways back to his lane on the road and reminds himself to tell the security guard he is relieving, to give the guy a hand when he gets off of duty.

Daniel parks his pickup, loyal with a constant sputter of an
~~~

over-extended lifetime of service, in the security personnel space. He scurries along to the front gate post to begin his shift for the day. In a routine semi-formal ceremony, he receives a pass down of the expected daily events and updates from the off-going guard. He gets a status report of the facility, reviews a list of expected visitors, maintenance personnel, and deliveries scheduled for the day. Foreboding lays heavy in the air this morning, but is largely ignored by the outgoing guard. Daniel shrugs away from the eerie feeling and displays a smile that says little more than 'today is not much different than yesterday.'

With the phrase, "I relieve you" and the corresponding "I stand relieved" Daniel assumes the duties of the guard. He tells his co-worker of the broken down van and asks that he provide help. As he surveys his post, he is greeted by a small birthday card signed the day before by the support staff and the fifteen scientists that work inside. It really brightens the early morning sunrise to see that so many people care; or so he would like to believe. Many of them are less than half his age. They often think too much of themselves to remember the guys, such as he, charged with a service that allows them to perform their self-indulgent duties. The card gives him just enough hope to feel that he is a more than just an early morning 'speed-bump' to a great parking space.

The final scientists herd in only minutes from 'late', crowd their vehicles back-to-back much like cattle. They occasionally 'moo' their distress with their horns, knowing each morning that it makes no difference to the one-at-a-time entrance gate that they must all pass through. Once beyond Daniel, there is usually a wave and a calming effect on each driver before they begin their day of researching rocks, minerals, meteorites, and rare metals. Daniel steals a moment from the attention given to the declining amount of vehicles entering his gate to wonder about the van that he saw earlier on the side of the road. A lull in security-gate duties offers a quick opportunity to call his co-worker. He feels the instinctive need to eliminate the uncertainty growing inside about the status of that broken-down vehicle.

The phone rings repeatedly as Daniel tweeds the base of the cord with his aged fingers before noticing a strong green light emanating downward from above his lone booth. The mysterious illumination is impressive enough to separate itself from the early morning sunshine. He circumspectly hangs up the phone slowly and straightens himself with intent to investigate the source of the strange, unexpected light glowing so intensely... glowing so determined.

The emerald brilliance expands in size, creeping in a nonlinear fashion, as though it is approaching closer. There is no one outside of the complex. It is as if the world had stopped; abandonment had become god. Realization is his only companion and it takes the time to remind him that he is completely alone.

Shaking slightly from apprehension, Daniel lowers his hand and unsnaps the retaining flap of his leather gun holster. He steps warily out of his gate post to investigate the source of the brilliance. Holding one hand above his brow, palm forward, he instantly experiences the sting of heat as his eyes squint against the intrusive brightness. Daniel, ignoring caution, struggles to focus on the light source only to have his attention diverted by the desperate screech of a vehicle engine approaching angrily.

Stealing a glance with poor perception, Daniel recognizes the blurry form of the steel colored van from earlier rushing towards him. Suddenly a surge of green plasma fire rips downward from the emerald light source hovering above the gate post creating a column of unadulterated molten energy. It is a living thing out of myth. The plasma blast engulfs Daniel Emma and the guard-post, swallowing them with arms of light and hellfire heat; the angry flames of green and orange, evil personified. The man and the structure simultaneously burst into flames and then explode. The faltered final breath of Daniel Emma is drowned out by this rage of perdition. Burning wood pieces and glass tinkle onto the surrounding concrete like rain making their own ambience. The acrid smell of burning flesh mixed with scorched wood wafts upward towards the source of the green light, which starts moving deliberately in the direction of the lab.

~~~

The stolen decoy van, carrying eight armed paramilitary soldiers, drives carelessly through the flaming debris and stops abruptly near the entrance of the lab building. Two of the soldiers anxiously exit the vehicle, which then retreats a hundred yards, providing a buffer of security. The two who had exited, move forward with haste and position themselves at either side of the security entrance doors. The mysterious soldiers are each dressed in khaki jumpsuits, identities hidden by the gas masks they wear. They gingerly but quickly unwrap and then place explosive charges along the outer edges of the doors, insert blasting caps into the explosives and attach radio-operated
~~~

triggers to the blasting caps.

The two move quickly and quietly away to safety, taking cover behind a nearby stone wall with the Udosion Labs' company sign embedded into it. The low click of a switch turning is immediately followed by the ripping noise of the entire entrance exploding, tossing the large steel security doors into the air as though they were mere confetti dancing in the wind. The compound shakes from the power of the blast. The van returns, reuniting the soldiers.

The smoke barely clears as the two, rejoined by their six compatriots enter the complex in a rapid and organized formation. They move with coordination and resolve, as though they were remotely controlled, leapfrogging each other to provide cover for the lead man. Lightly armored security personnel inside the building, reeling from the effects of the explosion and confusion are terminated with double shots from HK submachine guns. The group divides into two teams in the lobby area as the sprinkler systems engage. One team moves from room to room, gathering the scientists and killing their support staff. The soldiers' bodies move with unnatural ticks at the joints as though each motion is forced. None of them speak even as some of their victims beg while grabbing the legs of their executioners. The second team enters each vacated room after the scientists are moved out. They search for their prime target, a large chunk of metallic meteorite that pulses with a deep-arcane indigo energy when touched by anything organic.

CHAPTER 2

GREEN GRASS

"Battles will always be the children of war and Marines are their toys."
–Senior Drill Instructor Staff Sergeant Hines, USMC

0747 Eastern Standard Time

An unmarked black helicopter slices through the sky at top speed, flying a low approach towards the Udosion Labs complex location. Its cargo is the silent fist of the nation and the punch of its government, a tactical team of six black-clad United States Marines. The Marines are driven and intense with a look of grim determination, each one imprinted with the classic 'one-thousand yard stare' into nowhere. The heat of expectancy and adrenaline causes beads of sweat to run down each of their faces. Their contrasting leader stands near the helicopter doorway; he is spartan and aware staring through the open door, while rubbing a 'Y' shaped scar on his forehead, each time he briefly releases the ceiling grip. His other hand is poised by his side holding his index finger out while grasping a well-worn rubber gripped PDA unit... He is Captain Jonathan James Edwards.

Piercing the flickering dance between light and shadow caused by the helicopter's rapid approach, the Captain reviews the encrypted data on screen one last time before depressing the 'Delete' button as he has done so many missions before this one.

< **OPERATION: STONE MIST** >

Assigned Operators: United States Marine Corps, Force Recon Squad – Taskforce-7: The First Factor

Mission Parameters:

• (Primary Mission) Precious object retrieval – Indigo Stone (code named: 'Green Grass')

• (Secondary Mission) Hostage Rescue – Key laboratory scientists (code named: 'Sheep')

• (Optional Mission) Capture or elimination of enemy hostage takers (code named: 'Shepherds') / insurgents (code named: 'Wolves')

• (General Mission) Information Acquisition

< **PRESS DELETE EN ROUTE** >

The mahogany streaks from the Captain's camouflage paint blends with the deep complexion of his sweaty flesh pulled tight against a stern squared jaw anticipating the hell below.

"In all chaos, there is opportunity." He thinks to himself as he intently holds on to what makes his team the masters of chaos... CONTROL.

His eyes scan across his men, the savages of combat, as each one of them double-checks their equipment. His Sergeant, Mark Daldgerin, slaps the side of his M249 Squad Automatic Weapon. He balls his fist and tenses his arm with a motion of approval and motivation combined while returning his Captain's intense look for action. Sergeant Daldgerin is a short stocky man always seeking to be judged by his actions. The rest of the team nicknamed him 'Doll' because of his height and last name. Doll has always cherished being the heavy gunner in the group. The fury created by the ravenous chain of firepower created by his tool of war made him a 'toy' not to be ignored.

"Ready to get 'sum, sir!" He shouts, refusing to be drowned out by the helicopter's rumble.

Captain Edwards' attention drifts back to the open doorway to view the landscape outside. He's proud of his motivated savage. The whooping sound of the helicopter blades offer a repetitious song of intrusion to the beautiful scenery of the northern New York landscape passing beneath them. The open area and scattered woods join in deliverance of a sensation of peace that his gut will not allow him to enjoy.

The helicopter decreases speed as the pilot signals to the Captain by pointing forward to the police vehicles about a mile away setting up a roadblock on the exit off of the highway leading to the Udosion Labs complex.

"They'll keep the media away for a while, sir! Get your men ready!" Says the pilot as Captain Edwards shoves the PDA into one of his harness pouches.

He spits onto the floor next to the First Aid kit and lowers his hand extending his index finger. "It's time for us to go back into hell, Lieutenant! It's time for us to go home!" The Captain comments before removing his helicopter transceiver.

The pilot then redirects the helicopter to a wooded area about a mile from their goal. Flying over the treetops the pilot drops his speed once again as the small door light changes from a dim red to a piercing green. The leader spins his index finger a single time in a clockwise motion and each Marine locks and loads their weapons; each one customized based on their respective jobs within the team. They prepare to move, action is the only food capable of satiating their hunger. The five Marines and their leader, move to the open doorway as the helicopter comes to a final hover over the edge of the woods bordering the complex. Captain Edwards looks over his team of savages. They are his family. A final glimpse of his men stops with focus on the youngest Marine, Corporal Joseph Gonzalez, 'Gonzo', looking around at the others nervously before kissing the crucifix around his neck and shoving it down into his uniform. He didn't have 'the stare' which was ingrained into the others; he did not carry the same hunger that nourished their drive, but he had an attitude that was each of their equal. Edwards knows to watch the kid closely. Confident that things are under control, the Captain gives the 'GO' signal to his brothers-in-arms.

The Marines drop a rope from the open doorway and slide down one at a time. They are led down the rope by Corporal Andrew Young who is the second oldest in the group. They nicknamed him 'Young-Old Man' and respect him for being one of the fiercest fighters in the group, but that same reason is why he has been busted in rank and pay multiple times. The others joke with him calling him the 'Eternal Corporal'. Overall he was just a backwoods redneck.

Each member strikes the ground and takes up a defensive position, each facing in a different direction until the Marine behind them is on the ground. After the last man lands, the helicopter disconnects and drops the rope before whisking away as silently as it approached.

The Marines pause for a single minute focused on their task while melting into their surroundings. Captain Edwards holds his weapon towards the ground leaning his shoulder against a tree. The tallest Marine beside him, Gunnery Sergeant Leander Lewis, moves into the forward position, taking the role of point-man. It is this position that he favors, the one with the greatest danger. It is not that he believes that no other can do the job, it is simply because he believes that it is the ultimate test of faith. Gunnery Sergeant Lewis' father was an old-styled Southern Baptist preacher while he was a tool of war. Being a point-man allows his father's sermons to be spoken under his breath from the front of his patrol where no others can hear. The rest of the team simply sees him as their 'war-chaplain'.

Distant birds chirping through the forestry feed the perception of normality as the eastern sunrise slowly begins to swallow the lingering cold dark of night. Only then does the preacher's son feel confident to move forward. He searches forward by moving his head from left to right slowly then raises his right open hand sweeping it forward a single time directing the squad to move. His lips move softly against the morning air as his father's sermon comes to life.

The wooded area has a deadly silence and an inscrutable elegance that challenges the hushed movements of the Marines traveling through it. Leaves and branches, moist from the early morning dew, yield instead of snap to each fast paced step from these warriors passing over them. The mile to the complex is covered in minimal time.

Each Marine directs and responds to his companions as though they can read each other's mind. Doll, the stocky machine-gunner, brings up the rear while keeping an extra watchful eye on the kid, Gonzo. He does it because he knows that his Captain wants him to without ordering him to. Edwards knows that this is the level of control that makes his Marine Recon Squad the best. Lessons learned from their missions in Afghanistan and Alaska has made his team fiercely independent from base command and blood brothers to each other in the field. This simple knowledge of squad loyalty is what assures the Captain that there is no task that they cannot complete.

The recon squad approaches a small cliff jutting out above the eastern side of the complex about 50 yards below. The squad members kneel when signaled by the point-man, with each of their weapons pointed towards the rear of their position, each covering a different fire zone. The sermon of the point-man ceases as the Captain and another member of the squad, Staff Sergeant Shawn Livingston, low crawl to the edge of the hill cliff. There is not much that any of the team members can say about the grim chill that comes from the personality of this Staff Sergeant. He is alone in so many ways and yet a brother to this team. Of all the members of this covert family, he is their truest form of decisiveness. None present want to have his observation and attention focused on them.

Captain Edwards studies the complex, briefly looking for any obvious combatants before using his binoculars; once again the sunrise works his advantage as it lies behind his back. In the distance a stream of smoke dragging through the early morning air rises from the area near what should have been the front security post. The glare from binocular lenses can be detected almost a mile away and he knows this. He surveys with his naked eye first then slowly raises his binoculars to validate his observations. The Udosion Labs complex is exactly the same as the satellite photos that he was given during the briefing. The only immediate difference was the missing security post replaced by a pile of debris and what appears to be a twisted corpse smoldering along the entrance to the parking area. This was expected based on the briefing that the Captain received on his way over.

The building is smaller than normal labs of its caliber and shaped like a large 'L' with the longer section pointed towards the west. This was the area holding their primary objective, a mysterious indigo stone the size of a concrete block – code named: "Green Grass". The shorter end leads to a large cafeteria/auditorium used for announcements and meals. Behind the loading area on that side, an unoccupied steel gray van sits. Security cameras litter every angle of the entire building except for the front where they were all destroyed from the earlier blast. The government had been secretly funding the lab ever since its construction and designed it to appear simple. According to the briefing, all of the walls are reinforced with steel and silo-grade concrete. Captain Edwards knows that the only viable entrance will also be the most dangerous... past the charred remains of the security post and through the front doors.

"There's an empty steel gray van in back near the pasture where sheep should be, take note. Got a single body, south-by-southwest, 10 paces from the security gate; no sheep visible – no shepherds, no wolves. Zero visual activity. Too many cameras in back, we have to go through the front." He whispers softly as his message is relayed to his team through their communication earpieces.

The accompanying Marine Sniper, Livingston, waits until the light tap on his right shoulder by his Captain before directing his .300 Winchester Magnum sniper rifle on to the cliff and opening his scope protectors.

Covering his transmitter, Captain Edwards whispers to the sniper, "I don't want that van to move, Liv."

It is said that all forms of the being called Death must carry their tools, for this Recon Marine his .300 Winchester Magnum is his scythe. "I got it, Captain," responds this islander, separated and alone from his other warriors.

Once the sniper takes up his position overseeing the complex, he lightly taps the left shoulder of his Captain who then low crawls backwards towards the others while repacking his binoculars. He looks into each of their faces.

With hand signals Captain Edwards informs the team that the

major threat zone is the front of the building and that they would approach from here. The point-man would lead off first with his tactical cover being provided by Young-Old Man. Gonzo would go next with Captain Edwards covering him. Doll would be the tail of the formation by running as the rear.

"Radio when a visual on the Green Grass has been confirmed," the captain commands with a whisper.

Like a well-choreographed group of dancers, the squad descends the hill under the watchful eye of the sniper above. They advance towards the side of the secured complex heading towards the smoldering front entrance which is the only unsecured entry point. The point-man pauses near the entrance and raises his fist, directing the team to halt behind him. The point-man begins his sermon once more.

The sniper presses the button on his scope three different times changing the view types. Livingston studies the area intently then whispers a single word into his transceiver. "Clear." His voice is ghostly.

The team enters the complex taking up defensive positions in the lobby area at the fork of the northern and western corridor.

Young-Old Man sniffs hard and turns to the Captain, "Sumptin' ain't right, sir. No wolves to greet us."

The hallway delivers a feeling that is more similar to a school than a research center. Young-Old Man notices the dead before anything else. He keeps his voice low and rubs the bottom of his chin with a stiffed-fingered open hand.

"Wet gun powder, Captain. Not a gunfight, more like a slaughter. Security didn't have a chance to respond, their barrels are still oiled on the ends, and I bet their magazines are still fully loaded." He then looks over the corpses of scientists strewn out across each other as though they were caught in escape.

"These sheep were killed by controlled bursts of gunfire into their chests and heads," states the point-man before moving towards a body. He releases one hand from his weapon to exam the wounds. "Tight shot groups, these wolves are well trained." He realizes.

The Captain is not surprised. His team has fought enemies ranging from religious zealots to Russian Spetsnaz in the past. This type of professional killing is expected, especially when his team is activated.

He watches his point-man closely who peers across the room while holding in his battle ready position. He looks back towards the Captain and points his two fingers towards his eyes then down to bloody footprints on the white tiled floor. He then holds up four fingers, balls his fist, then holds up five, this informs the Captain that four to five men went this direction. He follows the same procedure for the other side of the hallway and informs the Captain that two men went down the western corridor.

Captain Edwards presses his earpiece signaling the sniper, "Six, I need validation… wolves, shepherds, and sheep."

Staff Sergeant Livingston once again goes to work surveying through concrete and steel. After a few seconds he speaks in a low clear tone with a Southern accent, "Five shepherds north guarding sheep and two wolves confirmed west with a possible third but the scanners show his image as unclear. Leader, they're near the Green Grass."

"Understood." Replies the Captain.

The leader points at two of his Marines, Young-Old Man and Doll, the stocky machine-gunner, and then points towards the western corridor. The appointed men move down the hallway while hugging the walls. The leader moves with the other two Marines, Point-Man and the youngest Marine, Gonzo down the northern hall towards a large break room. His team of five savages is split into two teams, with the two most experienced trusted to work on their own to recover their primary objective. He and one of his best friends, the point-man, would watch over their newest member. This decision was not made lightly; the preacher's son and the Captain both have younger brothers.

The point-man feeds a fiber-optic cable containing a camera under the doorway. "Sheep and five shepherds confirmed, Leader," he says softly, "They're in a scattered star formation six to eight feet apart in overwatch. Sheep are scared and exhausted, but alive."

Captain Edwards turns away to request a status check from his other two Marines, but is interrupted by the point-man.

"Wait up, sir, something's going on"

Suddenly the sniper comes in over the radio, "Hold on, Leader."

Two of the enemy soldiers stand beside the doorway at the opposite end of the room as another one goes outside to move the jeep to the exit doors.

"It appears that tha shepherds want ta move the flock, Leader. He's pulling tha van up for pickup. Keep time," commands Livingston.

Captain Edwards acknowledges, "Time kept, Six."

He signals his team and opens his hand wide covering his face. He then positions himself in the center and points to the kid, Gonzo, on the left clenching his fist twice vertically. He points to Point-Man and turns his fist sideways pressing it against his chest twice. He then raises his M4 assault rifle towards the doorway, kneeling as Corporal Gonzalez prepares a cylindrical grenade and Gunnery Sergeant Lewis prepares a similar flash grenade. Each Marine then pulls out a gas mask and positions it on their face while awaiting the snipers signal.

The enemy soldiers gather the scientists at the doorway as the van pulls up to the exit doors. The driver signals the others with a single beep of his horn. The sniper calmly places the crosshairs of his scope on the chest of the driver. He inhales, then exhales partway and holds his breath. A decisive end beckons. He caresses his trigger and feels the familiar buck of the finely tuned rifle sending a round down the barrel and then towards its target. The doors open while the single well placed shot from the sniper's bolt action .300 Winchester Magnum interjects itself into the plans of the enemy as a sudden reminder of the brief whisper of death. His scythe has swung. The driver jerks backwards then slumps forward over the steering wheel, leaving the other enemy soldiers in the doorway momentarily stunned by the grim and unexpected end-breath of their comrade.

Captain Edwards and his team hear the shot and spring into action. He uses the barrel of his gun to push the break room door open slightly as his teammates toss in the two grenades. For each of the grenades, the spoons pop off and release the spring-loaded triggers igniting the timers. The enemy soldiers close the exit doors leading to the van outside with their dead team member in it while speaking in a coarse robotic tone, "Sniper." They try to force the screaming scientists back into the room. The timers burn down for a timed three seconds and ignite the grenades' loads. The flash grenade explodes first, blinding and disorienting everyone in the room, the next grenade fills the room with a thick fog of tear gas causing everyone to cough and vomit. Kicking the doors open, the tactical team fires in short bursts at the enemy soldiers dropping them in their tracks. Skull fragments find their way through each of the gas-masked opponents onto the walls behind them. The kills are precise, instant, and professional. Eight seconds of intensity from the first shot provides memories of a lifetime to the fear-filled scientists witnessing the actions. Confident and something a little less-than godlike, the leader stands guard as his teammate opens the exit doors again allowing the tear gas to filter out with the scientists.

He then contacts Livingston for an update on the others, "Six, what's the status of Four and Five? Have they acquired the Green Grass?"

The sniper returns, "No radio contact, Leader. I can't find their biosignals. You're going ta have ta do a visual confirmation."

"Acknowledged." Edwards orders Gonzo to stay with the rescued scientists while taking the point-man with him. With a total of five Marines on the ground and two missing, he knows that speculation can quickly lead to chaos which is the enemy of control. The sniper is the sixth savage, acting as their angel in overwatch; uncertainty is a bad breath whenever he is blind.

The choice of whom to search for the others with was instinctive for the Captain, knowing that this was Corporal Gonzalez's first operation with this squad. He chooses his point-man, the preacher's son.

"Two, you're with me. Three, watch over the sheep and hold security," he commands.

Point-Man, looks into his Captain's eyes with agreement and moves out, headed briskly down the hallway. The two Marines glide through the halls at top speed retracing their steps to the main lobby area and towards their target, the indigo stone.

Moving with utmost caution the two Recon Marines enter the longer of the two corridors, the western hallway. The hallway is filled with greenish-gray smoke and debris. The sprinkler systems had been activated and the water flow is almost depleted. Carbon rubber on the outer soles of their combat boots slides marginally with each step as the soil between their tracks mixes with the water creating mud. Edwards and his point-man slow their progress making sure to step with a flat foot until the mud is removed.

The end of the corridor leads to a double-door laboratory entrance in which the doors are burned off, laying on the ground smoldering. The Captain recognizes the familiar atmosphere of battle by the bullet holes on the walls and the stifled stench of gunpowder and death.

"Six, I got a firefight here with 5.56 caliber rounds in the walls." Reports the Captain before locating two dead enemy combatants in the center of the room.

Another body is found beneath one of the doors to the room. It is the body of one of their missing team members, Sergeant Mark Daldgerin, 'Doll'. His assault weapon was not taken and is still smoldering from heavy usage. His skin is charred in multiple locations making his face all but a mess other than the distinct features of his dimples, hairline, and spaced teeth to identify him as their teammate. The stocky machine gunner was known for his fearlessness and yet in death his body is contorted in a sense that conveys terror.

It strikes into the heart of the preacher's son causing him to linger for a brief second. A thousand thoughts and memories ask to become active before refocusing on the mission; he does not allow them presence. Only the hurt makes it through.

"Doll... Daldgerin... damn..."

He then angles his head downward and looks to his Captain who responds with a single nod, pointing toward the doorway leading to the back.

"Let's go." He says, in an attempt for strength to keep his man moving.

Edwards endeavors to maintain control.

Point-Man carefully enters the far side of the doorway as the Captain moves forward with his rifle pointed down the hall. The preacher's son begins his father's sermon once again, but this time his utterance is accompanied by voice. For the Edwards, this voice, although low, is invited. He then uses two fingers to press against his earpiece contacting his sniper, Livingston.

"Six...two wolves down and..." his breath stirs through the transceiver, "...Five is gone - man down. We're moving forward."

No matter how professional the Captain tries to sound on the radio, Livingston senses his gap of vulnerability through his weakened words. His response is clear and reserved forcing his strength through voice to his leader.

"Five is down – KIA. Understood." Silence becomes a pausing hard reality.

The back of the lab leads to a large vaulted room with melted steel doors, red hot and smoking. There is a green glow through the dimness of the room. Captain Edwards's attention is redirected to Point-Man who points to his eyes with two fingers then towards the side wall opposite the green glow. This signals the Captain to look in that direction. Edwards searches frantically with his vision through the haze of the smoke and stops abruptly on new charred remains of their final missing team member, Young-Old Man. His body is almost totally burned into the very wall behind him with his bones showing on various parts.

Captain Edwards dry heaves and spits before wiping his mouth with his sleeve. His team has been together since their birth as Recon Marines. Young-Old Man had been a strong link to the team with his rude jokes and redneck ways. They loved him and his body was barely recognizable. Bones from one that is loved was never meant to be seen scorched. Flesh blackened into broken ash was never meant to be witnessed; nor metal fused into the human frame.

Anxiety is accompanied by a searing streak of rage within the Captain. They have lost only one member in all of their missions before today. They felt invulnerable as a team and untouchable as family. The Captain's secret has always been faith in his training and control. Today it seems that his faith is falling short and control is slipping away from his grasp. He feels violated. He is not used to this feeling and icy tendrils of fear seize his subconscious as his hand begins to tremble while pressing his earpiece, once again, to deliver the information.

"Six, Man down... Four is fucking gone."

When Livingston responds by clicking his receiver, the Captain realizes that the words that he had just spoken were nothing more than the thoughts that he was refusing to accept.

He swallows slowly and tries again, "Six, Four is KIA."

The preacher's son looks to his Captain and understands as his very heart drops. He breathes in slowly and watches as his Captain carries on, concentrating on their mission. The point-man wants to stop so badly, but watching his Captain move on drives him to follow from the opposite wall... and he does.

The two Marines enter the vaulted room and step lightly through the area towards the light. A murmur can be heard which leads to an unlocking sound then a scream. Captain Edwards struggles to gain control and signals to the point-man to move forward to get a visual, since he was closer, as a light, bright and verdant, emanates through the darkness. Gunnery Sergeant Lewis goes around the corner leading off with his assault rifle and stops. The Captain sees a stunned look of shock crawl across his face. The point-man, one of his closest friends, stands totally erect lowering his assault rifle as if he is looking at the devil himself. Captain Edwards calls out to him in a loud whisper.

"Two...Two, what do you see? Wake up! What do you see?"

For Gunnery Sergeant Lewis his uttered sermon stops. His mouth opens as he calls out in pure panic.

"JESUS... JESUS... JESUS!!!"

Suddenly the entire vault room fills with a powerful rush of viridian fire which engulfs the awed Marine killing him instantly. His screams are muffled by the rumble of the walls, shaking from the sheer force of the flame blast. The Captain is blown backwards into lab equipment, dropping his assault rifle. The new fire source once again causes the sprinklers to resume their deluge. This results in him sliding around on the ground while struggling to regain his senses.

All control is lost.

Wiping ash and water from his face Captain Edwards lunges for his assault rifle, turning in time to see a living inferno of jade flames, moving through the laboratory towards him. It is almost as if it is walking. His earpiece radio crackles on as the sniper attempts to contact him though the madness.

"Leader…zzzz…Leader, w-what's going on?"

Captain Edwards clutches his rifle with no reply and retreats at top speed back through the lab. A piercing bellow followed by a maelstrom of emerald tongues of fire erupts from the inferno causing the wall beside him to explode. The concussion knocks him to the other side of the corridor on his shoulder, ejecting the earpiece from his ear. He falls and scrambles on the ground backwards, splashing water and debris through his fingers while turning towards the approaching mass of emerald fire. He then sees what his point-man saw. He sees that this living inferno has eyes.

Scrambling once again to act, the Captain attempts to regain control and opens fire with his assault rifle into what he is sure is the devil coming for him. There is another piercing bellow as the flames around this devil increase in intensity. The water beneath each one of its steps sizzles as it transforms into steam, creating a mirage like effect around the entire base of it.

Streaks of gunfire scream through the short hallway stuttering their intent to aid the frenzied Marine Commander. Captain Edwards wrenches around to see that his young teammate down the hall is firing into the mass of flames.

"Sir, we have to move! We have to move now!!" Shouts Gonzo.

The Captain gets to his feet while reloading his rifle then runs down the hall towards Corporal Gonzalez who is providing cover fire. He ducks to the side of the corridor as a shaft of green fire strikes the wall behinds him annihilating it. The Corporal screams into his transceiver desperate and afraid.

"Six! Six…we need back up! Staff Sergeant we NEED backup NOW!!"

The young Marine ducks back to reload, as Captain Edwards grits his teeth, swallows down, holds his breath, and leans into the corridor firing his rifle into the devil of emerald flames. He then aims at a fire extinguisher on the wall beside it, causing it to erupt into the heart of the flaming mass.

The fiery mass shrieks out in agony while lurching away. This is when both Captain Edwards and Corporal Gonzalez notice the indigo stone, their primary mission, pulsating brightly with energy, being held by the creature. The flame smolders down showing the clear form of a jade being with white eyes and a mouth. It shrieks a final time, points its free hand upward, and fires a blast from it through the ceiling. It then reignites its flames and rockets through the ceiling escaping into the sky.

~~~

<u>Three days later</u>

A mission that began with six highly trained United States Force Recon Marines is now ending with the funerals of three, Gunnery Sergeant Leander Lewis, Sergeant Mark Daldgerin, and Corporal Andrew Young. This day, a mournful gray drizzle gives visible voice to the grief of the group made up of family members and close friends. There is a lone blond woman gripping her child in her arms. She has buried her happiness next to her endless worries over her Young-Old husband; for now she is alone. There is an elderly couple stricken by the burden of the unfairness in life as they watch their grandson go into the ground. He has been their 'Doll'. The final loved one, a large slim man draped in black and sorrow, whispers his own prayer to God for his son. He promises to meet him again soon and releases the anger held in his heart for his son's choice to be a Marine; for his choice to be a point-man.

An honorable speech is given by the commanding officer and the last rites are given by a man-of-the-cloth. Captain Edwards stands over each coffin stern with tears swelling in his eyes. These were his blood brothers and they relied on his leadership. His point-man was a preacher's son. His machine gunner personified courage. His Young-Old Man would be loyalty and wisdom lost. For the Captain, it was a burden of grief and guilt that he would have to live with, a loss that he is forced to accept.

Control was not lost, but stolen.

Without it, his confidence in battle was tested against fear. Anger ripples through him. These were his brothers of secrecy and now they are gone.

The words spoken are drowned by the rain along with the tears for those they loved. Just as the final blessing leaves the mouth of the Priest and his hand falls releasing a small handful of soil, Staff Sergeant Livingston approaches the coffins. He opens his hand with
~~~

three bullets in it and places a bullet on each coffin, sitting them upright.

These were his brothers also. He struggles to choke back his tears and says a single broken comment under his failing breath that can be heard by all.

"All Hail the Heroes! Semper Fi!"

CHAPTER 3

GENERAL BLACK
AND THE SKY GHOST

"To die on the battlefield without a mission is to die in vain!"
-Staff Sergeant Crawford, USMC

Time has been standing still for the last week. There is an irrevocable hurt that goes with losing a team member and Captain Edwards stands alone on this cool April morning reflecting; he can't wait for the warmth of summer to return.

For civilians, to speak about the deceased is to keep their memories alive; for Marines it is a quiet reminder of the friendship between risk and death. Marines speak of the dead when they are no longer warriors on the battlefield embraced by that friendship... risk and death. The sky is gray on this brittle and frosty morning. The overcast atmosphere adds to the misery felt and dulls all colors into muddy hues.

The Captain stands on the outside far edge of a hangar bay. He stares at the towering aircraft entry doors briefly before walking through the personnel entrance beside them. The inner area jars memories of his Citadel college football field due to its depth and scope. Sound desires to echo within this hollowness, but the distant rumble of jets passing over steal the opportunity away. His fingertips hurt from the cold; as does his heart.

His memories are his own and he rarely opens the door to them because of his desire to forget. He wishes to forget his few visits to prison to see his father. He wishes to disremember the men his mother brought home. He wishes to unlearn a broken family and to not hate his own mother for her drinking binges and lack of love.

I couldn't control her. I couldn't stop her. He thinks to himself. Then he thinks grimly about the last mission. I couldn't control it. He reluctantly accepts as a thought more than as the truth.

He remembers slapping his mother on the day he left for college. She was bitter over his future as well as her own the lack of a future. Her drunken comments wished for his failure, cursed his father, and ignored the presence of his younger brother. The slap hurt him more than it hurt her; the pain confirmed the shattering of his family, as did his failure with his men.

He promised to never let his future family fail no matter what the cost; it has been his goal ever since. He knows in his heart that he has to regain his strength and move on. With that he speaks to God and himself at once.

"I will not lose control," he promises sullenly, stubbornly bridging the gap in his confidence.

Now he stands on a new threshold, knowing that his men depend on his decisions in battle. The Marine Corps and his brother-marines are his new family.

The inside of the hangar cloaks him in darkness until his eyes adjust from the outside morning light. He is greeted by his commander, Colonel Bishop.

"Morning, Captain Edwards."

"Good morning, sir." The loss of his men is felt in the Captain's reply to his commander.

He wonders if the commander truly understands what he is feeling and realizes just by the touch of his commander's hand resting on his shoulder that he does.

"Son, losing men under your command is never easy. It happens, but it is not easy. I have lost many Marines under my command, but I pride myself on those that I have saved by not giving in to the desire to quit."

The large open hangar and dank cool air creates a stunted echo of each word leaving the lips of Colonel Bishop; finally the echo has its opportunity and takes it. He removes his cover and runs his fingers through his thin graying hair before returning it to position. He faces the young captain and reassures him.

"This is Recon, Captain, and we are the first factor that matters on the battlefield. Ever since our birth, Marines have always been the children of war. It is all that we know... and loss is a part of this game. It is the necessary part of the game that we all truly hate. We have to learn how to lick our wounds, heal our hearts, and commit to going forward, protecting this country and the people in it. We are the point of America's sword and it gets dinged from time to time by fighting her foes. All we can do is re-sharpen it and push on." The colonel rests against the rails of the walkway looking down over the interior of the hangar. "We stand watch over the ungrateful and the unknowing as their guardians and unsung heroes. We never surrender, we never quit and we always honor our fallen comrades by carrying on their traditions and memories. That's what makes us Marines."

Captain Edwards raises his head and nods to his commander. Colonel Bishop responds with a firm gesture of agreement built upon the battle-wear on his face. He directs the Captain to walk with him.

"The United States of America cannot take any military actions on American soil unless it is a part of a national emergency, in which our actions are limited to humanitarian rescue. We are the most technologically advanced organization in the world and yet because of our own laws we can't use any of our technology in our own land. The Posse Comitatus act of 1878, which restricts the use of the military within the United States, could not have possibly foreseen today's circumstances."

Colonel Bishop escorts the Captain to the side of the hangar and raises his finger to signal the controllers above to open the far double doors.

"The local authorities are asking a hell of a lot of questions about that last operation, Captain, and to be honest with you…it has become increasingly more difficult to answer them with a captured video camera showing our Marines in action. Just to think, all of this was because of a blasted space rock!"

"The meteorite, sir?" Questions the puzzled Captain.

"Yes, Captain… That damn space rock. I'm no scientist, but I fail to see how that big, blue pebble is worth even one Marine's life and much less how it's supposed to save the world. But I'm a Marine, the same as you and this wasn't my call to make. Speaking of saving the world… our guest is here."

The hangar begins to rumble as a strong gust of warm engine exhaust envelops the two warriors announcing the arrival of a uniquely designed, all-black aircraft.

The aerial vehicle is the size of a small personal jet but moves and hovers like a helicopter with no propellers. The underside of the craft has long, glowing glasslike strips that change in illumination intensity to balance out the craft against the pulls of gravity. The aircraft then lands with a silent, velvet touch and sits. It looks like a UFO from pictures that the Captain saw as a child.

Captain Edwards and his commander then turn around to the sound of the personnel doors of the hangar opening behind them. Coming through the doorway are the final two surviving members of the Captain's tactical squad, the sniper and the youngest Marine. They both report to the commander with their eyes irresistibly drawn to the mysterious jet craft sitting in front of them. The youngest member has a million questions that he fears to ask. The sniper is the first to hold his stance, cross his arms and speak.

"What's going on, Captain? What is…that?" He questions, refusing to assume without the application of basic logic.

There are no words spoken or responses made as a low click signals the opening of the side door of the craft. A uniformed man passes through the open door and approaches the team. There are two shiny silver stars on each shoulder of his uniform. Colonel Bishop calls the men to attention.

GONZALEZ
U.S. MARINES

"General Black, Tactical Squad-7: The First Factor has been mustered as ordered, sir."

The General carefully studies Captain Edwards and his two Marines standing at attention then takes a step back.

"So, you three are the last Devil-Dogs left in your team, huh?"

"Yes sir." The Captain responds boldly, all the while privately interpreting the general's question as abrasive. He recognizes the general instantly from his classes in Officer Candidate School.

"Aren't you the former commanding general of the entire Infantry Division at Camp Lejeune seven years ago...sir?" He questions the general directly in a manner which could easily be perceived as insubordinate.

The general rubs his chin and gives a smirk to the Captain. He chooses not to verbally respond to the question. Instead he stands erect and begins to admire the team.

The sniper is a slender black man with a slightly receding hairline. Sharp facial features and thin lips add to his character, making him somewhat near the flavors of acute and surreptitious; trust is alien to him. His demeanor is expressionless, with battle experience to back up the solemn assurance in his stance. He sways almost imperceptibly away from the general's stare with a total awareness of his surroundings. His wariness is obvious.

What attack does this sniper wait for? The general muses to himself. He'll make a great addition to the team.

The young Marine is Hispanic with a boyish appearance. The smooth skin on his face makes it obvious that he struggles to grow facial hair. Round eyes begging for maturity reinforce his youth. His facial features are a cross between handsome and cute while the corded sturdiness of his neck and sinewy, muscular frame display his adherence to athletics. He is the shortest of the three, but the subtle swagger of his movements boast the stalwart confidence that is shared by all Recon Marines.

The final person the general studies is the Captain.

Finally, he thinks to himself, the one that I have heard so much about.

Captain Edwards stands three inches above six feet and has a dense form with strong features. He has the classic officer appearance that is expected in the Marine Corps, but there is hauteur in his watchful eyes that belies the disciplined words that come from his mouth. His widened nose flares against the system as do his proud lips and scarred forehead. The most notable thing about this beast of a leader is the breadth of his shoulders. Everything about the Captain is strength; his only true weakness is his compassion, but then again, this has already been calculated.

The general stands before the men in a casual parade rest position; his feet shoulder length apart and his hands behind his back.

"I want you Devil Dogs to stand at ease. I am very impressed by your actions and I offer my condolences for those Marines lost. They are heroes."

He then turns to address the team's commander, standing beside the Captain.

"Colonel Bishop, I am here to take command of your team. With your permission, I would like to load them up for their first situational briefing. You will be debriefed on everything in two days."

Colonel Bishop agrees and looks over his men for what he knows might be the last time.

The young Marine nudges the sniper with his elbow and whispers, "Hey yo, is that a spaceship?"

"We call it the Sky Ghost, Corporal Gonzalez," responds the general, interrupting the intended reply from Staff Sergeant Livingston.

The sniper waits until the senior officer's attention shifts.

"Hell, nah. It's another top secret toy of tha white man." He says softly to his young teammate. The sharp comment reeks of sarcasm.

The General, having taken command of the team motions them to board the Sky Ghost. As the team enters, the power strips on the underside of it begin to glow. Captain Edwards stops before passing through the doorway and looks back to the commander.

"Will we ever see you again, Colonel?" He asks.

The commander shakes his head. "Probably not, son."

The Captain walks back to Colonel Bishop, holds his hand out to grasp the commander's. "It was a pleasure serving with you, sir." He salutes, and then runs back to the Sky Ghost.

The jet craft rises to a silent hover, then rockets out of the hangar.

CHAPTER 4

THE INVITATION

"An invitation into the world of secrets leads to a room of darkness with only one way in. There are no exits... There are no exits at all."

–Slogan written on the first door into the 'Ghost-Train'.

The interior of the Sky Ghost is designed with an executive appearance of total luxury. The seats are Italian leather with a couch on the opposite wall. Near the front of the fuselage is a large cherry oak desk with a small box of cigars in the corner.

Edwards looks back at his teammates and says, "Looks like a little version of Air Force One."

The sniper, having little desire to being noticed by a General Officer, smiles. Gonzo moves his hand along the leather on one of the seats, massaging it before sitting down. Then Livingston's cynicism overcomes his apprehension and he follows up with a sardonic taunt simply by deducing the value of the quality items within the interior of the craft.

"Yeah, look at our hard earned tax dollars at work."

The general seats himself at the desk in the front, opens the cigar box, and gently extracts one from inside. He then lights the cigar and inhales deeply before exhaling slowly, adding a sleek haze of blue smoke accompanied by the warm aroma of black cherry tobacco to the inner atmosphere of the aircraft.

"We have been ordered to disband and restructure the tactical squads of your Recon division in light of the results from Operation Stone Mist in the Udosion Labs complex. This has caused some complications with the civilian sector. When the silent alarm was tripped by the vault, local law enforcement became involved. That created problems for us."

The General presses a button and a small ashtray swings out from the side of the desk. He taps his ashes into it.

"The FBI was contacted with barely enough time to stop those local policemen from going to their deaths. Department 13 of the FBI then contacted us, which activated your team for direct action on this mission. We didn't receive the intel on the living flame until you were all in the building.

"What you encountered within that lab is what we refer to as an E.M.D., Enemy of Mass Destruction. That living inferno was an individual with abilities far beyond that of a normal human. He is what we have categorized as a N-ionically enhanced human, affectionately referred to as a N-ionic. He is not the only one of his type. That meteorite that you were sent to recover is used to create beings such as him."

The general inhales again slowly he places the cigar into the ashtray. He then opens a drawer and extracts a manila folder labeled as Top Secret. He carefully opens the folder and removes some of its contents. He places documents and photos on the desk and motions to the team members to come closer and see the classified material.

"The United States has known about N-ionics since the end of World War II. This is when the first confirmed N-ionically enhanced human was encountered."

The team members look at an old black and white photo of what appears to be an elaborately clad Nazi soldier floating. He was engaged in a fire fight with an American Special Forces squad led by a man with a full-face hardened mask, a Thompson .45 cal submachine gun, and a war-torn uniform with a dingy eagle on the chest and shredded cape. The sniper studies the photo longer and more intently than the others, observing minute details that others would normally miss. The general then takes out another sheet, titled The Elite Force Division, and slides it forward on the table.

"The President of the United States ordered the organization of a unit whose sole purpose is to address these types of individuals and to establish their threat levels to our nation. A cabinet made up of military members and civilians has been created to head the division. The cabinet was called OMEGA. The division that was created under their command is called the Elite Forces Division and classified as Top Secret. We call it the EF-Div. The entire OMEGA Cabinet is carried on the books as a special advisory team to the President and does not have to be confirmed by the Senate, but has direct access to the National Command Authority."

The general leans back in his seat and grabs his cigar again. "The EF-Div was placed under the authority of the Marine Corps so that it doesn't have to go through the red tape of Congress before every action. It was also given the authority to act on American soil so long as a minimum of one-third of the staff is made up of civilians and all support products and services come from American-owned civilian corporations. Even we have to play the game of politics occasionally."

Rolling the cigar between his fingers, the general continues, "Just to make things a tad bit more complicated, we also work directly with the FBI's Department-13. There are only 12 official departments of the FBI so this one does not exist...it handles these types of 'special' cases."

Captain Edwards swallows and takes a ragged breath while building up courage to ask a straight question to the general without offense. "Sir, why in the hell are we here?"

The general cracks a smile. The last group of files that he pulls out is made up of documents and photos of the Captain, his tactical squad, and individuals classified as Public Operators from the late 1940's, 1950's, 60's, and 70's. The photos of their lost team members sting each of the Marines viewing them. General Black opens the bottom folder first, passing around pictures of some of the popular Public Operators of the past. Captain Edwards holds up two of the pictures and almost forgets his pain as he speaks.

"Ultra-Max and Atum-Ra…I used to watch their cartoons on television when I was a kid. Are you saying they were real, sir?" Asks the Captain.

Sliding recent photographs from the bottom of the stack displaying an elderly man in the hospital, the general responds, "Ultra-Max died eight years ago after a long and painful battle with cancer. Atum-Ra disappeared sometime in the early 70's."

Livingston, astute sniper that he is, grabs the first photo they were shown and rests his fingertip on the barely legible masked man with the Thompson submachine gun. "Who is this, General? Why is he dressed like that?"

Careful with his answer and even more careful in dealing with the sniper, he responds, "All we know is that he was called The Patriot's Ghost, Staff Sergeant Livingston. Everything about him was shrouded in secrecy. His identity was only known by a select few… and I wasn't one of them."

General Black holds up a final sheet and summarizes it briefly.

"Captain, your five man squad has seen action in Afghanistan, Iraq, Africa, and Alaska. Before the operation a week ago, you and your sniper here," he says, pointing at Livingston, "had lost one man in all of those missions. Your team member's replacement Corporal Gonzalez may be young, but he has already proven his professionalism and value in last week's operation. The men you lost on Operation Stone Mist will always be remembered as heroes."

The general places the paper down on the desk along with his cigar. "Captain, I have been a Marine for damn near forty years now. If there is one thing that I know, it is that if you want the best…and I mean the ABSOLUTE best, you go to the Marine Corps and you look to Force Recon! That is why you and your men are here today. I need the best! I need you and your Devil-Dogs to join our Elite Forces Division, Captain Edwards!"

The Captain leans back with an uncertain look on his face.

"Sir?"

A small yellow light flickers on the corner of the general's desk. The jet begins to prepare for its landing approach at the United States Marine Corps Reserves base in Camp Sparta, New York. The general puts his cigar out and latches his seat belt while relaxing with the same smile of anticipation that he displayed minutes earlier.

"Look out the windows at the wings of the aircraft."

Each Marine moves towards a separate window and looks for anything unique about the Sky Ghost's wings. The General then begins to speak in a low gruff voice across the radio to the pilot, "Myth, take us to the Daylight."

"Yes sir."

Suddenly a light energy field surrounds the plane and the entire surface begins to reflect light and becomes invisible. The Marines gasp at the transformation of the appearance of the Sky Ghost.

"How does that work?" Says Gonzo, murmuring quietly. General Black hears the tone of awe and explains. "It is a lot like a computer screen, but done with red, green and blue Light Emitting Diodes. The LEDs are in an array and connected to an advanced computer built into the heart of this craft. They're hooked to miniature high-speed video cameras opposite the array separated by millimeters. The video cameras stream live images of the Sky Ghost's immediate surroundings and the computer routes the signal from the camera to the panel, making just the right color and brightness. If you are more than ten feet away... the whole aircraft looks invisible."

Gonzo stares at the general with a confounded appearance and a twitch in his top lip. Livingston instantly notes to himself the technical prowess of the general's answer. He won't forget.

The plane lands on one of the rarely used landing strips near the back of the base. The entire area is surrounded by armed guards and electric fences. The plane taxis into one of the older standard hangars as the doors of the building open and shut automatically for the craft.

Once the Sky Ghost stops, the Marines disembark into a large darkened hangar with multiple types of crafts similar and yet different from the one they had just exited. The general excuses himself and answers a cell phone call while walking towards the front of the Sky Ghost. Captain Edwards takes the opportunity to speak with his teammates. He calls them by their nicknames.

"Liv, Gonzo...I want you to speak freely. How do you feel about all of this? This guy is supposed to be one of the greatest commanding officers in the entire history of Marine Force Recon. We learned about this guy when I was in school!"

Gonzo responds first in an anxious tone, "I don't know, Captain. This crap is scary! When I first went into Recon it was a dream; it was exciting. I have always wanted to be a Devil-Dog, a Leatherneck, and a Marine, but this here is just plain and simple SCARY! Sir, I still collect comic books with some of those guys in them! Hell, I have da Hero Federation issue number one with most of them in it!"

The Captain turns to his oldest and best friend, Staff Sergeant Livingston, and waits for his response.

"I don't really care who he is, Captain. It's not like you can say no. This ain't nothin but another white man's game. Take a look at how carefully we've been prepped for this. Did you notice the details in tha files that he had on us? Tha most you can do is suck it up and play it!" says the sniper. His tongue is as accurate as it is sharp. "The mask on that guy was a hockey mask of some sort."

"What are you saying, Liv?" Asks his Captain.

Livingston lowers his voice before speaking, "The first hockey mask didn't show up until the 1960's."

"Who's to say the mask wasn't wood?"

"Wood splits along the grain, Captain. Check the photo carefully... the cracks on it were diagonal. It had to be Fiberglass."

Gonzo becomes antsy. "I don't get it, Staff Sergeant."

"I understand what Liv is getting to, Gonzo. Fiberglass was created in the 1930's and mostly used for aircrafts. This guy the general called the Patriot's Ghost wore a hockey mask over fifteen years before the first one was technically created. In other words, the U.S. Government had a hand in his creation and existence."

Livingston smiles, "Of course they did, Captain. Fiberglass was developed by a white-guy named Games Slayter out of Indiana. He got rich and tha government acquired a new resource for war."

"Hunh?!? What the hell? How d'you know all of this stuff, Staff Sergeant?" Asks Gonzo.

"Because the handful of blacks in that town caught hell during that era, Gonzo."

The youth becomes quiet.

"Consider this: you think they can let us go after telling us that stuff on tha trip over here? The way I see it is we do it or get ready to fight our ass outta here!! Either way, I'm with you, Captain."

Gonzo looks at Livingston and pauses for a minute to scratch his chest before asking, "What d'you fight for, Staff Sergeant? You know that sometimes you scare me."

Livingston looks towards the Corporal, "I believe in tha rules, laws, and policies set forth by this 'all-endearing' Nation, Gonzo. Tha same laws that white people created to put them in power is also hurting them because they were meant to serve all races! America ain't evil…it's just tha handful of redneck white men holding on ta tha old ways that are. Why d'you think we needed a black president? What in-tha-hell do you think we're a part of here? I fight for tha facts, Gonzo. I truly believe in the creeds recorded into the doctrines of this country and the fairness of them will not be denied to my people. Hell, 'Doll' said that you read tha bible the whole night before our last mission, you should know this crap!" Staff Sergeant Livingston turns away from the youth, disgusted by the pain he is forced to remember for mentioning his dead teammate's name. He was close to Doll and he really didn't know or have patience for this new kid.

Captain Edwards begins to rub the 'Y' scar on his forehead while contemplating the proposal. His military life has been about control, belief, and faith which were achieved by the trust of his men, trust in the nation, and trust in the Marine Corps; not to mention intense training. His men are family and he wonders to himself what this will do to that relationship. Will this be a prison in itself? He saw what it did to his family growing up. His apprehensions were quickly growing into anxiety, but his sniper made sense. He's already in too deep.

The general greets a man dressed in a suit exiting a large black SUV. He returns a salute to the military driver and shakes the hand of the person in the suit who is obviously a civilian. The civilian points at the captain and his team and is then escorted over to them by the general.

"Have you Devil-Dogs thought about my proposal and come to an agreement?"

Captain Edwards looks back at his men as Livingston crosses his arms and Gonzo nods. Edwards responds to the general, "Yes, sir. We gladly accept the honor of joining your division."

General Black then steps slightly to the side and introduces the civilian that he is standing with. "Captain Edwards, I would like for you and your team members to meet your new civilian coordinator, the Operational Commander of Department 7. His name is Michael Webb."

OCD7-Webb stands just less than six feet tall and is distinguishable by his obviously darkened red hair, which he wears slicked back. He has an enthusiastic look about him that instantly makes Captain Edwards

leery. The general then introduces the captain and his team, "Commander Webb, I would like to introduce you to the members of Tactical Squad 7. Their field name will now be the only name that they will be using. It is The First Factor."

The general then stands at attention and salutes Captain Edwards and his men. "Gentlemen, welcome to the Elite Forces Division!"

The general drops his salute and allows OCD7-Webb to take charge as he walks over to a second black SUV with the driver standing at attention. He says something to the driver, enters the vehicle and leaves the hangar.

CHAPTER 5

THANKS FOR THE RIDE

"What's Going On?"

–Marvin Gaye

Antiquity, New York is a community that has the outward appearance of living within the lazy days of the past. The small town is built upon the generations of military servicemen that have simply chosen not to leave. The youthful Marines smile and salute the higher population of elders, sure to refer to them as 'Sir' and 'Ma'am' when engaging in casual conversation. The blue sky complements the red brick buildings and amber halls. Pearly-white churches, corners bordered by bronze ageing, thrust towards the clouds to display the common pride of religion for the few visitors that the town has every year. This town is all but awake and proud of it. This is also why it is perfect for the covert nature of Camp Sparta and the Elite-Forces Division.

Two and a half weeks have passed since Captain Edwards's tactical squad known as the First Factor has agreed to join the division. In that time Captain Edwards's family has moved into Camp Sparta's base housing while Staff Sergeant Livingston and Corporal Gonzalez have moved into the barracks. Each has been given a separate room, as a matter of course for Staff Sergeant Livingston but, surprisingly, also for Corporal Gonzalez.

Upon joining their new division the Marines have been put on a strict diet and given "vitamins" to be taken every morning at 0500. Each morning the three participate in vigorous physical training and various classes on hand-to-hand combat which last until lunch time. Their afternoons are mostly meetings and briefings on events that are occurring throughout the world. There is a strong emphasis placed on events within America and the Middle East. The evening liberty usually begins at 1800, after a custom-prepared dinner, made by cooks who wear deep blue uniforms with no names.

~~~

Livingston is driving to the Marine Corps Exchange, the Marine version of a department store, as he passes Gonzo, who is running in the same direction as he is headed. The young Corporal is wearing jeans, boots and a pull-over shirt with an Eagle, Globe and Anchor embroidered on the chest. He is obviously not out for a jog. Livingston slows the government car that he is driving, opens the passenger side window and calls out to his squad mate, "Corporal Gonzalez!" He stops on the side of the road as local military traffic find their way around him with rude horn beeps displaying their annoyance.

"Gonzo! Get over here!" Barks the Recon sniper. The young Marine
~~~

flings himself into the passenger seat. He wipes away his sweat, "Thanks for the ride, Staff Sergeant. It's kinda hot out today."

The senior enlisted Marine looks narrowly into the face of his comrade and eases the car back into traffic. He asks, "Where're you goin?"

"I was tryin' ta make it to da store before it closed. You a damn blessin' right about now! Thanks for da pickup." Answers the corporal.

"When you getting a car, Gonzo? This ain't gonna happen again," Livingston responds with an acerbic but serious smile.

"Don't got da money right now, Staff Sergeant. I gotta take care of mi familia over in Mexico." Gonzo begins in amusement but quickly resolves into truth. "I was born in El Paso, Texas, sir."

Livingston interjects, "Don't call me 'sir,' boy. I work for a living. Save your 'sirs' for officers and old white men."

The young Marine leans back in his seat, away from the acidity of the sniper's comment. Disregarding the corporal's disconnect, Livingston speaks candidly, "I'm going ta be honest with you, Gonzo, I didn't get ta go over your files, but I do know that you were tha best in your class from training. That carries weight with me."

This was the warmest compliment that this cold-hearted assassin could muster. Noticing little reaction from the reserved youth, the Staff Sergeant tries again.

"Mexican hunh? White people probably think that you set a good example for your people, don't they?" He chuckles before continuing, "That's how they treat the captain. Hell, I just sit back quietly and observe things. How 'bout your parents? What do ya momma think, Gonzo?"

Connecting with Staff Sergeant Livingston's comment and question is something more felt than understood for the Corporal. He opens up to answer, "Mi madre was in labor when she snuck across the Rio Grande. She got caught by Immigration, and was rushed to the hospital because I was REALLY on my way."

The corporal giggles at the broken memory, merely reciting what he has been told. "Imagine that, a mom who would risk everything to give her child the greatest gift imaginable, American citizenship."

Livingston glances over at Gonzo, debating his last statement within his mind while flashing through the history of blacks in comparison.

"Hell, we came as slaves and ya'll are fightin' ta be here."

Gonzo responds based on his personal feelings, "I don't know nuthin' else, Staff Sergeant. I was born in America, I was raised in

America, and I am American. Don't have much of anything else. I have a grandma and a beast of a dad in Mexico I ain't never met." The youthful Marine leans forward with swollen pride, "Mi madre wanted to be American, but never really got da chance."

The car stops in the parking lot to the MCX, and Livingston gazes at his new team member. With the loss of his other teammates, he didn't want to know this kid. "Mexican hunh?" He repeats. "At least you ain't no corn-fed white boy wearin' a Confederate flag tryin' ta prove he ain't trash," says the sniper while pointing to the corporal's door with his thumb. "Now get out the car 'fore they come arrest me for taking their vehicle for too long."

Corporal Gonzalez diffidently exits the vehicle, "Thanks for da ride again, Staff Sergeant Livingston,"

"Yea... Yea, whatever. Did I ever take the time to welcome you to the team, Gonzo?"

"No," the youth responds, hanging on for an expected "Welcome."

"Good. We'll see how things go. I'll see you tomorrow morning at Zero-Dark-Thirty," says Livingston as he drives away, leaving a light billow of dust in his wake. Gonzo's earlier smile returns. He spends the rest of his day shopping for his favorite video games and drinking in the local bowling alley. His desire to prove his place on the team becomes a zealous fervor.

CHAPTER 6

THE BREAKFAST BEFORE

*"The funniest jokes are often about race.
There once was a Black guy, a White guy, and a Mexican..."*

–Chris Rock

This morning breaks the routine they had followed since their transfer to Camp Sparta. It is the morning of their enhancement process. This process was explained to them on their first day as a procedure that would naturally enhance their bodies' abilities. Yesterday and this morning are the only times that the men are allowed to eat and drink anything they chose and to go without their "vitamins."

At 0700 Captain Edwards knocks on the door of Staff Sergeant Livingston. The door is unlocked and the Captain walks in, only to be enveloped by the aroma of scrambled eggs and turkey. Motown music fills the room as Gonzo rambles through Livingston's music collection picking out the best CDs. Livingston is in the kitchen, fully dressed in his fatigues, cooking breakfast while eating an apple. Captain Edwards takes a seat at the small folding dining table.

"Turkey bacon, Liv? Do you ever get tired of that?"

"I ain't touchin' no swine, Captain," responds the sniper-cook with a 'you-knew-that' grin.

Gonzo whoops from the background, "White people eat pork!" His sarcasm pokes fun at Livingston's black pride.

The captain releases a small chuckle and massages the scar on his forehead, engrossed in deep thought. His thoughts race over the lost members of their team—Point-man, Doll the machine gunner, and Young-Old Man—but he does not mention them. He does not desire to decrease morale, but his thoughts recycle their memories and that last fateful day within the Udosion Labs. Livingston notices it and removes the apple from his mouth to speak. "You think too damn much, Captain. Did you tell your wife about today? You know that Alicia's going ta worry." The Captain tries to smile but ends up making a peculiar look with the worry wrinkles on his face, "Nice music, Liv. You love your music." He pauses briefly then finally responds to the question asked. "No, I didn't tell Alicia. I didn't want her to worry."

Gonzo hollers from the background. "White people eat mayonnaise!"

Livingston pauses to watch the young Marine's rummaging process and dismisses it as a lost cause. He continues to scramble his eggs, taking care to use light salt and oil to replace the heavy use of butter. The sound of the food cooking makes its own conversation in the silence between the Captain and his best friend.

Gonzo interjects with an elated display of mission accomplishment as he holds a CD above his head, "HAHAHH! I didn't know that you had this, Staff Sergeant! This here's a classic! This baby here has Afrika Bambaataa, the Sugarhill Gang, and Run-D.M.C on it! This is where rap began, Captain! Me and my homies in da' hood at home was still break dancin' to dis stuff when we was in high school. This stuff here never dies!"

Livingston brings two plates of food to the table and hands one to Captain Edwards, taking the time to comment to Gonzo, "Now you know you Latino-boys don't know nothin' about that stuff. Those beats have roots in music that reach all the way back to the tribes in the motherland."

Gonzo enters the kitchen to make himself a plate of food. "Yea, whatever, Staff Sergeant. All I know is that the beats are hittin' and the music is live! You guys may have started it, but us 'Latino-boys' perfected it! Man, when we add our twang to it, da' women go crazy! You know that you can copy most of this stuff on to your computer... like modern day people, so you don't have to have all of these CDs."

Captain Edwards studies one of the CDs on the table beside his plate titled 'Golden Oldies.' He used to listen to music of the same sort when he went to visit his father. It reminded him of his brief days as a child playing with his dad before his father went to prison. He glances at the Staff Sergeant. "You do have some good stuff here, Liv. Marvin Gaye and the O'Jays? These are some great oldies."

Shoving a fork full of eggs into his mouth, Livingston answers in short blurts, allowing crumbs to escape his lips onto the table below. "Marvin Gaye and the O'Jays ain't oldies, they're classics! Soul music don't get no better than that... which is why I keep my CDs." He devours half of his plate of food before he notices that the Captain hasn't touched his. "You ate already, Captain? Oh, I know what's wrong with you...you're worried about the experiment they plan on doing to us today, ain't you? What do you fight for, sir?"

Captain Edwards studies Livingston's face for a moment before reluctantly taking a bite of his breakfast. A part of him feels that submitting to the breakfast would be easier than providing an answer to his question. It is the second glance into the sniper's eyes that remind him that nothing will get past his attention.

"This is my career, Liv. I made an oath." Resolves the stalwart Marine captain before gulping down his eggs. Livingston merely rests his fork and bobs his head with a light nod. He then reaches back to the end table beside his chair and opens the drawer to extract an old Time magazine. The headline on the cover is about the super-hero Atum-Ra and the picture is that of the black superhero battling a group of white-robed Klansmen attacking a church. He places the issue on the table in front of Captain Edwards. It is dated 1957.

"My Pa gave me this when I was a kid and it changed tha way I saw everything, Captain. I want to help my people and to be a hero just like Atum-Ra and my Pa. If I hafta play tha White-Man's game to do it…then HELL, they can experiment on me. My Pa kept this from when he was young and passed it to me. I'm gonna pass it to my kids someday and teach them never to forget that our nation's heroes weren't all white."

Captain Edwards holds his fork straight while pressing them into the eggs, "It's not an experiment, Liv. It's an Enhancement Process… nothing else." He then stares at the magazine cover and wonders to himself about their destiny.

Gonzo yells from the back, "White people can't dance!" He changes the music in the background to a mix CD starting with the Temptation's "Just My Imagination." The song strikes the youth emotionally, bringing private reflection about his sordid history. The harmony becomes magic. Slowly he starts to dance around with a piece of turkey bacon hanging from his mouth, "Hey, Staff Sergeant, can you make me a copy of this? It was the last song me and my Momma danced to before she died." The comment is spoken quickly and softly by the lonely young corporal, mostly hoping to show that he is over the pain while failing to prove it. The loss of his mother was not mentioned to the Staff Sergeant the day earlier on the ride. It did not have to be.

Livingston reviewed Corporal Gonzalez's file when he came back to his room the evening before. The youth are the results of their parent's achievement, identity, and loss. The deportation of his mother made his teen years increasingly difficult while growing up in the system. Many of the private notes indicated that his alcoholic Mexican father might have had a hand in her being discovered as illegal. A list of marked returned letters received by the youth from Mexico was the first hint that something happened to his mother. A fight with Immigration, two court appearances and six months of Juvenile Delinquency imprisonment resulted in the confirmed knowledge of her death. With nothing left upon freedom from juvenile incarceration, home was found in the Marine Corps.

Splitting his attention from the Captain for only a second to acknowledge his other teammate, Livingston prepares to give him a canned answer to the question of making him a CD and notices Gonzo's face with each slow spin of his dancing. The youth has his eyes almost completely shut with small tears coming from them while he is chewing his bacon with a distant smile. "He's dancing with his mother," thinks Livingston as he answers in a voice that can no longer be heard by the lonely youth, but it is felt. "I'll make you a copy of it when we get home tonight, Gonzo. I promise."

The music changes to Louis Armstrong's "What a Wonderful World" as Livingston swallows his last gulp of food looking directly into the eyes of Captain Edwards. He speaks in reference to the 'enhancement process,' with sarcastic amusement, "What we have here, Captain, is two blacks and a Mexican...I am quite sure that you know what they're doing. We're perfect candidates. Heh, it's always been like this whenever it came to tha government. Follow tha history...it's called the Tuskegee Syphilis Experiment."

Captain Edwards stands up slowly with a discerning smile and shakes his head while rolling his eyes upwards. He absorbs the majestic movements of their newest teammate dancing in the background to his memories and appreciates his inner struggle to let go of his own. A small laugh escapes him as he comments to his best friend, "Liv, you are the epitome of 'Black Power.' Why did you ever join the military?"

Livingston grabs his gym bag and cover, "I come from tha deep South, Captain. A place where my people ain't goin' nowhere in life. I ain't never had much but the wisdom that my Pa gave me and a good trigger finger from huntin'. I'm going to be a Sergeant Major someday and I'm going to have tha power to help other brothers and sisters that want to make it out of their placements. Just like our black President and just like this cat, Atum-Ra, in tha magazine. If I have to go on missions that are suicidal, take pills with no name, and be a guinea pig for tha white-man to accomplish that...then it's just like I said earlier, I'm going to do it, Captain. Someday when I do make it...stuff like this won't just be happening to us no more."

The Captain looks at his friend as the music ends; Gonzo grabs his gear in the background to hurry to the door. Livingston locks the door as the team embark quietly on the day that they are sure to change their lives. Captain Edwards will be depending on Livingston to be what he has always been to the team, the harsh reality to each mission as well as the backbone of motivation for himself – after all, it's two blacks and a Mexican.

CHAPTER 7

THE ENHANCEMENT PROCESS

*"Pain is a vehicle traveling on the road to hurt.
For some, the road is one-way."*

–Colonel Ronald Estep

The team leaves the barracks and drive over to the security entrance. Speech is absent among the trio while their thoughts rage with the noise of concern. They meet with a security guard, solitary and aloof, who greets the Captain with a salute. He informs them that OCD7-Webb was on his way up to escort them into the lab. "Up?" Asks the captain.

"Yes sir. He's coming 'up' in the elevator from our underground facility." Answers the security guard.

Corporal Gonzalez moves his finger instinctively along his neck and pulls his crucifix from beneath his uniform shirt. It is his small courage and it is precious. "This is sounding more and more like that one-way-in, no-way-out spy stuff, Staff Sergeant." He then turns to his captain. "Sir, do you know what da Enhancement-thingy that we're supposed to be doing today is?"

Captain Edward's shakes his head as he and Staff Sergeant Livingston remove their bags from the vehicle, "No, I don't Corporal," he replies, then briefly pauses. "Look, everything is going to be alright. They're not going to kill us. That would be dumb. Anything less than death, we can handle. We're Marines! Oorah?"

The Corporal swallows, his face a mask of comical bravery, "Oorah!"

Livingston throws his bag over his shoulder and approaches the gate first as OCD7-Webb arrives and immediately orders the guardsmen to open it. He welcomes the team and escorts them into a small entrance that leads to an elevator which scans each of their retinas for access. The doors close as an ominous feeling engulfs the team before the elevator moves. OCD7-Webb then faces the team, "Today you will be entering the Daylight Labs underground complex for the first time. This will become your new home away from home, gentlemen."

He types in a five digit code and presses the button for level 5. The elevator shifts slightly, then moves fluidly backwards and subsequently down through the floor. The sides of the elevator open, exposing crystal clear windows which offer a full view of the interior of the complex. It is nothing less than awe inspiring.

The Daylight Lab's layout is almost identical to that of a large cruise ship embedded into a skyscraper sized cavern with a crystalline stone sky made by the top of the cave. Each level that the group passes through offers a view into each department's common area. One area has a large park, surrounded by thin, towering street lights, in the center of which people are walking and talking. One level has two barracks and Marines organized into units, exercising and training.

The pool that sits in the middle of the track is more of a small lake oasis surrounded by landscaped foliage. The windows of the elevator darken to an opaque black as they pass the next level. On the fifth level the windows once again become clear as the elevator comes to a halt. The team is met by a small group of scientists.

OCD7-Webb introduces the head scientist to the First Factor. His name is Dr. William Sharpe. He stands 5'8" with a pronounced belly. His unkempt hair and bushy beard directs focus to the darkened frames surrounding his eyes which are exhausted from an obvious lack of sleep. He greets the team with a "Welcome" that trembles on the verge of complete fatigue. He directs them into the lab as though he is racing time.

The first thing felt as each member of the team enters the room, is a frigid wave of air, desolate and forsaken. An air of dread dominates the lab, gripping each team member with glacial fingers. The scientists separate these docile savages of Recon and direct them to medical examination tables. The stainless steel tables are topped with a sheet-covered mattress and are ringed by restraints, reminiscent of medieval torture devices. The walls are all sterile, bleached white. The floor is kept at a cold forty-one degrees in order to aid in the control of this room's internal temperature. The room is the size of a large classroom and filled with technology that will not be spoken of outside of this lab for at least another decade. The strange-looking and unfamiliar technological devices add a feeling of trepidation to the Marines' experience. It floods over each of them worse than when they were behind enemy lines. Normalcy is instantly missed as it becomes a source of homesickness. "Uh... I'm gonna hafta use the bathroom, Staff Sergeant." Says the young corporal.

"I don't like this either, Gonzo. This is nothing like I expected. This is some mad-scientist white-people shit," whispers the sniper in response to the youth.

"I think I gotta take a dump," utters Gonzo. His stomach tightens from nervousness as the team is led deeper into the room.

Next to the vaulted, titanium, auto-activated double doors that the team entered through is a retina scanner for the scientists and guests of this level. There is a barrier wall with a large shatterproof window designed to protect witnesses from the processes carried out in this room. Instantly, Captain Edwards begins to think about Livingston's earlier statements about this being an experiment. He knows this feeling all too well; it feels exactly like the prison where he used to visit his father.

He peers at the three large examination tables and notices that each seems to be plugged into over a hundred different sensors. The scientists direct each team member to a separate bed, tugging on each of them more like laboratory animals rather than humans. Disgruntled apprehension is the response from the sniper as he rips his arm from a scientist and shoves him back, shouting, "Get your damn hands off-a-me! Captain this shit is crazy!" Livingston instinctively grabs the scientist's throat, squeezing it to block his air - the frail masked man falls to his knees. He is released with a short toss away from the Marine. "What in-tha-HELL are you planning to do to us?"

Gonzo nervously rips away from his scientists also and moves to the center of the room, placing his back against Livingston's. "Captain, this ain't right! It ain't right!"

Edwards glares at the scientists holding him with a controlled stern squint. He is released. The Force Recon Marine officer steps towards the center of the room joining his men - his family. "I stand with my men! Give us answers or you go to hell! It's your choice!"

Webb steps into the dank room with Dr. Sharpe beside him holding a clipboard. He positions himself before the Marine. "We are going to give you and your men power. We are going to change you into heroes greater than the norm. That is what you have been trained and groomed for your entire career, Captain Edwards."

Gonzo leans to the side to speak to Webb. "You're trying to turn us into da' burning thing that killed our teammates?!?"

Control of the conversation is secured by Dr. Sharpe, who works to reassure the team. "No, Corporal. What we are going to do is increase your natural energy level somewhere between 4 and 5 percent. It should make you a little stronger and faster, that's it. The entity that you fought had his energy levels increased to ranges that are way off of any charts. We are not authorized to do that and we never would because it could be dangerous."

Gonzo leans back with a slight reduction in his anxiety. Captain Edwards looks at Livingston's apprehensive expression, then readdresses Dr. Sharpe. "Sir, is this experiment safe?"

Webb holds his open hand out and places it on the chest of the doctor to stop him from answering. The boldness of the fire-haired civilian commander is second only to his confidence. He answers in place of the doctor, "Captain, this is an 'Enhancement Process' and it is perfectly safe. You have my word on it. We have taken every precaution to ensure the welfare of you and your team members. I promise."

The Marines, feeling more than a little sheepish because of their fears, which have been assuaged by the reassurance of their senior civilian commander, relax. They confer and silently agree to undergo the procedure for which they have been preparing.

Each of the three Marines moves to his respective table, and is secured to it by the restraints. The lab assistants fasten the straps on to Gonzo after he reaches for his crucifix and kisses it one last time. An IV is inserted into the arm of each patient with a drip-flow of a fluid labeled 'Andrionic-4.' Dr. Sharpe visits each Marine's table and performs a close, meticulous examination of the wires and sensors connected to their bodies. Webb leaves the lab and proceeds to the witness area behind the shatterproof glass to observe the procedures.

Dr. Sharpe completes his checks and goes over the paperwork on each of the clipboards at the end of each examination table. He knows that the team's strength and fortitude comes from their leader, so he makes it a point to visit him first. "How are you holding up, Captain Edwards?"

The captain lifts his head up slightly making sure not to jar the connector flat against his temple, "I'm alright, Sir. How long should this take?"

The scientist works to ease the trepidation within the captain by placing his hand on his shoulder and speaking firmly. "It will be over before you know it, Captain. Hell, you will probably be looking at the newest dirty magazines before me. Heck, I'll treat you to some, myself."

The captain relaxes his shoulders as he tries to smile through his uneasiness. He has to be strong for his men.

A large five-inch titanium tube coils down from the ceiling with a branch connection to the main power conduit feeding the other tables. The Captain is a field combat Marine above all else and to him the tube carries the appearance of a large snake stabbing from its hole. The weight of the steel-ringed tube head is felt upon his midsection as two assistants twist it clockwise onto the receiver ring on top of his chest, above his heart. He speaks to himself, each made up excuse justifying his cooperation, followed by a determined resolve for control. The quick scribble of Dr. Sharpe's pen against the extended checklist on his clipboard jolts the captain's attention back to focus.

"So what's it going to be, Captain Edwards? Do you like Penthouse, Playboy, or one of those raunchy small brands with foreign women?" Asks Dr. Sharpe.

"I can't do that, Sir, I'm married," replies the Captain.

Two tables over, the youngest member of the team, Corporal Gonzalez, turns his head with a large smirk on his face and anxiousness in his voice, "Hey yo, Captain, if you don't want them I am always here to lift those sinful burdens from you! I'll add them to my comic book collection."

Everyone in the laboratory laughs except for the final member of the team, Staff Sergeant Livingston. He holds his poise; for him each falsely smiling face in the room, other than his team mates – exists between unwelcomed and damned. He studies each person and each item in the room as though he is stalking another one of his targets. His response to the joke is the same as his response to everything else, stoic silence.

Each of the scientists exits the room as the technology begins to spring to life with blinking colors, blips, and beeps. The procedure is about to begin.

OCD7-Webb stands in the observation room waiting on Dr. Sharpe to begin the 'Enhancement Process.' Behind the duo other figures with as much anticipation as them stand wrapped in shadows. "Did everything check out, Dr. Sharpe?"

The doctor takes a seat beside the commander and pulls out his clipboard of notes to show the leader of the shadowed group. He then faces Webb and answers, recognizing him as a direct member, "Everything is going better than we expected, Commander Webb. Captain Edwards will be given a five percent N-ionic increase because of his size. We have him connected to the main conduit. It is significantly less than the amount administered in the past to create Nimlok, but it is the most that we feel that a human being can survive. He is the largest of the three and hopefully this will increase his chance for surviving this level of increase."

OCD7-Webb shrugs off the technical callousness of Dr. Sharpe's comments and inquires about the other two Marines. The doctor notices his pause and continues, "Staff Sergeant Livingston will be given a 4.75 percent increase in his natural levels of N-ionic energy, while the youngest, Corporal Gonzalez, will be given the safest increase of 4.50 percent."

Commander Webb then sits down in one of the observation chairs and informs the doctor that he may proceed. Dr. Sharpe exits the observation room, dons his anti-radiation protective suit, and enters the lab.

With a loud buzz and a crackle of energy, the experiment begins. Livingston is the first to jerk unnaturally from the energy burning into his being. His teeth grind against the mouth piece as his eyes ignite with a cerulean luminescence. His restraints tug tightly around his wrists as he churns in opposition. He has no more fear as hatred engulfs him, forcing him to witness what consciousness begs him to forget. The youth beside him shudders as his muscles tighten and his very blood begins to boil from the inside. Even through Gonzo's heaves and gasps he can smell the acrid odor of his very fluids evaporating through his flesh. His head slams repeatedly as his eyes roll backwards.

"HYDRATE HIM! He needs hydration now!!" Shouts Dr. Sharpe as his staff, also clothed in radiation-suits, shove IVs into the young Marine's arm. His violent coughs remind them that he lives as the pain sharply returning is a reminder to how fleeting life is.

"STOP!!! PLEASE STOP!! JESUS HELP ME STOP!!!" Gonzo cries out as Dr. Sharpe casts a glare to his staff member manning the overall energy output for each of the Marines. His nod is so slight that most would miss it because of the blinding lights created by the discharges of energy dancing within the room. A light twist of a dial and the press of a button increase the effects on each of the Recon Marines. This time, no screams can be heard as the process of DNA corruption, destruction, and rebuilding takes it place. Each Marine screams in pain from the agony of the change occurring in their physiology.

Corporal Gonzalez's body stiffens, his sensors begin to peak out as his flesh begins to ripple from the emerging veins pulsating beneath them. He gurgles without response as Dr. Sharpe waves his hand to drop the power on him. The limp patient breathes frantically as consciousness escapes him.

Livingston pulls and pulls as his back arches and releases. He refuses to scream as his ears, nose, and eyes begin to bleed. Dr. Sharpe holds his hand up waiting for the Marine's consciousness to give out. He steps alongside the medical tool table for a closer look only to discover absolute determination. The sniper's skin burns to a deep char-black as vibrant dashes of electricity begin to jump from his sweat; he does not scream. His skin begins to glow and swell before pulling tight; he still does not scream. His flesh ignites into a brilliant blue flame which explodes, knocking Dr. Sharpe back into Gonzo's table, then to the floor.

"Drop the power... cough, drop the power!" He calls out, only to go unheard through his wheezing. Meanwhile, the flames surrounding Staff Sergeant Livingston's flesh begins to change from blue to deep blood crimson. It is his eyes which will never be forgotten by the doctor, "His eyes..." he whispers; for they are the only contrasting radiance within the crimson swelter to remind him that the sniper is human. They glow a piercing blue towards the doctor as his staff cuts the power allowing his body to go limp. Consciousness finally escapes him and yet he did not scream.

The stench of burning flesh and the clanking of a large, coiled energy tube against the braces directing it from the ceiling to the final Marine's chest is the somber reminder as to the one destined to receive the highest output of energy. Captain Edwards cannot scream anymore, for the N-ionic energy fed merely as doses to the others was being delivered directly into his chest. His heart has already failed and his internal organs are in the process of following suit. He attempts to gasp, but with a heart burning and compressing from pure energy, it can't be determined if he is in need of air. His lips motion as his body lurches frantically for freedom. Between the intended screams of pain, his silent words utter, "Alicia." Dr. Sharpe knows not how to react to him as he stares as his digital pad displaying his life signs and failed organs. His screen is interrupted by a hasty written message coming from the observation room outside.

"Increase the power."

The message comes from OCD7-Webb. The doctor moves slowly away from the glowing captain and hesitates to raise his finger giving the order to his staff.

"Do it now, Sharpe! Don't play with me! Increase the power!"

Dr. Sharpe raises his finger as the lights dim and the coiled tube from the ceiling slams harder against its braces in response. Captain Edwards agonizes as his chest burns into a small sun of power. The light is so bright all vision is lost as his fireproof restraints catch flame and the very table beneath his body begins to melt.

"GODDAMN IT!! TURN IT OFF!! TURN IT OFF NOW!!" Shouts the doctor.

No controls respond as the powered tube rips free from the brackets and pushes all of the coils straight by slinging the large Marine's body into the display glass causing it to crack. Pure N-ionic energy pumps harder than ever into the heart of the captain as his voice returns, "AAAARRRRGGGGGHHHHH!!!!!"

With the heat rising drastically, Dr. Sharpe orders his staff to remove the other Marines while struggling with his exploding equipment to cease the experiment. He fails, as the captain instinctively grabs the edge of the tube connected to his chest to pull away from the source of his pain. His garb ignites and disintegrates as did all other cloths and leathers in the now empty room. Glass begins to shatter as metal warps and melts from the heat; amazingly, the naked Marine continues to pull against the tube.

Outside, Dr. Sharpe orders emergency fire suppressant release, which has limited impact on the chaos within the room. Instead, the captain's chest explodes, causing the entire floor to shake and the display window to shatter, exposing the onlookers, including General Black and Commander Webb. A secondary bomb shield slides down in place as the small group immediately engages in evacuation procedures from that floor.

As things begin to subside and the smoke begins to clear, the staff stands as amazed as their leader, staring at their final patient sitting upright in the corner of the lab. The tube is finally disconnected and laying on the ground before him while low-level energy remnants travel from the tube end to the 'heart' of the Captain. His chest has a large glasslike window on it with swirls of N-ionic energy dancing within.

"Uh... Dr. Sharpe... have you ever seen anything like this?" Asks one of his staff members.

"Never in my life," he responds, before checking the area for radiation and heat levels. Captain Edwards breathes slowly and steadily as he glimpses the approaching scientists, before falling unconscious. For him, his new life is about to begin.

CHAPTER 8

WAKING UP

Evolution is born from need and honed through time.
Change is born from want and honed through choice.

–Dr. Melvin Dalton

To: Members of the Omega Cabinet
CC: General Black

Subject Classification: Top Secret

Assignment 32A69: The Ministry Project
Scope: N-ionic development for immediate field deployment operations
Title: Enhancement Process – test 13

Dr. Sharpe's personal notes:

Standard scientific analysis teaches that the body creates electrical pulses which stimulate the nerves that control all body movements and functions. Very little research had been performed on the type of electrical pulses the brain produces until 1995.

The discovery of Particle-N ionic energy by Dr. Melvin Dalton has changed the entire path of all genetic science. It must be noted that I was honored to work with him during this discovery.

Particle-N ionic energy is the bio-energy created by the brain used to stimulate the nerves that control basic body movements and functions; it is NOT electrical at all. We have also discovered that the base form of this energy also controls the advanced functions of all living cells within a body, the chromosomes, the DNA, etc. in short, the full range of the genetic building components.

The scientific code name issued to this new found Particle-N ionic energy was 'N-ionic Energy.'

We performed a total of 13 controlled experiments of N-ionic Energy manipulation on volunteer Marines over the last decade in an effort to perfect the enhancement process. All have failed to achieve anything close to our expected or desired results; that is, until now. Other than this enhancement process, we have only had one other in which at least one of the candidates survived. Our greatest achievement quickly became our deepest nightmare, with the 'incident' resulting in the creation of Nimlok; he became death incarnate. All mistakes and sub-routine miscalculations, along with proposed solutions have been recorded in Assignment 32A12 for review.

Each test has provided us with crucial data that we have used in order to permanently increase the basic N-ionic Energy output levels of an

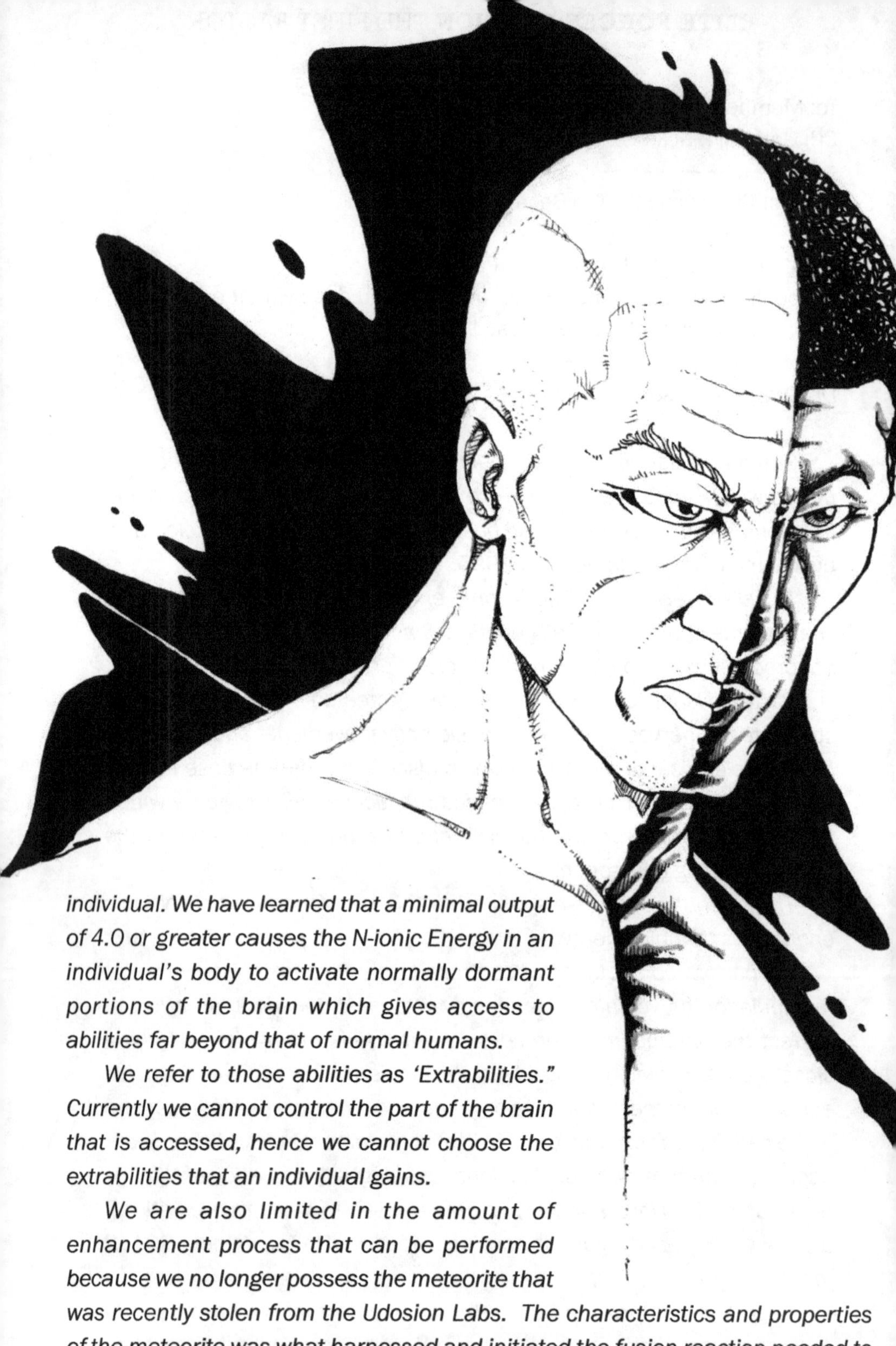

individual. We have learned that a minimal output of 4.0 or greater causes the N-ionic Energy in an individual's body to activate normally dormant portions of the brain which gives access to abilities far beyond that of normal humans.

We refer to those abilities as 'Extrabilities." Currently we cannot control the part of the brain that is accessed, hence we cannot choose the extrabilities that an individual gains.

We are also limited in the amount of enhancement process that can be performed because we no longer possess the meteorite that was recently stolen from the Udosion Labs. The characteristics and properties of the meteorite was what harnessed and initiated the fusion reaction needed to *perform the experiments.*

We currently have enough of the meteorite for one more 'enhancement process.' It is CRITICAL that the original meteorite is located and returned in order for our entire project to be a success.

-Dr. William Sharpe

With a single click, the email is sent through one of the most encrypted networks on the planet. The portly Dr. Sharpe stands up in the dimly lit room and rubs his eyes while stretching. He turns to grab his clipboard beside his computer and stares at the names of the three Marines and the date of the procedure, which was a week ago. Today is special because the last two Marines are finally awake from the enhancement process. The doctor is anxious to discover what extrabilities have been gained by each of his subjects. With that in mind, he exits his office and heads down the hall.

Scientists scurry through the hallways while Elite Forces guards vigilantly protect each subject's door. The first room that the doctor enters is Corporal Gonzalez's. He awakened two days before the others and has already been through a comprehensive group of tests. His attitude is positive and physique is perfect. When Dr. Sharpe enters the room Corporal Gonzalez greets him before he can say a word.

"Hey yo, Doc, I feel GREAT! I don't know what you did but I will tell you that it feels good!"

Dr. Sharpe reviews his paperwork then presses his fingers against the Corporal's neck. "Are you telling me that you don't feel any pain at all?"

Corporal Gonzalez leans back with a raised eyebrow and a smile, "Not a bit. Am I supposed to? Where are da' others? When am I going to see them?" The youth displays a mischievous grin, then winks. "Oh yeah, I didn't forget about the nasty magazines you promised back in the lab. You still have them... riiight?"

Just as Dr. Sharpe begins to answer, the door swings open and a scientist enters in a hurry telling the doctor that they have an emergency and he is needed. Dr. Sharpe speeds out the room into the hallway with Gonzalez following behind him.

They enter the hallway just in time to witness a scientist being thrown through the doorway, from the neighboring room, to the other side of the hall.

Out of the doorway comes an unknown white male with another security person on his back. He twists around and charges into the wall, ensuring the security person receives the brunt of the impact and forcing the guard to release him. He looks across the corridor at Dr. Sharpe. The doctor tries to calm him down. Two Elite Forces guards stand prepared at the side of the doctor waiting on his command.

"Staff Sergeant Livingston, please calm down. Your loss of control is causing unnecessary injury and damage!"

With sweat rolling down his forehead, the white male takes a step forward, grabbing the sleeve of his ripped shirt and tearing it off to reveal more of his flesh.

"Look at what you've done ta me, you bastard! I'm WHITE! You've turned me into a goddamn white-man!!"

Corporal Gonzalez stands shocked by what he is witnessing. He can see pure rage growing in the blue eyes of his teammate. The sharpened features of his staff sergeant's face appear almost blazing against his new peach-hued skin. He tries to speak and yet there are no words to leave his mouth. The white man, Staff Sergeant Livingston, stands face to face with Dr. Sharpe and clenches his fist. Suddenly a strong voice is heard through the hallway which causes everyone to turn around.

"Stand down, Staff Sergeant!"

Captain Edwards stands in the middle of the corridor shirtless, wearing only medical trousers. His body is surrounded with a thin soft crimson glow. Over his heart there is a large glass-like circular opening in his chest. There appears to be energy within it swirling around like a reactor of some sort. The Captain rubs his fingers across the car on his forehead then across the glass opening on his chest. "You're not the only one that went through changes, Liv!"

Livingston watches his best friend turn around and slowly fall against the doorway of his room, causing the very edge of the frame to crack and crumble. Edwards's nose begins to bleed as two scientists rush over to aid him. He staggers groggily into his room with blood all over his chest and trousers. There is an eternity of silence for all of the rest standing in the hallway. The staff sergeant turns a final time to look at Dr. Sharpe and then Corporal Gonzalez and walks back into his room, disgusted. His door closes behind him with a swishing sound. There are no more words spoken as the entire corridor clears.

CHAPTER 9

FIRST AMERICAN ACCEPTANCE

"Evil has always been a point of view."

In downtown New York there is a thirty story building in which seven of the floors are leased by one of the most successful financial companies in the nation. The company is First American Acceptance. The CEO is extremely popular across the United States. He has three weekly shows and one daily show broadcast on seven different television stations. He currently earns ninety million dollars a year. His father resides as head of the board of directors for the entire corporation. His family name alone is worth well above a hundred million dollars. This company manages ninety percent of the financial transactions of the United States Government's Special Operations and Elite Operations divisions; this is held with the utmost confidence for each one of these clients. The CEO has been serving a darker master for the last two years because of this information and today he is going to receive a surprise visitor. This day will change the CEO's life forever. His name is Andrew Joseph Schwartz.

It is Friday and it is 4:40 p.m., twenty minutes before the formal start of New York's infamous rush hour. Above the building a helicopter surrounded by a small swarm of flying mechanical beetle-like vehicles lands on the roof. Each vehicle carries a single, uniformed paramilitary rider wearing a gas mask to hide his identity. A figure clad in blue and gold insect-like armor exits the craft. The sheen of his armor reminds one of the wing effects of a horsefly. He raises his hand and commands all of the flying "beetles" to land as the soldiers surround the craft. A massive framed warrior, carrying a large war-mace, steps from the craft, followed by twenty additional soldiers in light armor carrying M-16 assault rifles. They move, robot-like, in quick, short bursts to form a perimeter around the roof of the building. The only soldier moving with a smooth, human-like gait wears three stars on his chest and multi-colored stripes on each of his shoulders.

The final person to debark the helicopter is the leader, escorted by an unlikely bodyguard, a nonchalant and slouchy man in jade raiment fitting his soft-toned body like a second skin. Moving with a purpose, the leader stands four inches above six feet and his slender frame carries a startlingly light weight of no more than a hundred and sixty pounds. The slim man pauses for an instant to correct the sleeves on his tailor-made Huntsman business suit. Each of his movements is with the occupational prestige of a business executive. His saturnine and striking appearance is attributed to a powdery white skin tone with each vein and wrinkle deeply etched in an unearthly electric blue. His gleaming obsidian hair, freshly trimmed and groomed, sharply contrasts the pale border of sunken cheeks and jutting, cleft chin.

The leader faces the massive-framed warrior, who stands an intimidating height of somewhere near seven feet, and speaks in a calm commanding tone, "Shrine, disable all security and cameras."

Shrine's solid leg muscles bunch and bulge as he lumbers with great force towards the rooftop power center, causing small tremors with his eight hundred pounds of weight. His hair is close cut, curled into small angry fists of fiery wool. An obliging snarl escapes his lips just before he rends the security gate with his bare hands. He then proceeds to the building's security data panel, breathing like a beast through his animal-like nostrils, and tears the front panel off of its hinges. He shoves his calloused hand into the open circuitry and grabs all of the wires. Connectors begin to spark and sear against his dry, metal-like flesh; an electrical fire erupts briefly then smothers into a thin char that indicates the eradication of the entire circuit board. Shrine removes his hand slowly and raises his other hand, the one holding his war-mace. The staff of the mace is made from a compressed titanium alloy wrapped with durable leather in the center for grip. The head of the weapon is made of a black, dense metal known as osmium; embedded in the head are four flat, rectangular, ruby-colored gems. He smashes the entire security box with a single swing from his two hundred-pound weapon and then approaches his leader, the slim businessman. Speaking in a deep baritone voice, his words crack slightly, making his speech sound accented as if in an old world Romance language. "Security, cameras, communication, and power have been discontinued, Lord Syphon." The giant is soothing in his simple unquestioning obedience.

The leader, Lord Syphon, nods with approval then turns to the insect man and the general leading the soldiers.

"Warbug, send your beetle riders down to the twenty-ninth floor of the building. General, I want all exits on the twenty-ninth floor blocked with half of the men from your group. Contain all of the people there and I want you to personally hold Mr. Schwartz until I arrive."

The general turns to his soldiers to relay the orders but stops briefly to correct the leader, "Lord Syphon, I am a true follower of my faith and a soldier to her call. I am an Apostle of her service and I expect to be acknowledged in that fashion. The same goes for my comrade who controls the very technology that protects our escape."

Lord Syphon nods in agreement with the experienced soldier and apologizes with a prudent respect. He then restates his previous command, referring to the soldier as Apostle General the second time.

The soldiers then divide into smaller groups and take different routes down to the twenty-ninth floor.

Lord Syphon turns to the slouching man in jade and raises one hand, opening it palm up with a maniacal smile on his face, "Stalker, if you would, indulge me with a flaming entrance to the twenty-ninth floor. Straight down through the other floors, if you please."

Stalker smiles as his eyes turn yellow and green flames erupt from his body, creating incandescent heat; an eerie green wave of energy burns through the rooftop. The radiant emerald flames slither and crawl over his body before answering his compelling command of destruction. He burns a molten cylindrical tunnel of passage straight down to the desired floor.

Lord Syphon waits a couple of minutes for the smoke to clear and raises both of his hands as a bright, white aura begin to emanate from them, causing both he and Shrine to float. While the duo levitates downward through the newly created hole to the twenty-ninth floor, the advance team gathers the entire staff as terrified hostages. The Apostle Warbug grabs Mr. Schwartz and brings him over to the leading soldier. "Apostle General, this is the individual that we are seeking."

The Apostle General scoffs with derision, then places a handgun to the temple of the man and guides him to the center of the room. Lord Syphon lands softly, then walks forward while peering deeply into the eyes of Mr. Schwartz. "I have been informed that you have asked for an increase in compensation for the information that I seek, Mr. Schwartz."

Stalker walks up to one side of Lord Syphon while Shrine takes a station on the other. Lord Syphon turns around to face Mr. Schwartz's staff and says, "We do not negotiate with Americans, Mr. Schwartz. This is because their greed has no limits. They would lay with a family member and betray all that they love for money. America is a prostitute and you are the married man driving around seeking her services. The morals within this whore do not exist. I despise her and the bastard children that she bears."

Lord Syphon directs his hand forward, surrounding one of the older secretaries with energy which paralyzes her movements. He then steps towards her with a casual elegance and fondles the skin on her face with his cold pale fingers. He continues his conversation with the terror-stricken CEO as his focus on the woman offers a hollow form of compassion.

"When are they moving the weapons, Mr. Schwartz? Convoys cost money and if you follow a dollar, it always tells the sins of the owner."

Broken arrogance stutters information from the CEO's lips in almost a repetitious pattern of ambiguous tones between swallows. "I-In about t-two weeks...In a-about two weeks...I'll get you all of the details for free, Lord Syphon. Please, don't kill me...the convoy is moving in about two weeks...please..."

Lord Syphon gently removes his hand from the woman's face and releases his energy around her, causing her to drop to the ground. He continues to survey the woman's elderly beauty while delivering his comments to the cowering CEO contemptuously. "I will not kill you today, Mr. Schwartz, for you are a necessary evil for my endeavors. You are my personal American leech and I will treat you as such."

He then whisks his face around quickly staring at Schwartz once again while sneering with evil. "Apostle General, order your men to kill every person in here!"

The Apostle General looks at his men, then looks at his comrade, the Apostle Warbug, and raises his right hand, making a slicing gesture across his neck as the masked soldiers open fire and hack into Schwartz's staff, killing each of them. Many of the cries in agony are cut short by the gurgling of blood. Person after person falls before their boss, some attempting to beg, as all do in situations such as this, but to no avail. Death is delivered to them with a systematic approach. Stalker stands beside Lord Syphon and struggles to hold back his giggles from his amusement at the carnage. The body of Schwartz's personal secretary falls in front of Shrine, twitching from the blood lost through her slashed throat. Shrine drops to one knee and uses his finger to create an arcane symbol with her blood on her forehead. He mumbles a final prayer to his lord of darkness for the delivery of her soul and stands once again beside Lord Syphon.

Schwartz screams out with tears in his eyes and fear in his heart. He collapses to the ground, then scrambles to his knees, shaking and with sweat running down his face. Lord Syphon grabs his face and raises his head up, forcing him to survey the loss of life within the room. "This is power, Mr. Schwartz. In the next three weeks, two of your board members will die in car crashes, one will be killed in a home robbery, and your father will die in five years from the disease that he contracted from one of my whore-assassins...that happens to be a beautiful American actress. Do not ever think of failing me again."

Lord Syphon then slaps the kneeling man as he cowers back in horror against his desk, "We are the Third Nation, Mr. Schwartz."

The Apostle General looks at his comrade The Apostle Warbug and the soldiers a final time, then points to the doorway as they follow his unsaid order and begin to disperse to the roof for pickup. Stalker goes to the middle of the floor and looks back toward Lord Syphon waiting on his command. Surrounding his body and Shrine's with his aura, Syphon levitates upward back through the tunnel entrance while speaking down to Mr. Schwartz.

"I suggest that you evacuate, my little American leech. The police and the FBI will have nothing more than a pile of ash to investigate after Stalker is finished. Oh, yes, please don't get too upset over the incidents that have just occurred, after all...it was just business!"

Schwartz stumbles to his feet and then runs awkwardly through the emergency exit, half falling and slipping in puddles of blood as he races down the stairs. Stalker grits his teeth and begins to strain while screaming out, causing the entire room to explode into viridian and amber flames. The explosion blows out all of the windows, causing debris to fall twenty-nine floors to the ground below.

The traffic jam caused by the falling debris makes it nearly impossible for fire trucks and rescue vehicles to reach the building. Lord Syphon and his team enter their helicopter and escape unconcerned.

Andrew Joseph Schwartz sits in the stair well on the twenty-first floor, shaking, sweating and crying from the trauma that he had just survived. It is going to be at least another twenty minutes before fire and rescue reach him. He knows that his entire staff will be nothing but ashes swirling in the wind.

He joined this organization for money and power, just as Lord Syphon stated. The price for his arrogance and fame was the loss of his soul and the death of his staff. The deliverers of his punishment would be a name that he will never forget... The Third Nation.

CHAPTER 10

TEST RESULTS

The conference room is dim and cool as the team takes their place at the side of a long black lacquer table with OCD7 Webb and Dr. Sharpe at the head of it. At the far end of the conference table sits General Black. One wall holds several large HD monitors. Hidden in the shadows at the periphery of the room are other figures, identified only by a soft luminescent number below them. General Black stands to speak, "Good afternoon, Gentlemen. We are here to review the results from the N-ionic human enhancement experiment carried out a month ago. Please hold any questions you may have until the end of the briefing. Presenting the results of the procedure will be Dr. William Sharpe, the lead scientist in this project."

Dr. Sharpe stands. Like most people, he feels apprehension about speaking in public. The shadowy nature of the room and the purposefully obfuscated audience reinforces this natural fear. He does not know exactly who is in the room, but he knows they all wield a tremendous amount of political and financial power. He nervously picks up the remote control for the projection device on the table. He feels the buttons on the remote and depresses the control that starts the presentation. Three displays come on simultaneously, one for each team member. He then turns to address the general: "We have been monitoring all three of the subjects closely and we have some collected preliminary but still significant data...positive and negative, sir."

"Give me the details," commands General Black.

"The experiment caused each subject to enter a coma-like state as their bodies recovered from the effects. Corporal Gonzalez recovered consciousness in about three days and proved to be in excellent health. The other two didn't awaken until about two days after him. Their recoveries did not fare so well."

General Black interrupts, adding to the doctor's nervousness, "I want to know everything that happened, get to the point! Tell us something good." General Black sternly places his fists on table.

"Yes sir! First, Captain Edwards has a glass like opening on his chest in the shape of the connector for the cable that was attached to him. We believe that it burned into his chest, causing the flesh in that area to transform into this clear covered shape. We have tested it and it has most of the properties of normal flesh. The main difference is that it is almost impenetrable. In fact, that was the main issue we had with Captain Edwards. We did not have any devices that would penetrate his flesh, except for gladium-lensed, high-powered lasers."

"This is remarkable, Doctor," comments one of the shrouded

onlookers.

Captain Edwards sits attentive to the words spoken, but critical of the responses received. The mere elation heard in the last comment makes him wonder about the end goals of this project. Trust is hard to come by in his line of work, but he holds to his decision to serve his country by serving this command.

"Staff Sergeant Livingston went through the most drastic change of the three. The experiment caused all of his natural pigmentation to change and diminish. His hair has thinned out and his eye color has changed from a dark brown to a very light blue. His skin has changed from brown to white. Staff Sergeant Livingston appears to have literally changed from an African-American to a Caucasian. This also opens up another area in racial research."

"That is very interesting, Doctor, but we're not here for racial research. What have we learned about their capabilities?" Asks the general. "We want to know if they have gained any 'extrabilities'....or if all of this has been in vain."

Dr. Sharpe raises both palms in front of him, shrugging anxiously. He steps towards the Marines as if to protect them and himself.

"No, sir. No, sir, this was not in vain! Each one of these Marines has changed in amazing ways!"

"Now, this is what I want to hear...don't make us wait any longer, Doctor," states one of the shrouded inquisitors.

"We have not completed all of the testing yet. Here is the information that we have acquired so far. Corporal Gonzalez has registered an exponential increase in certain natural functions and abilities within his body. His bone and muscle durability have increased to somewhere near two to three times that of a normal human. His organs currently function approximately three times more efficiently. Corporal Gonzalez bench pressed five-hundred pounds in the weight room yesterday and held his breath for ten minutes in the pool while exercising underwater."

The creaking grin on Corporal Gonzalez's boyish face crinkles with the wildness of immaturity as he lightly taps Staff Sergeant Livingston under the table. The look from his blue-eyed responding elder slaps the smile from the youth's face without moving a muscle.

The general lights a cigar, adding the aroma of black cherry to the cool air inside the room. He knows that smoking is prohibited in government facilities, but he is, after all a general. Besides, it always helped him to think more clearly. He looks down towards the table at a small stack of manila folders containing information about each Marine. He briefly glances over Corporal Gonzalez's folder then, pleased, turns back to Dr. Sharpe.

"This is outstanding."

Dr. Sharpe's poise becomes more self-assured as he directs his attention to the sniper. Clearing his throat, "Staff Sergeant Livingston is once again probably the most amazing change that I have seen in an individual. His reflexes are registering as twice the normal reaction time of a normal human. His brain functions have also been changed. Staff Sergeant Livingston now has an uncanny ability to focus and calculate distance. He can see a little over six times farther than a normal person with crystal clarity. His accuracy is near faultless now. We literally watched him throw knives into fruits from twenty-five yards."

From out of the shadows, a seemingly disembodied voice emerges, "This is what we are looking for."

I feel like a stinkin' guinea pig, sitting here, Livingston thinks to himself. Disregarding the kid beside him as ignorant of the capabilities of 'white-government,' he looks to Captain Edwards. He searches his best friend for a reaction and possibly confirmation that they were nothing more than lab rats in a successful experiment. It is the slight glimmer of the reflecting shadows riding along the captain's clenching jaw that confirms the sniper's belief.

Guinea pigs we are, he resolves to himself as a light shimmer of energy jumps from his hands under the table.

The doctor, now excited, interjects more information to the general before the silhouettes watching can take over. "I'm not finished, Sir. Staff Sergeant Livingston has demonstrated the ability to create N-ionic energy in his hands."

Many of the shadowed figures begin to speak amongst themselves. General Black stands from his chair, leaning forward with both of his hands bracing him up on the desk.

"What?"

"He can not only create the energy and control its power level and intensity but he can stretch it and use it almost like a slingshot. We are still testing the range and limits of this ability."

One of the shadowed figures speaks again directly to the doctor, "What happened with the captain?"

"Captain Edwards...well...ummm...the simplest way to describe his change is to basically consider him a nearly impenetrable living generator of N-ionic power. His potential strength, endurance, and stamina extend beyond our ability to measure! Each day of his recovery has been marked with an increase in his strength and raw power. We are hypothesizing that every time...and I mean every time Captain Edwards moves, his body is storing N-ionic energy and converting it into pure power. A normal human dissipates used N-ionic energy, while he appears to store it. Although he is increasing his power only a tiny percentage at a time...it is adding up. Currently, because of the changes in his body, it appears that his true storage capability could be limitless. We are still testing this hypothesis."

"Exactly, how strong do you think that Captain Edwards is right now, Doctor?"

"Yesterday during testing he picked up a small car and threw it. Monday he held an exploding grenade in his hands and suffered no harm."

There is a short pause creating an eerie silence in the room. It is broken by the voice of General Black.

"Does he have any side effects that we should be concerned about at this time, Dr. Sharpe?"

The doctor points at the manila folder on the table labeled 'Captain Edwards.'

"The most moving side effect of his new found extrabilities is that he has lost his tactile sensations. This causes him to crush objects that he's holding and break things without knowing it. We are working closely with him on this issue. He is damn near invulnerable, General."

"Thank you for your report, Dr. Sharpe. Please continue to monitor and prepare these Marines for action. Give them one week of liberty and get them started on a training program ASAP, under the command of Sergeant Major Hannibal Tyr. We need these Marines in the field. Our enemies won't wait!"

CHAPTER 11

TRAINING

"Train. For what you practice, is what you do best!"

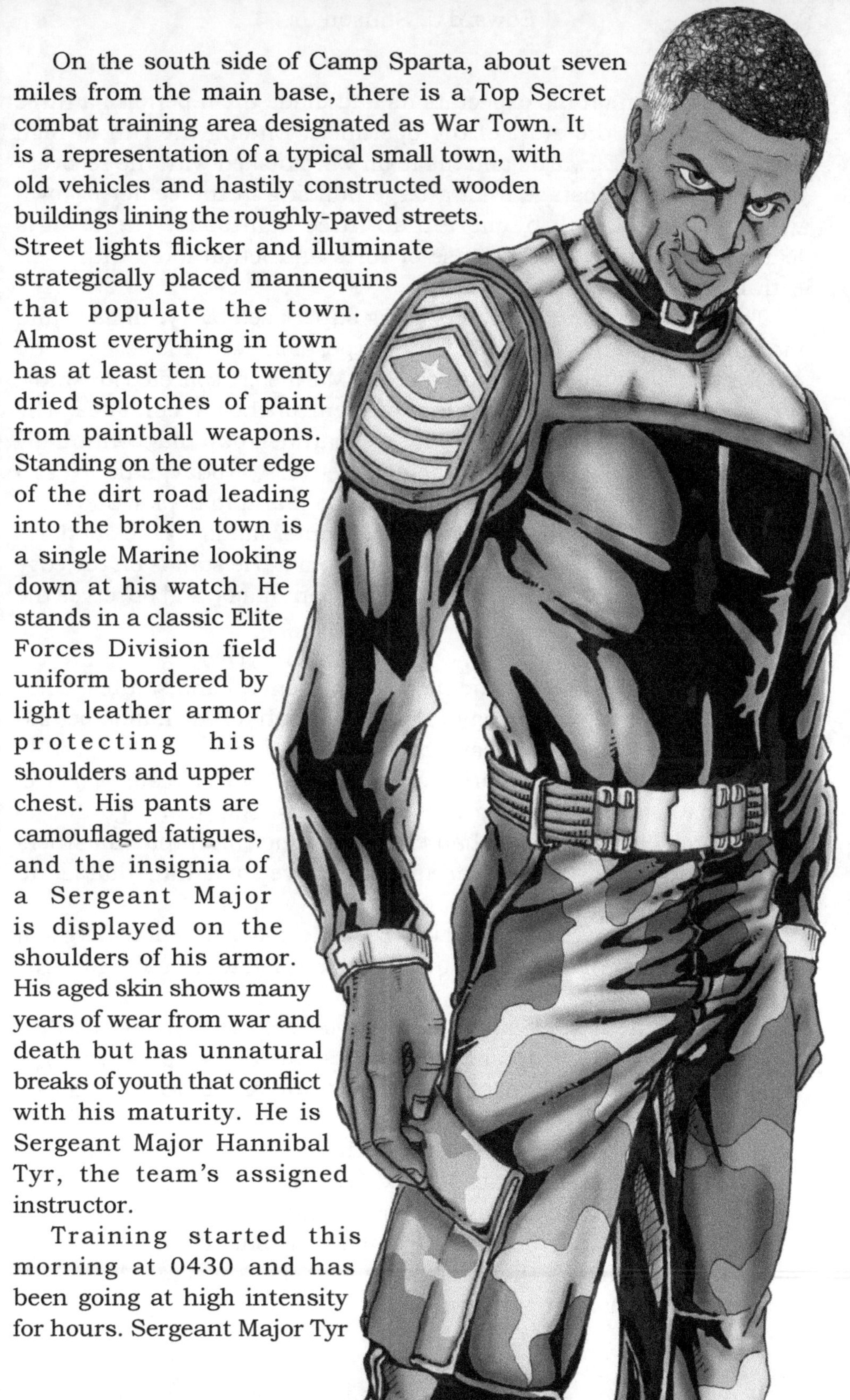

On the south side of Camp Sparta, about seven miles from the main base, there is a Top Secret combat training area designated as War Town. It is a representation of a typical small town, with old vehicles and hastily constructed wooden buildings lining the roughly-paved streets. Street lights flicker and illuminate strategically placed mannequins that populate the town. Almost everything in town has at least ten to twenty dried splotches of paint from paintball weapons. Standing on the outer edge of the dirt road leading into the broken town is a single Marine looking down at his watch. He stands in a classic Elite Forces Division field uniform bordered by light leather armor protecting his shoulders and upper chest. His pants are camouflaged fatigues, and the insignia of a Sergeant Major is displayed on the shoulders of his armor. His aged skin shows many years of wear from war and death but has unnatural breaks of youth that conflict with his maturity. He is Sergeant Major Hannibal Tyr, the team's assigned instructor.

Training started this morning at 0430 and has been going at high intensity for hours. Sergeant Major Tyr briefed the team on his expectations and made them perform a three mile run before the start of the operation. Ending the run in high spirits, Captain Edwards and his team were tasked with the recovery of a mannequin hostage from a large building in the center of town without being struck by more than three paintballs. The team is learning how to replace the use of rifles and lethal force with their extrabilities and wits.

The entire training session is being supervised by Tyr himself and monitored by OCD7-Webb and Dr. Sharpe, along with his select group of scientists. Thousands of notes on each Marine are collected for study, analysis and ultimately, the improvement of their techniques. The commander stands on the side with a separate group that continually photographs the team during their maneuvers. Today is their third week of training and the anxiety of the command to deploy this team in the field becomes obvious when a helicopter lands on the outskirts of the war town and General Black exits from it. He stands on the edge of the broken paved street beside the sergeant major and observes the Marines in action.

"How are they performing, Sergeant Major Tyr?"

The ebony-skinned Marine turns to the general and salutes. Once General Black returns the salute he places both of his hands behind his back before answering candidly.

"It is good that Recon Marines were chosen for this team, General. The adjustment from killing the enemy and using heavy gunfire to solve a problem was easier than expected. I have been pushing them hard for the last few weeks and today we have something that is fun for them, if inconvenient."

General Black jerks his head in a brusque nod of assent to Sergeant Major Tyr. The general then returns his attention to Captain Edwards and his men.

Each Marine is soaked in sweat and covered with paint and dirt. The general watches Captain Edwards use his enhanced strength to rip off the top of a small car off to make it into an improvised shield.

"This is good. He improvises, I like that," states the Sergeant Major.

The captain protects himself and the other two members of his team from swarms of paintballs fired from automatic weapons being held by the simulated enemy soldiers in the surrounding buildings. Staff Sergeant Livingston creates small, light blue energy balls with his hands and throws them at enemy soldiers, knocking them back whenever he can get into range.

Sergeant Major Tyr takes notice of the staff sergeant's limited range and approaches Dr. Sharpe, who is already noting it on the paper on his clipboard. The sergeant major looks at the doctor's clipboard and points his finger at one of the entries scribbled under 'potential weapon aids.' Dr. Sharpe acknowledges the sergeant major's choice by asking him if he is sure. Sergeant Major Tyr responds, "His accuracy is uncanny. His limited range will create longer times to close in on the enemy and cost lives. The bow option you have written can be the improvement that he needs." With that being said, Dr. Sharpe uses his cell phone to contact the technological research department.

Once Captain Edwards and his team reaches the front of the building containing the hostage, Corporal Gonzalez goes into action using his enhanced agility to scale the outside of the building by hopping from floor to floor. There are hundreds of paintballs shot at him and two strike him before he makes it to the third floor, where the hostage is located. Just as he enters the room and grabs the hostage, the inside door bursts open, revealing three enemy soldiers who start blasting paintballs at him. Corporal Gonzalez throws the mannequin out of the window and yells to Captain Edwards before getting shot multiple times by paintballs. Dr. Sharpe approaches Sergeant Major Tyr, now trusting his judgment, and shows him the paper on his clipboard with weapon entries under Corporal Gonzalez's name. The sergeant major points at the shield and tells the doctor to change the design by shrinking it and making it more mobile. Dr. Sharpe agrees and steps away from the sergeant major to make another phone call.

Captain Edwards drops the car roof he is holding and jumps into the air. He snatches the mannequin like a center fielder grabbing a fly ball, while crashing into the second floor of the neighboring building. Staff Sergeant Livingston throws multiple energy orbs at the enemy soldiers to distract them and to provide cover for the Captain. This is in vain; the sniper is taken down in seconds by a hail of paintballs. He is a sniper and this makes it obvious that he is being used wrong.

Captain Edwards stands with the mannequin under one of his arms and hears a small group of soldiers gathering outside of the door. He then does something unexpected and punches downward into the floor, causing it to collapse and giving him a quick escape to the first floor. He lands on the first floor and darts across the street into another building. Once inside that building, he decides to push his invulnerability to the limit and charges into the side wall, exploding through it and into the building beside it. He repeats it over and over until he bursts through each building leading back to the starting point of the mission.

Captain Edwards makes it to the end roaring with the voice of victory while holding the mannequin above his head. He then pauses with everyone staring at him and notices the missing right leg on the hostage. Corporal Gonzalez starts to giggle as Dr. Sharpe shakes his head with his pen at his lips, "Failure."

Everyone begins to laugh out loud as the Captain drops the mannequin to chuckle in between breaths. Staff Sergeant Livingston stands dourly for a moment then turns and walks away. Sergeant Major Tyr stands before the scientists and the team. "Laugh all you want. Two of you would have died if this was real. Clear your heads and fix the problems with this mission."

Everyone takes a break as General Black approaches Sergeant Major Tyr and Commander Webb and directs them away from the hearing distance of others. He pulls out a black cherry cigar and lights it, causing a smooth stream of smoke to outline the side of his face. "Gentlemen, I am going to make this quick. The President of the United States and the Omega Cabinet have reviewed the summaries of your notes and plans for this new strike team. They have both approved the tactical use of this team. They want us ready for action as soon as possible and have allocated a budget of a billion dollars for your next year of operations. Commander Webb, you will be totally responsible for budgetary transactions. I want these Devil-Dogs ready to go ASAP."

The general rubs his thumb along his cigar and inhales while watching the excitement on Webb's face. "The entire seventh level of Daylight Labs has been designated for the team's use. You have full access to it, Commander Webb, along with the members of your new marketing staff. Sergeant Major Tyr, you already have placement on another floor of the complex, but you will be given full access to the level. Dr. Sharpe and selected members of his team have limited access to sections of this level."

General Black gives a manila folder to each of them. He then leans forward with a grim look on his face. "Commander Webb, the strike team will be going public just as proposed by our superiors. This will be the first time the general public will have any idea that The Elite Forces Division exists. You are the main gateway of information control to the public."

Standing straight the General looks over at the Marines taking a break from training and focuses in on Captain Edwards. Without changing his view he speaks to Commander Webb, "You must have faith in the leadership abilities of the Captain." He then redirects his attention to the sergeant major. "Sergeant Major Tyr, train them right, oorah?"

"Oorah," responds the Sergeant Major.

General Black turns to walk away. He stops to flick the ashes from the tip of his cigar and says a final comment to both of the men. "Oh, I almost forgot, the tech department created new uniforms and codenames for these Devil-Dogs along with some toys. Get the men acquainted with them."

OCD7-Webb looks at the sergeant major, who is looking back at him. Both men shift their gaze to watch the general leave in the helicopter that brought him. Sergeant Major Tyr marches over to the gathered group of Marines and scientists. He gives them the rest of the day off. Webb informs Captain Edwards that tonight will be their last night sleeping in the labs on the fifth level and that they are now authorized to eat in the main cafeteria on the second level for dinner.

The team is excited about the news and leaves the training area, keeping all questions to themselves. A van arrives to transport the men. A skinny, bald driver steps out of the vehicle and introduces himself to the men. "How are you guys doing? The name's Worm; I'm your ride back to base. Go ahead and hop in."

The team enters the van and begins their ride back. Almost the entire trip is spent in silence with each person gazing out of his window deep in thought about the things said by their new trainer, Sergeant Major Tyr. Corporal Gonzalez is the first to speak when the ride is near its end. "Hey Captain, how long they gonna have us doing this stuff? It's been a month already and we ain't been able to leave da base yet." The youth ponders in an appearance of amusement and associates their situation with what he knows best: "You know that this is just like da guys in my Hero Federation comic, they're like stuck in their building for da first month training how ta be a team."

Captain Edwards looks at the driver and notices that he is wearing the single bar of a first lieutenant on his collar. He hesitates with another officer present, and becomes careful of his professionalism. He responds to the corporal, "I don't know, Gonzo. We're going to have to make the most of this and try to stay motivated. They have put a lot of trust in us by gifting us with these pow... er, uhm... 'extrabilities.'"

Staff Sergeant Livingston speaks to the first lieutenant driving, ignoring all respect for his rank. "No. They made us weapons. I ain't a fool, Captain, I know white folks all too well." The direction of the sniper's conversation shifts abruptly to the driver. "They call you Worm, hunh? What in-tha-hell's going on around here, sir? What are they going ta do with us?"

The driver smiles with a quick look back at the sullen staff sergeant and says, "You guys are the future! The people around here don't see you as weapons. They see you as heroes. Hell, you're Super-Marines!! You have no idea how important you are to the entire division as a whole. You guys will be like the superheroes from the past. There are only a few departments that even know that you exist right now. Wouldja believe, the EF-Guardsmen platoons have been whispering about you guys for the last two weeks. Now that you're here there are all kinds of rumors going around about how great you are." The first lieutenant reaches out with his words and uses an analogy similar to Corporal Gonzalez's.

"You're going to be bigger than Atum-Ra and the entire Hero Federation!" Youthful excitement swallows Corporal Gonzalez – Worm is nearly as excited as the youth. "I've been around the block and trust me when I tell you that it is a big deal for you to be trained by Sergeant Major Hannibal Tyr. The guy's a living legend and you guys work with him every day. That guy is the ultimate Leatherneck. He can fight a war alone. Even high ranking officers stay away from him. The guy is that good!"

Corporal Gonzalez's face illuminates with a grin from ear to ear while the captain is apprehensive. Staff Sergeant Livingston rubs his fingers against the glass as though he is testing it and stares at the white skin on his hand. He thinks about his racial change and keeps his feelings to himself. He continues to question the driver. "You still ain't answered my question, Worm. What are they going ta do with us? They gave us all of this power....for what?"

The transport van pulls into the Daylight Labs surface garage, then parks beside the entrance elevator.

"I have no idea what's planned for you and your teammates, but I do want you to know that there are a lot of us out here who believe in you guys. Don't hesitate to contact us if you need us!"

The team exits the van, which drives away promptly. They are more confused now than when they first entered the van. Standing in gloomy reserve, Captain Edwards speaks freely. "We are their tools. They gave us power as easy as they gave us guns. Nothing comes for free; I don't believe that you're far from the truth, Liv. The only thing that we can do is have faith and stay in control. The mission should always come first."

Corporal Gonzalez leads the way to the elevator and presses the button while trying to hurry the others. Captain Edwards rubs the 'Y' scar on his forehead as his best friend watches him, knowing that action means he is deep in thought; Captain Edwards does not like to lose control of a situation. The secrets surrounding the team remind him sorely of how little control he really has. The elevator doors open as Corporal Gonzalez stands in the doorway to keep the doors ajar then watches the others with a feeling of inadequacy.

CHAPTER 12

THE OFFICIAL WORD

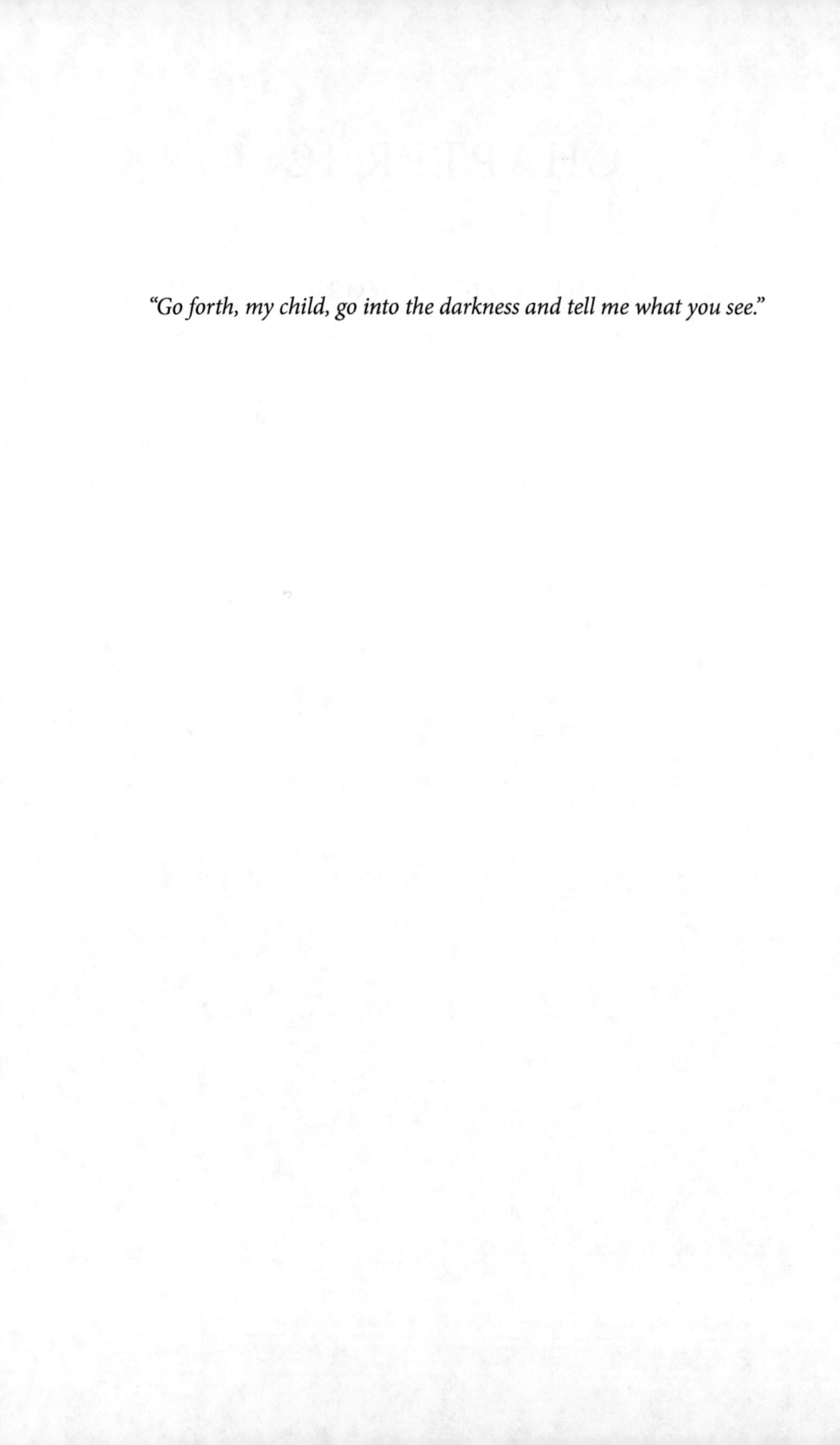

"Go forth, my child, go into the darkness and tell me what you see."

<u>Camp Sparta (USMC Reserves Base), Antiquity, New York</u>

"Ready…Aim…fire!" Shouts a masked Marine with light armor; he is an experimental weapons tester.

Bright yellow blasts of energy erupt from the barrels of three different rifles. The first blast strikes a mannequin outfitted with bulletproof armor that lacks the ability to stop the searing penetration of force. The blast goes through the front of the armor, the mannequin, the back of the armor, and into the concrete wall approximately 50 feet behind it.

The second rifle's blast is more intense than the first. It penetrates the entire engine block of a small jeep and goes through the full length of the vehicle, also striking the concrete wall. The third rifle blast is a continual stream of energy which strikes the side of an old, retired tank. The stream burns through the armor plating on the side of the tank and eventually through the tank, before it makes it to the backstop wall.

Twenty-five yards behind the Elite Forces Guardsmen firing the weapons is a small observation booth, a light stream of aromatic smoke rising from the shaded awning. The aroma is that of black cherry and interest.

Standing with a cigar between his index finger and thumb, General Black observes the testing of this new batch of experimental plasma rifles. Beside him stands a young lieutenant, a gray-haired lieutenant colonel and two civilian corporate executives. With an impressed appearance, the general nods his head in acknowledgment of the successful tests and inquires for more information from the seasoned veteran in charge of the operation. "These weapons will change the face of combat, Lieutenant Colonel Watson. How many do we have in all?" The rugged officer double checks his list and hands it to the general, saying, "We have a batch of 20 fully assembled rifles, but only 7 of them are functional, Sir... We are going to send the entire group to Jett Future, Inc. for analysis in two days."

The General reads the lists and flips to the final page, which outlines the transport plan for the rifles. "Am I to understand that we are going to use regular Army personnel for the transport of these rifles, Colonel?"

The Lieutenant Colonel points to an entry on the sheet. "General, we are going to be traveling with soldiers from the 10th Aviation Brigade; these men are very professional."

One of the civilian executives steps in front of the lieutenant colonel and addresses the general, "General Black, I do not have to stress to you the importance of these rifles making it Jett Future safely. I strongly recommend that you assign Elite Forces Guardsmen to the convoy as added security. Professionalism is one thing, gentlemen... practicality is another; we would rather have Marines guarding something as important as this."

Hiding his slight resentment of being spoken down to by civilians, the general agrees with the recommendations and orders Lt. Col. Watson to restructure his transport plans to include a small team of Marine Elite Forces Guardsmen to travel along with the Army soldiers in the convoy.

~~~

<u>Daylight Labs Underground Complex, Department Level-7</u>
The elevator door opens, creating a smooth whisking sound. Dr. Sharpe steps off of the elevator first, escorting the three members of the First Factor. The men step out into a lobby area that is as elaborately decorated as a five-star hotel in Las Vegas. The center of the room has
~~~

a large fountain with a waterfall pouring water into a circular, open pond filled with beautiful Oriental fish. Directly above the fountain is a large chandelier made up of pristine crystals and soft lights.

The carpet is designed with intricate patterns of a patriotic persuasion and the walls are lined with pictures of monuments, wars, and Marines awarded the highest honor that can be bestowed upon a soldier of this nation for their actions, the Medal of Honor.

Sergeant Major Tyr stands beside Commander Webb, who is leaning on the front desk with an innocuous smile on his face. "Welcome to your new home, guys! This is level seven and this entire floor is ours."

Each teammate stands wordless and awestruck. Webb continues to speak but is tuned out as sight becomes the primary means of sensory perception amongst the men. A small support staff is introduced as the caretakers of the entire floor. They are led by a young woman with short brown hair and a small space between her front teeth. She has an exotic beauty and introduces herself with a relaxed tone from behind the front desk.

"My name is Melinda Teller and I am the senior receptionist and caretaker of your department."

A powerful but invisible blow is struck upon the professionalism of Captain Edwards as his very senses become quickly confused. He instantly sways from the aroma of this woman's sight and the succulent smell of her vision. He is a loyally married man, but above all... he is a man, first.

She's attractive, he allows himself to think.

He's handsome, she taunts within her mind.

Her mouth dries from the ambush of nervousness created by this massive Marine before her. He towers a few daring touches away with dark skin and ferociously determined eyes. He instantly threatens her controlled manner and it has only been mere seconds. She has never been attracted to skinny men; and this, he wasn't. The young woman had a long speech prepared, but now she decides that ending it quickly would be her best decision.

"If you gentlemen have any issues with your comfort or how well the area is kept, please feel free to let me know." She forces herself to share her focus with each member of the team. She ensures that the final person that she locks eyes with at the end of her introduction is the captain.

She leads the men to each room, explaining the purpose and design of each one. The team is shown a meeting room filled with video conferencing monitors, a war room connected to holographic location imaging devices, a training facility with the most advanced machines that science has to offer, a medical facility that supports full reconstructive surgery, and many others. It is the plush dining room and the private quarters that impress the men the most.

Each team member is shown their respective room and given an access key by Melinda, who hands each key off with a small, seductive smile. It is to Captain Edwards that she delivers a flirtatious look to accompany her smile. Inside each of their rooms, on the bed, are two boxes with a sheet of paper on top of them. Webb orders each man to follow the orders on the paper and to report to the lobby in five minutes.

Five minutes later the three Marines gather in the lobby. Each is dressed in a unique new battle uniform. Captain Edward's has a large, golden, medallion-like eagle on his chest on top of his Retro N-ionic Amplification Core. His scarlet-and-gold uniform is brazen and classically heroic. Staff Sergeant Livingston has a full face mask and a custom designed sleek compound bow. His uniform is the most different of the trio. It is made up of blues and grays; there is no scarlet. Corporal Gonzalez wears a one piece mask similar to that of a ski mask and carries a rectangular shield. The three look at one another in amazement. Their commander stands before the group once again smiling with ambition and anxiety.

Sergeant Major Tyr addresses the team in a somber voice. "Each of you will begin to train in these uniforms to get used to them. You will also get used to your new 'field' names, which will be used when referring to one another whenever you are wearing your uniforms. Corporal Gonzalez, you will be known as Knight. Staff Sergeant Livingston, your new name will be Islander and, Captain Edwards, you are Pharaoh."

Corporal Gonzalez holds his shield out towards the captain, then says to the sergeant major, "Hey, Captain, what d'ya think of this? Excuse me, Sergeant Major, but what am I supposed ta do with this?"

Sergeant Major Tyr opens a folder that he is carrying in his hand and shows him the information in it. "You will be doing a lot of melee fighting and you are not bullet proof. Although you heal fast, you can still be killed. This small shield was designed by the technological research department to absorb 80% of all impacts received and to protect you without hampering your mobility, Corporal."

The youthful Marine then looks over to his staff sergeant, who is closely studying his new bow. "How ya like your bow, Staff Sergeant?

Why are you staring at it so hard? You look like you've dropped something."

The sniper runs his fingers along the bow's frame slowly, stopping just above the stabilizer and the cherry-wood grip. "I'm looking for a GPS chip," responds the elder Marine.

"What? Why would they put a GPS chip on a bow?" Questions Corporal Gonzalez while dislodging his shield to inspect it closer.

"Why wouldn't they?" Retorts Staff Sergeant Livingston, upon discovery of a small notch drilled into his bow in the exact place that he expected. "Found it," the sniper comments. Gonzo locates his notch just beside the leather grip clasp attached to the bottom of his shield. "I got one, too, Staff Sergeant. Anyone ever tell you that you're scary?" He inspects it for less than the few seconds it took for him to find it then quickly goes back into dreaming that he is just like the characters in his comic books. Corporal Gonzalez grins while nodding his head and makes another request. "Can we come up with our own names and call ourselves The Hero Federation like my comics? Da Captain can be Ultra-Max, Staff Sergeant Livingston can be Atum-Ra, and I'll be Da Blind Flame! We'll be cool... Sir."

He bounces up and down in place moving his shield around like a comic book character.

"The women are going to go crazy when they see this!! When I grow up...I wanna be me!"

Everyone stands deathlike and soundless as the sergeant major shrugs with disregard. He then pulls out another sheet of paper and hands it to Islander (Staff Sergeant Livingston). "This is a specially made bow that has the ability to not only withstand your new N-ionic energy levels but to allow you to pull the energy back into arrows which can then be propelled ten to twenty times further than you could throw them. This bow actually conducts your power, Islander...not to mention that it is also extremely durable. It is the first model; we will continue to upgrade it as we learn more about your power levels."

Webb then steps forward taking out three smaller boxes of his own and hands them to the team. Inside each box there is a black Rolex Submariner watch, an elaborately designed platinum ring, a gold necklace, and a cell phone. "Each of these items is an emergency communication device that has direct access to the front desk. You must wear at least one of them every day and everywhere you go." He clears his throat with pride. "Each one of these items was chosen by me. They are top-of-the-line products that will increase your prestige around… others." The team studies the items, with the most intense scrutiny coming from the actions of the sniper, whose interest in their weight, structure, and material types raises an eyebrow from the commander for his perceived paranoia.

Stepping next to the marble counter top Webb waves his hand over two more uniforms, identical to the ones currently donned by the team but with darker blue-and-gray designs. Pharaoh is the first to lift his uniform up before commenting, "Blue-and-gray? I think I like this one better than the one I'm wearing now, Commander. It looks like the one Staff Sergeant Liv… uh… Islander is wearing right now. Are you giving us a choice of attire?"

The commander's answer is abrupt, "No. Islander wasn't supposed to wear that uniform." His eyelids relax, closing halfway as his upper body curtails away with an expression of annoyance. "These darker uniforms are your 'Utility' uniforms. They are to be used on missions or operations out of the public eyes and/or requiring some form of stealth. Personally, I don't like them! They're a distraction to the brand that I'm trying to create for this team."

He moves towards Pharaoh and runs his hand down the royal blue portion of his uniform above his golden eagle medallion, stopping on the deep red portion below the medallion covering his abdomens. He then whisks his open hand around, palm up, as though he is giving an introduction. "I designed this uniform; Red-White-and-Blue to grab the attention of our public, with the red just dark enough to be considered scarlet. The gold was added in homage to your Marine Corps traditions. I call the uniforms that you are currently wearing, 'Dress-Blues.'" His self-pride is anything but subtle.

"The utility uniforms were ordered by my superior. I… do as I am commanded, Captain. But you can trust me when I say that you will spend more time in your Dress-Blues rather those dreadful utility… costumes."

The fire-haired commander raises his chin and inhales, enlarging his chest with anticipation. "We will be going to two 'meet-n-greets' per month in your new uniforms… your Dress-Blues. You will have one training session per month publicized on television and every quarter one of you will serve a random police district or fire department for a day."

Corporal Gonzalez's smirk creeps along his face as he feels one of his greatest dreams becoming a reality. "Dude, we really are superheroes now. If only mi Madre could see me now."

"We will start as public servants, Corporal. Becoming 'super... heroes' depends on how the team is marketed and presented. That is the job of my marketing team," states the commander while running his fingers along the side of his head.

The youth circles Islander excitedly and inspects his utility uniform. "Why didn't you wear your Dress Blues uniform, Staff... oops... Islander?" The sniper's glare through his mask stills the movements of his questioner. "Because it's ugly," he replies.

Turning towards Pharaoh, offended by the sniper, Webb commands the captain to follow him into one of the private rooms, leaving Sergeant Major Tyr with the other two in order to go over their new weapon designs. Webb changes his tone from a light-hearted, excited tone to that of a more serious manner. "Listen, Pharaoh, because of your unique physical change some concerns have been created about the protection of your identity, especially with you being married. The superiors have agreed to debrief your wife and to give her limited information about your new 'physical differences.' Information control is going to become slightly difficult but not impossible."

Pharaoh rubs the golden eagle on his chest and faces his new commander, "Commander Webb, when are we going to be able to leave this facility? When can I speak to my wife?"

OCD-7 Webb steps back and turns away slightly from Pharaoh, breaking direct eye contact. "As of today, each of you will be granted phone privileges again. You must understand that these separate identities created for you and your men have been created to protect your personal lives. You must protect them above all else. Your team will be allowed to leave the complex after you have been medically cleared by Dr. Sharpe."

Pharaoh gives a slight nod of acknowledgement and begins to leave the room when he is suddenly stopped by his superior. "There is one other change to the team that I forgot to mention, Pharaoh."

Sensing the inevitable collision of truth and politics, Pharaoh turns to his commander.

"I am quite sure that you have been informed of the magnitude of this team going public. I have been appointed to head up all of the marketing to control our image to the nation. There will be a full staff of marketers attached to us under my command working day and night on our reputations, image, and placements in politics," says the commander.

Stepping away even further from the captain with a slight twist of his body to face him, OCD7-Webb continues to speak, "When this team was first proposed your squad was not my first choice and I am going to be honest with you...I voted against you and your team. As a group, you did not have an image that would be easy to market to America. I lost the vote and now we have been bound together for this new adventure into the public's eye. I am hoping that you understand some changes that I am recommending for the team to aid in our new marketing strategies. I would like to change the team's name to Islander and the First Factor. This would work better for public acceptance. I feel that it would be best if we focus on Islander as the team leader."

Pharaoh pulls his mask off, showing a disgusted expression combined with disbelief. "What in the hell did you just say....Sir?"

Webb pulls out a magazine in the design phase with various splashes of electrical blue in the background and Islander on the cover with his thumb up and an American flag behind him. The

computer-designed image is a close-up of Islander's face and torso, and the shadows on his face give the impression that he is smiling. Through his mask, there is a strong emphasis on his blue eyes and his Caucasian skin surrounding them. He hands the magazine over to Captain Edwards.

"I'm not going to lie to you, Captain. You and your men are going to be the nation's premiere super-team that all others will follow. It is critical that we do this right and give the public what they want in order to build trust."

Captain Edwards grips his mask in his fist and drops his other hand holding the magazine. His face and body tense briefly with paralysis at what he is hearing. His eyes are the only thing that moves as they roll slowly to the corners to stare deep and hard at his commander. "Stop beating around the bush...Sir."

OCD7-Webb rubs behind his ear then kneads his eyes with his index finger and thumb. "Listen, I don't think that the public is ready to have a person such as you in charge of something so important right now, Captain. You are...uh...large and possibly too intimidating."

Pulling his mask back onto his face, Pharaoh hands the magazine back to his commander, shoving it into his hands.

"Intimidating? I'm a Marine, Commander. Why don't you just say the truth, that the nation isn't ready for a black man to lead their very first super powered team - or maybe you're not ready! It was hard enough getting a black president and now it's just too much having a black 'super' hero. Our team name stays! We are not a comic book super hero group lead by some big guy with blond hair and blue eyes and a cape. We are Marines! We are not The Hero Federation, we are The First Factor!"

He walks out of the room to join his other team members. OCD7-Webb grits his teeth as the door closes behind Pharaoh.

CHAPTER 13

THE AMBUSH-PART 1

"Lament, worry, and fear tomorrow…act today!"

The morning drive for the eight Army-vehicle convoy from Fort Drum is clear and smooth. The convoy is being led by Lieutenant Colonel Watson with soldiers from the 10th Aviation Brigade and the Elite Forces Guardsmen. While everything about this trip is supposed to appear routine, a select few know that this mission is far from that. The mission is to transfer a new batch of prototype plasma rifles to the company Jett Future, Inc. for final approval and analysis.

The convoy is made up of thirty soldiers, of whom twenty are normal Army drivers and the final ten are Marine Elite Forces Guardsmen from the EF-Div. The cargo vehicle transporting the rifles is a heavily armored, six-wheeled tanker van. It is the fourth vehicle in the column and the most heavily guarded.

The sunrise breaking the horizon is the signal of commencement on this day as the convoy passes through the 178 West Church Street overpass. Lt. Col. Watson raises his left hand above his brow to block the sunlight while he stands halfway up in his quick moving Vietnam-era classic jeep. It is his vehicle of preference which inspires the men in his convoy as they receive motivating horn-beeps in traffic by Vietnam veterans passing by who receive the vision of this old open-topped 'warhorse' as an honor.

Clutching onto the windshield with his right hand, he notices what appears to be a trail of smoke headed directly towards them through the oncoming traffic. It is his years of battle experience that forces his bellow of warning before his mind knows what to do.

"RPG! Get down!"

The second vehicle behind the Lt. Col. explodes from a direct hit into the side window, killing the driver and the passenger instantly. The lieutenant colonel is blown out of his hard braking jeep onto the pavement as machinegun fire begins to riddle his driver and his seat.

With bloody patches of uniform scrapped into his skin, he staggers to his feet only to dive to the ground again as the final two vehicles in the convoy explode from another RPG and thrown grenades. Covered with glass and blood, he tries to regain control in order to think straight. Leaning against the side wall of the freeway, Lt. Col. Watson rests while trying to catch his breath as he watches the EF-Guardsmen return fire into the oncoming traffic on the far side of the freeway.

Through the smoke and fire he gets a glimpse of the enemy. They are lightly armored soldiers wearing helmets and gas masks. Their

movements are methodical and robot-like; their enemy appears to be well organized.

One of the EF-Guardsmen squad leaders runs over to the lieutenant colonel, bringing him a rifle and a radio. "Sir, we have men dead and wounded and need to call in backup ASAP!"

Lt. Col. Watson picks up the radio to call in to headquarters when he notices the direct attack onto the tanker van.

The tanker van is under assault by what appears to be a large humanoid carrying a war mace surrounded with energy. Bullets strike his body, leaving light imprints of their impact before bouncing off of him onto the ground like pebbles thrown at a charging bull; his strength is phenomenal. The lieutenant colonel changes the frequency on the radio to the top secret channel. "Postman 23 to HQ... Post 23 to HQ, This is Chief Mailman on delivery and we are taking fire! We have KIA and an EMD on premises!! Need support, 'other than normal!' I repeat, we need support other than normal!"

The lieutenant colonel's bloodied radio chirps with life as it crackles back a response. "Understood Postman 23, support 'other than normal' is on the way!" With a hasty wipe of blood and spit, the senior officer waves his hand in command to fan his men out while throwing down the radio to return fire across the highway. He calls out to his men, "Hold your ground!! Backup is on the way!"

~~~

<u>Camp Sparta (USMC Reserves), Antiquity, New York</u>
<u>The Daylight Labs Hangar Bay</u>
Pharaoh, Islander, and Knight are on stand-by waiting to see if their team is going to be activated for this mission. They are all nervous because they have never seen action in their 'new' forms, they have only trained. Pharaoh is apart from the others speaking with his wife on his cell phone, their words are private and yet his look of concern speaks volumes. "I'm going to be home soon, honey. Tell Tre to wash the dishes before he goes to bed. I miss you both and I love you," he concludes before disconnecting his phone to stare at the screen showing his home number.

Knight sits with Islander trying to have a conversation with him but receives very little response. "Are you nervous, Staff Sergeant?"

Islander adjusts his mask, ignores Knight and grasps his specially designed fiberglass and light-metal bow as Sergeant Major Tyr exits the
~~~

Humvee and approaches the team in a hurried fashion. Pharaoh packs his cell phone into the duffle bag going back to their rooms, while taking care not to crush it with his still newfound strength. His strength has been increasing incrementally from the growing anticipation of their mission. Even with his tactile training, he still struggles to balance this unique extrability by applying his training. He approaches the rest of the group as the sergeant major speaks.

"This is it, Marines! We have a convoy ambush with men down and wounded. There has been an Enemy of Mass Destruction reported and confirmed on the premises that can't be stopped by any conventional means. Those men down there need something 'other than normal' to be interdicted into this fray. The First Factor will be that interdiction! Captain, your team is needed!"

A second vehicle parks as OCD7-Webb steps from it with two photographers that instantly begin to capture images of the team preparing to leave. He brushes arrogantly past the sergeant major and addresses the team.

"News crews will be arriving at the scene within minutes. Watch your actions out there, Marines. We need to put on a good show on our first time out, try to make the nation proud!" The fire-haired commander stands before the group and squeaks out his best attempt at a charismatic smile while pointing forward as his photographers begin to hastily snap more pictures.

"Make sure you send these photos down to the graphic design department to have them touched up for release as soon as this incident is over," commands OCD7-Webb.

The door of the waiting jet craft opens as the pilot steps forth. His voice is less than welcoming; in fact, it is raspy with a veteran's tone.

"I'm Myth. I will be taking you on the battlefield today. What in the hell is the delay?"

He is not startled or flattered to see superheroes or uniforms; in fact, he looks beyond them to go over tactical details with the sergeant major.

"The radio is blaring with gunfire, Sergeant Major! What is the damn hold up? We have men down!"

"I apologize, Myth. Commander Webb is in charge of this mission. He has need for images of the First Factor before the launch of this operation," answers Sergeant Major Tyr in a stoic tone.

"You've got to be kidding me!" Whispers the pilot in an angry, low growl.

After handing a small sheaf of papers and maps to the pilot, Sergeant Major Tyr directs the First Factor's attention to a lightly armored medic also stepping from the craft. He uses OCD7-Webb's photo session as an opportunity to introduce the medic to team. "This is Dossman. He's a Phantom Hawk Corpsman." The young medic fumbles with one of his belt pouches before nervously waving his hand.

In the background, OCD7-Webb shouts at one of his photographers while pointing at his laptop with images on screen. The sergeant major ignores the commotion and continues with the introduction,

"He is a medical specialist and a technology guru rolled in one. Pharaoh, he will aid the wounded, so take care of him. The top brass has chosen not to send in anymore of our Elite Forces Guardsmen ground forces because of the civilians and cameras. They want to see you guys in action."

Myth barges out of the Sky Ghost, "Commander Webb! We need to leave now!"

Everyone pauses as Webb stares at the war torn pilot, who is very much ready to behead him with the closest thing to him that can be made into a weapon.

"Sorry… Myth. Th – They're yours. You can go now," he responds slowly.

"Thank you, Commander! Marines… load up!" Says Myth upon his return into the craft. The doors pull shut as the glass sheaths below the underside of the Sky Ghost dance with brightness to move its mass against the natural tug of gravity. The entire sight is a merging of elegance and speed as it darts out of the hangar with a light whisper of air.

The commander becomes enraged and attempts to suppress it until the Marines leave. He looks into the face of Sergeant Major Tyr, who ignores him. He then confronts the sergeant major. "Who gave you the authority to include that medic with my team, Sergeant Major?!? He's has no experience with public relations or with my team! If he harms the image that I have created for us, I will have both of your heads!"

Sergeant Major Tyr looks towards the photographers who receive the subtle hint to leave and answers in a professional tone, "With all due respect, Sir…this is combat. Each Marine entering combat comes back in one of three ways: healthy, wounded, or dead. These Marines need every advantage they can have on their first time out. This is not a game and it is certainly not television, Sir. I apologize if I stepped over my boundaries. You're correct about him not having experience, but we mitigate that risk by the faith we have in our training."

Webb looks behind him to ensure that there are no others in the listening range of the two of them, then steps forward, pointing his finger into the sergeant major's face. "I know why you're here, Sergeant Major, and I don't like it or you one bit. This is my team and they are under my command! As soon as you are finished with their training, I want you out of my department, is that understood?"

Sergeant Major Tyr agrees, once again in a professional, even tone, and walks pass the commander to enter the Humvee that he arrived in. The vehicle leaves the hangar as OCD7-Webb joins the rest of his marketing team to review the photos and to track the progress of the mission.

The jet craft turns invisible once its prep is completed, then rockets out of the hangar to the convoy at top speed. Pharaoh sits up front with Myth, while the newest member, Dossman, sits in back with the rest of the team.

Fiddling with his headset transceiver, Pharaoh says to the pilot, "Myth, right? Uh, what do they expect from us?" Myth turns slightly to look at Pharaoh. He clutches the end of the headset transceiver cord and connects it to the dashboard socket.

"They expect you to save those men, Marine! You and your men are the last line of hope and defense. Whenever you are called in action, know that Hell itself must be on Earth."

Pharaoh looks down, then faces forward, lifting his head as though he now understands. Myth and Pharaoh listen to the screaming, gunfire, and explosions from the ambush on their radio. Pharaoh knows the familiar sound of combat and the deep pit that swells in the stomach before an operation. He promises to himself not to lose control this time. Myth speaks with the soldiers and Marines on the ground to gather broken information on what they are flying into. He delivers information updates to Pharaoh without doubt of his capabilities. "There is an overwhelming enemy force made up of over fifty enemy soldiers. They have reported an EMD with the strength to rip steel with his bare hands; apparently, he is carrying a mace or weapon of some sort that is crushing our forces. Do you have a plan, Pharaoh?"

Pharaoh grits his teeth and stares out into the clouds rushing at the windshield of the Sky Ghost, "We win, Myth."

"Nice answer," Myth puts his right hand up with his thumb pointed towards the back. "The men need you."

Pharaoh goes in back to see the others. Knight has his mask off and is holding onto the small crucifix that he normally wears on his necklace. He glances at the captain with a familiar grin of false bravado and kisses it while saying a prayer. He nervously places it into one of the small pockets on his belt. Dossman sits with an eerie firmness of pre-battle experience by the details placed in his review of his med-pack. He taps his foot uncontrollably while doing so without notice. The captain knows that if the sergeant major assigned him to the team, then he must be one of the best in his field.

"Who are you with, kid?" Asks Pharaoh, aiming to relieve some of the building anxiety.

"S-Sir?"

Pharaoh repeats himself to the medic, "Who are you with...what department?"

"Oh, uh, Department Level-4, Sir."

Dossman's hands scamper over his equipment with a shallow confidence that is familiar to the Marine Captain. It reminds him of Corporal Gonzalez on their mission at the Udosion Labs complex, which was his first.

"Is this your first time going into action, Dossman?"

"N-No, sir...I've d-done over 200 hours in training and...," the young medic drops his head, "Yes, Sir. It's my first real mission. Sir...I won't let you down. I will try my best!"

Pharaoh acknowledges Dossman's courage. "You're going to be alright, son."

Islander appears to be staring out of the window deep in thought, with his mask and glove removed from his face and hand, exposing his Caucasian skin. It takes a little more than a willed desire for sapphire-hued energy to glow between his fingers, rippling from tip to tip.

Does the white skin protect me or is this an intentional curse? He thinks to himself. Clenching his fingers together into a fist, he concentrates only a bit harder and the energy alters into a deep crimson, producing heat.

Seconds later, he releases and the energy dissipates, leaving cool pink flesh and relaxed fingers. He stares at his reflection in the window glass with ocean-blue eyes of ice.

Where is my black skin? Those bastards took it to change me, but I won't let them.

The silent promise is his alone. He keeps to his thoughts and pulls his glove into place. He scans the other members on the team and locks eyes with his leader.

Pharaoh says to his team, "There is only one peace that combat Marines know in all their existence...it is the precious few minutes after battle, just before the birth of their next conflict. We will fight and we will not yield! We will fight and we will not quit! We will never fall back; no-matter the cost! This is nothing new to us, we are Marines! We are Force Recon! We are the First Factor! "

The comment jars Islander, making him lift his face to listen intently but there are no other words spoken amidst the sound of the aerial vehicle's muffled engine. Staff Sergeant Livingston has been with Captain Edwards longer than any other Marine he knows. That bond between them gives him the ability to read his movements as his actions speak to the team.

Pharaoh stares into the eyes of each of his men as his deep mahogany skin pulls tight across his squared jaw. Slight ripples of his jaw muscles roll in the dim cockpit light as his expression bleeds determination through action. He drops his right hand to his side as a single finger points downward indicating to the team to prepare for action.

Pharaoh's eyes begin to glow as his entire build tightens through his uniform. "Now follow me!"

Knight puts his mask on, then fits his shield onto his arm. Islander straps on his mask, and then pulls his gloves on while standing up to move near the side doorway. Pharaoh rubs the scar on his forehead through his mask.

The lights instantly go to a dim red as the jet craft becomes visible. Myth tells the team to get ready because they are now coming up on the ambush site. The first thing that can be seen through the windows is the smoke and the traffic jam that stretches for miles.

Everyone is wordless as their first mission as superheroes is about to begin.

CHAPTER 14

THE AMBUSH - PART 2

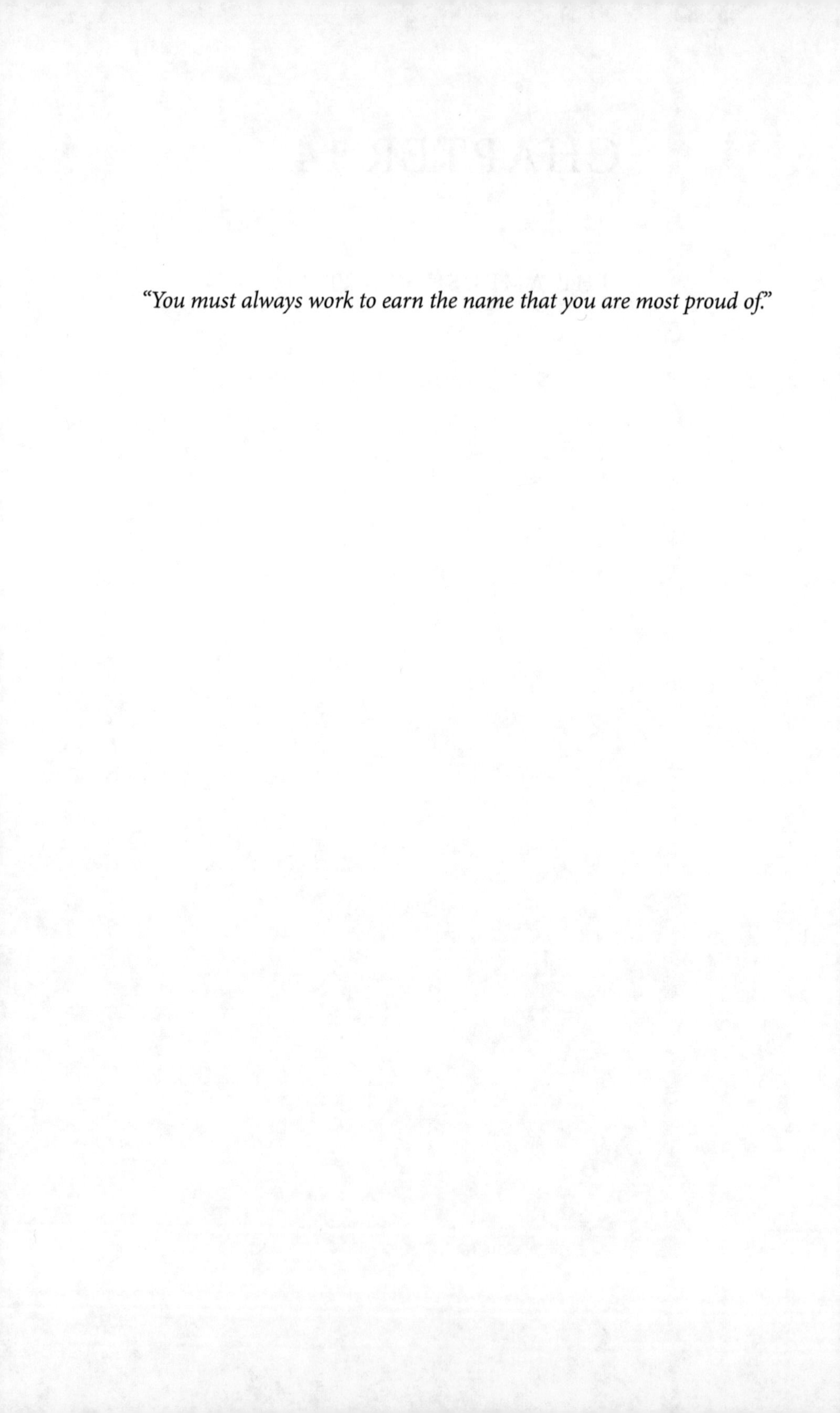

"You must always work to earn the name that you are most proud of."

<u>Operation Quick Save</u>

It is a scene of carnage and mayhem. The freeway is lined with blood, oil, and other twisted fragments of wreckage; soldiers and Marines – dead – have no courage or concern for the living. Destroyed vehicles define this landscape. Highway guard rails are chewed into abominable shapes from frenzied civilian drivers hoping for escape. Gunfire seems to be coming from all directions as vehicle occupants cower in their cars. The dirt, broken into thick clumps, seems to punch through the husky plumes of battle-smoke as a professional fighter against a child. Breathing has become a task for all except the robot-like enemies adorned with bizarre gas-masks. They are as disturbing in appearance as they are in action.

Army infantrymen and Marine EF-Guardsmen under the command of Lt. Col. Watson battle for their lives. Life is taken without guilt or pause from the enemy, whose jerky motions instill terror in those glimpsing their approach. Protecting the innocent becomes a forgotten priority for the American warriors as both heroes and victims fall from emotionless attacks.

It is the dead children strewn along the pavement and trapped in their car seats that force this moment into realms beyond humane. There is no honor. One young body lies just in front of a burning black Volkswagen. It is that of a little girl who will never giggle at another cartoon or feel the joys of her first crush. Rubber burns from something within the engine and sends small rivers of molten streaks down the metal bumper dripping onto her lifeless legs. It is natural to expect a flinch and a jerk away from pain, but for this silent damsel it merely collects on scorched flesh and finds its way to the pavement beneath her. Her thin yellow sun dress flutters in the hectic air, slapping away wisps of smoke like a flag of surrender. It beckons not for the surrender of the enemy or the surrender of their opponents, but for the surrender of hope.

This attack is something that one would see on television in the Middle East or beyond. The reality is that is here in America... within her breast.

The enemy is well-organized and powerful. Even through the chaos of this ambush their movements have been tactical and patient. Their leader appears as a living shadow, reflecting only enough of the bothersome sunlight to highlight the tensed muscles beneath his dark, skin-tight suit which acts as armor; the material is of a technology that none have seen before. His soldiers refer to him as the 'Apostle

General' and he leads from the front.

He waited until his rocket propelled grenades destroyed the front and rear vehicles, trapping the tanker van in the middle, before unleashing his most dangerous weapon. This is the weapon that is upon them now and the weapon that follows orders without delay. The weapon is a large warrior carrying a war-mace with inexhaustible strength…'Shrine.'

The lieutenant colonel orders his surviving men back, regrouping beside the tanker van since it is the most heavily armored. His infantrymen begin to lay down dense rifle fire across the freeway, taking out some of the enemy troops as they try to push forward. It is at this time that the clear distinction between Army infantrymen and Marine Elite Forces Guardsmen is understood.

Elite Forces Guardsmen make up the highest echelon of professional warriors, with no member younger than thirty-five years of age. They are as wise as they are fearless, and they know war. Each member is drawn from ranks like that of Delta Force, Navy SEALs, Marine Recon, and the CIA. They must have years of field experience before consideration to join the Guardsmen. Those that make it are trained to be the type of warrior that all others hope to become.

Matted with dried blood and soil grime, two of the EF-Guardsmen, who were assigned to the front of the convoy, crawl alongside some destroyed vehicles and launch a flank attack on the enemies with gathered grenades from other fallen combatants. Army infantrymen witnessing them moving forward into this gate of hell cannot ignore the pull of heroism from their hearts created by these warriors. The enemies begin to scatter as the exploding grenades launch sharp pieces of shrapnel though their ranks like glass through tissue paper. This causes the enemy to develop a hesitant respect for these elite warriors.

The Apostle General orders Shrine to eliminate the Guardsmen; hesitation and respect for them cannot be tolerated. Lt. Col. Watson orders intense covering fire for the EF-Guardsmen as they try to pull back. Shrine reels back from the intense barrage, grabs a small vehicle from the stalled traffic without bothering to see if it is occupied, and throws it at the two escaping Guardsmen, causing another explosion which kills them both instantly. Respect may have survived but hesitation is now no longer necessary.

Knowing that the Army infantrymen are low on ammo, the Apostle General orders Shrine to attack the tanker van. The spiritual warrior slams his war-mace into the side of it, the shock alone knocking the remaining infantrymen back in different directions; the force... tremendous.

The enemy soldiers attack the scattered Army infantrymen, picking them off with machine gun fire and grenades. Lt. Col. Watson gets hit by shrapnel, and two gunshots pierce his thigh and stomach before he collapses with his rifle.

Shrine penetrates the side of the tanker van and rips the armor open with his bare hands, showing a full inventory of top secret plasma rifles. The Apostle General raises his hand and waves it in a circular motion as a delivery truck drives across the matted and bloody grass in the median. Enemy soldiers exit the truck and point their weapons at the American soldiers who were assigned to guard the experimental weapons. The enemy forces the American soldiers to unlock the weapons lockers and transfer the weapons to the delivery truck.

Scoffing with an evil smile, the Apostle General orders the surviving infantry men rounded up on the other side of the tanker van. He then orders his men to execute them as he walks back to the front of the tanker van where his other men are loading the plasma rifles.

The inevitability of the intended horror is reduced to an expected non-factor when compared to the blood and gore surrounding them. The infantry soldiers line up as their eyes expand and their vision focuses onto the weapons of their emotionless executioners. They are watched from across the highway by the wounded lieutenant colonel, who recognizes the sergeant in the middle of them as one of his most faithful men. Weapons rise against them as some crouch with broken nerves and anguish. There is no honor in dying like this.

Three large, blue bolts of energy from the sky slice through the rising plumes of smoke. Two vehicles on the other side of the freeway, occupied by enemy troops, explode. Another series of bolts sling out with deadly accuracy, knocking the would-be executioner soldiers into the side freeway walls, unconscious. A hushed whisper of change enters into the area as eye after eye scampers along the sky above for the explanation. Lt. Col. Watson releases a bloody sigh and says, "Thank you, God!" Tears swell in the old soldier's eyes as they clear dust from despair. "They are here. They are finally here..." he mutters.

The Sky Ghost becomes visible, swooping to hover just above the tanker van. It rides the air, alien in appearance with noble patterns made up of an American eagle placed on top of an American flag. The thin, flashing red lights running the border edges of the craft cut through the smoke and signal to the enemy that a shift in battle-tide

has come. The hanging doorway on the side of the craft introduces a new kind of warrior to those peering up from below. A bowman, masked with a full face plate and piercing blue-eyes that can be seen independent of distance, holds his weapon of choice as a methodical deliverer of promise—a promise that the enemy will remember his name forever.

He stands strapped into the doorway, firing blue bolts of pure energy down into the enemy forces, causing them to scatter in different directions. Each azure surge resembles the divine bolts from God written about in scripture.

Limber and quick with shield in hand, Knight emerges from the craft next, jumping down to the top of the tanker van as a blue blur, deflecting small arms fire with his shield while Dossman fast-ropes down and heads for the wounded. Dossman hits the ground, applying small single use bandages to the most critically injured civilians and infantrymen. The bandages cause wounds to heal at an immense rate, acting as artificial white blood cells, and then regenerating skin on top of the area. All before the material disintegrates into gnarled ash after use.

Surprise wanes, as it seems that everything pauses for the craft to curve into a hovering position. Islander drops his bow hand as the energy crackling from his finger tip recedes, making way for the titanic silhouette emerging from the interior of the craft behind him. A crowned eagle on the forehead-mask of the warrior moves into the battlefield sunlight first. Grabbing the drop-door structure, the massive frame of the team leader casts a determined gaze over his brothers-of-battle below. The golden eagle medallion on his chest shines from the rays of the sun, making him appear as one-above-man while only a little less than a god. His royal blue and scarlet uniform burns into the background of the jet craft and the sky beyond as fountain of faith offered to those dying from thirst on the battlefield below. Pharaoh looks at the beast with the war-mace.

"Islander, save these people! I'll take the brute!"

He jumps from the jet craft and slams into Shrine, causing a quake-like ripple of debris and smoke as the street pavement cracks under the pressure. Chaos churns in a brawling rumble as the first blow landed by the Marine is quickly returned with one of equal and possibly greater force. It is the age-old story of the battle between titans and gods.

Knight stands in front of the rounded-up infantrymen and

EF-Guardsmen. His full-faced blue-black mask holds opaque eyes of amber as he stares at the lead man. Most people find difficulty trusting those with concealed identities, but this time was different. The deep blue-sheen material making up the top of his uniform is bordered by the symbol of an eagle on his chest. That eagle is something that is in common amongst all American soldiers. Men have bled and died for it, and today was no different.

"I am Knight!" He shouts, "I'm an American warrior just as you and these bastards are terrorists! I need your help to take them down!'"

The staring soldier follows him almost instinctively. Knight throws a rifle into the arms of the exhausted Army sergeant standing before him. The bloodied soldier catches the rifle and stares once more into the eyes of the masked man. Knight grabs his shoulder and speaks in the most commanding tone that he can muster.

"Let's kick some ass!"

It takes all but an instant for the sergeant to survey the battlefield littered with his dead and wounded comrades. His face changes from fear and confusion to anger and determination. He raises his fist, reloads the rifle, and yells out, causing his other men to follow him behind the masked stranger. The attacking infantrymen, led by Knight, arm themselves with discarded rifles and begin to open fire across the freeway as Islander lands on top of the tanker van, firing explosive energy arrows deep into the enemy ranks.

The bowman quickly changes his position moving as the sniper that he is. Jumping down from the top of the tanker van, he is always one step ahead of his enemies, taking natural cover to peel away their ranks. Beneath his sweaty mask, the white man wears an expression of derision which adds up to a little more than a sneer. True aim delivers his ammunition to the rapidly dropping opponents and allows him a private chance to exercise his anger. He strives to protect his teammates.

Pharaoh comes crashing out of the shallow crater made by his collision with Shrine and flies into a small truck, crushing it. Shrine runs at him, his war-mace above his head, and slams it into the truck, missing Pharaoh by inches. Although the Marine captain has trained to fight with his new strength, it is the core martial arts skills from his military background that prevail as instinct for him. He twists to the side, shifts his weight and draws back for a mighty punch into the jaw of the savage warrior, causing his head to snap upwards to a side angle. Pharaoh swings with a second blow to the stomach of

Shrine, making him lurch forward and over. He then reaches back with his right hand, grabbing a five hundred-pound piece of concrete from the road and slams it into the back of his head, driving him into the ground.

"Fall, brute!" Commands the Marine captain.

The Apostle General observes the tide of battle turning by these new super powered warriors and orders his men to retreat with the weapons that they have. Knight flips onto the top of the tanker van and dives onto the top of the delivery truck with the Apostle General in it. Crawling on top of the truck, the Apostle General then swings at Knight. Rigidly trained instinct controls the hero as he uses his shield to shove the punch upward while countering with a crushing blow to the black skin-armored face of his enemy. The Apostle General turns with a snarl of rage and fires a pair of lasers from his glowing eyes, penetrating the shoulder of Knight and knocking him off of the truck. The delivery truck screeches to a halt as the Apostle General exits with a remote switch in his hand. He approaches Knight and punches him in the face, then lifts him like a ragdoll with his super-human strength and throws him into the tanker van.

Shrine rises from the debris with his face swollen and raises his war-mace, causing a wave of energy to emit from it knocking everyone back. The Apostle General yells out, "Now is the time to leave your enemy, Shrine! Let us go!" Shrine leaps away from the freeway as the General presses the button on his remote switch.

Seven chain explosions on the freeway cause the entire overpass to weaken, making a total collapse inevitable. Rising from the burning vehicles and crushed metal, Pharaoh calls out to the infantry men and EF-Guardsmen alike, "Gather the wounded! Civilians first! Get them into the tanker van!"

Dossman fires a grappling hook into the jet craft and pulls himself up while carrying Lt. Col. Watson. He enters the craft and grabs the cable winch controls, dropping four vehicle-carrying cables from the craft to the top of the tanker van. Islander and Knight struggle to connect them as the entire freeway gives out, falling onto the streets below.

The jet craft loses altitude slowly because of the sheer weight of the armored tanker van. The pilot, Myth, pulls against his throttle control to save the lives of those below his craft. The craft jerks against gravity and sustains, answering the commands of its controller. Myth manages to successfully set the tanker van down in a nearby clearing, saving all of the lives aboard.

Pharaoh and Knight step outside of the damaged vehicle as the others exit slowly behind them. Civilians gaze at the blue-and-scarlet frame of the massive hero in disbelief. They gaze at the shield on the other. The bowman glides through the ranks of wounded soldiers to join his leader and comrade, standing to their side. Those watching marvel at their uniforms, so much like... costumes. A term is softly spoken among those tapping one another and mildly in shock. Children dare to seek confirmation from their parents while those same parents dare not to answer.

"Are they...?"

"Could they...?"

"Mommy, is that a...?"

"Holy shit, those are real live...?"

The softly spoken term increases in volume as what they have witnessed today becomes an accepted conversation piece for the remainder of each person's life. Pharaoh, Islander, and Knight turn when the term is spoken aloud...

"Superheroes!"

The enemy escaped, but lives have been saved. Ambulances begin to pull up onto the grass to help with the wounded, both friends and enemies. The enemy casualties were separated and guarded.

News vans and reporters begin to show up as Myth orders the team to grab onto the cables for extraction. Before they leave, the sergeant to whom Knight threw the rifle earlier comes up and thanks him, and to ask who they are. With a chest full of pride, Knight responds...

"We are the First Factor!"

CHAPTER 15

THE DEBRIEF

"Know when to yield. All battles are not meant to be fought."

<u>Camp Sparta (USMC Reserves), Antiquity, New York</u>
<u>Daylight Labs Underground Complex, Department Level-7</u>
"Where is your team now, Pharaoh?"

The conference room is dimly lit. Video conferencing monitors display shrouded silhouettes of some of the most powerful people in the nation. A heightened atmosphere of stress and pressure is created merely by their online attendance. Pharaoh sits alone today, interrogated about the actions of his team on their first operation. He is bombarded with questions by his operation commander, and he answers each one briefly while sticking to facts. "Knight is currently a patient in our medical facilities having his shoulder attended to. Islander is teamed up with the Phantomhawk medic, Dossman, at Antiquity General Hospital. The most critical individuals had to be moved there in order to save their lives, and once they are stabilized, we will relocate them to our facilities. Currently, Islander is acting as security for Lt. Col. Watson and the enemy soldiers that we captured and Dossman is overlooking the medical processes."

Pharaoh sits at the head of the conference table with the video monitors at the other end changing silhouettes for each person that chooses to speak. On one side of the table are General Black and Sergeant Major Tyr, acting as witnesses to the interrogation, while on the other side OCD7-Webb is out of his chair, pacing back and forth. He has been the person controlling the entire interrogation with his barrage of questions about each decision made and action taken. Pharaoh has seen this type of action in the past, mostly by those anxious to prove themselves at the expense of others. He thinks before he answers each question directed to him. The commander points downward at a sheet of paper on the conference table in front of his chair and looks up towards Pharaoh. "Pharaoh, upon review of the actions taken in the last operation we noticed that one of Islander's energy bolts destroyed an enemy vehicle, killing one of them and critically injuring three other enemies, of which one later died from his injuries. Was he following your direct orders?"

Pharaoh looks at his superior, puzzled that he would ask something like this, as if he was trying to set him up. He then responds carefully, anticipating a verbal attack. "Sir, there were dead soldiers and civilians everywhere; although Islander's actions were extreme, I believe that they were necessary for the situation."

The fire-haired commander sits, slowly placing both of his hands together, and raises his fingertips to his lips as he speaks in an attempt

to gain control over the interview in front of his peers. "You see, Pharaoh, this is the main point behind your 'creation' as a super-hero. You are given extrabilities far beyond that of a normal human and, because of this, you are responsible for decisions that are not only greater but more extreme than normal humans, and your strengths are in actions, not thoughts—even if your trainer tries to get you to believe differently. If we wanted a casualty count in front of live television we would have sent in normal military soldiers instead of you!"

Pharaoh works hard to maintain his composure as he is struck by such a strong and belittling comment. Sergeant Major Tyr sits emotionless and professional, totally unaffected by the allusion to his training of the First Factor. Webb then turns to face the video monitors as his confidence grows. "With all due respect gentlemen, we all know the importance of our public image as well as the potential dollar value that this team will be responsible for in the near future. There will be movies, toys, and many other high profit items created because of these individuals. We are talking about multi-millions immediately, which opens the doors to a billion dollar industry; they will be a greater asset than the Hero Federation ever was. It is imperative that their actions reflect the highest levels of moral and ethical decency at all times."

Pharaoh noticeably clenches his teeth as the muscles in his jaw compress from his disappointment in his commanding officer. General Black watches Pharaoh closely to see his response to this new level of politics. Webb glances back quickly at Pharaoh, and then faces the group again. Before OCD7-Webb can begin to speak once more Pharaoh interjects: "My operation commander is correct. We do have a greater responsibility to those that look up to us and depend on us and because of this I will make it a priority from this point forward to always find a solution other than the termination of any individual whether friend or foe; after-all, we are superheroes."

General Black looks at Pharaoh and nods slightly with a small smile on his face as he lights a cigar. The sergeant major sitting beside him displays a slight relaxation of his eye brows as a cough escapes his mouth. OCD7-Webb sits back with a slight tilt to his face; he is left without a response to Pharaoh's statement. The aroma of black cherry cigar smoke acts as a warm sweet breeze of change.

The video conference monitors change to the silhouette of a mysterious woman with short curly hair. Her voice has very little emotion and is overshadowed by a frustrated tone. "General Black, what are we doing about those plasma rifles?"

The general takes the cigar from his mouth. "I have already met with the operation commander of Department Level 4 - Diantha Grante and her team. They have already launched a recovery mission. Actions have been coordinated with the Phantomhawks and the Knightcrawlers for support."

OCD7-Webb turns his entire chair around towards the general. "What? Sir, this was our mission! There is a great chance that the recovery of those rifles is going to bring a lot of publicity and my department is trained for it! General, we should be doing this, not Dian…I mean, Commander Grante!"

The general glances at Pharaoh, and then looks down at his black cherry cigar, flicking the ashes carefully into his ashtray. He slowly looks up at OCD7-Webb, with a noticeable smirk on his face. "Based on your complaints with the team, Operation Commander Webb, I feel that you should take this time to send your team back for more training in order to live up to your expectations. We don't want them to disappoint you in the field again, do we?" The trailing question is wrapped in a smug tone. "You should really take this opportunity to brief the sergeant major here on your personal techniques for 'improved' training." General Black's amusement lightens the dreary atmosphere of stress created by the fire-haired civilian operation commander.

As the debriefing comes to an end, Webb storms out of the conference room, walking past Pharaoh while grumbling to himself. General Black thanks the others and finalizes the meeting by setting another date for the briefing regarding the rifle recovery operation.

~~~

<u>Antiquity General Hospital</u>

Hospital security has increased three-fold because of the incident the day before. Dossman and Islander are sent to monitor the captured soldiers as well as Lt. Col. Watson, who is struggling to survive his wounds.

The local authorities treat the new 'superheroes' as celebrities as they watch them arrive in their technologically-advanced Armored Personnel Carrier driven by a new driver with his identity concealed by his helmet and goggles. Dossman referred to him as 'Worm.' Islander is quiet and observes the entire time. Once the APC stops, armored Elite Forces Guardsmen step out to each side of the van at Worm's
~~~

command as protection for Dossman and Islander.

The duo shows their security cards to the smiling police officers as they enter the hospital. While Dossman advances to the front desk to get the room numbers of the wounded enemy soldiers, one of the policemen gathers up his courage to approach Islander. "Excuse me, Sir. I-uh…I'd like to say that –uhm, all of us guys think you're awesome and the way that you saved those Army guys and those people really meant a lot. My sister was on that freeway that morning and you guys saved her. I just wanna say thank you."

Islander stands, statuesque, staring at Dossman then turns slowly to look into the eyes of the police officer. "You're welcome, sir," he responds. He looks at the white policemen and wonders. How many innocent black-men have you arrested?

The policemen grins as his friends stand in back, thumbs up and gesturing for him to ask for an autograph. Before the officer can speak, Islander grabs a small piece of paper and signs it for him. "When I was kid, all I wanted ta be was a policeman like you. You men are tha true heroes in my book." Sarcasm burns in his statement, but the excited officer does not perceive it from his blue-eyed hero. For the policeman, it is as if he had briefly experienced a childhood dream.

Islander then leaves to meet up with Dossman for the prisoner check. The sniper notices that there were no guards posted outside the door, "Shhh… something ain't right here, Dossman." The duo warily traverses the corridor, stopping short before the prisoner rooms. When they enter, Dossman instantly begins to inspect the two captured soldiers carefully and quietly while Islander waits at the doorway. He then pulls out a small pen-sized scope and runs a small blue light across the IV bags on each soldier. He then rushes to Islander silently and whispers, "Islander, these men were just poisoned! Their machines were all turned off and my bioscope shows fingerprints that are only minutes old. The killer is still here, sir!"

Islander reaches on his back and pulls his bow off while clicking it into shape. Dossman then pulls out the paper on which he wrote the room numbers and scans it for the next room number. "Lt. Col. Watson is in room 323B! C'mon, we've got to hurry!"

Both men run at top speed down the hall and bust the door open. Inside is a snake-like man with a doctor's coat on, standing beside the lieutenant colonel's IV, injecting it with poison. He is leaning forward in a bestial position; his skin is smooth and pulled back with shallow crevices making up his scales. His cheeks are high on his face,

connecting with the strong frame of his upper brow. He struggles to hold his saliva within his mouth.

Islander quickly fires a blue bolt of energy, knocking the snake-man into the wall and causing him to hiss in pain; loose saliva spills from the corner of his mouth. Dossman darts over to the IV and snatches it out of the lieutenant colonel's arm. He instantly goes to work trying to save his life.

The snake man runs in a slithering motion across the floor, dodging two blasts from Islander, and comes up punching him in the bottom of his jaw. His speed is uncanny and his strength is far greater than expected from one with such a small, lithe frame.

Islander flies through the doorway into the far wall of the hallway as the security alarms begin to blare. The snake man rises while crossing his legs together. He squirms from his pants with ease as the flesh between his thighs and calves begin to meld into one smooth form of an elongated snake tail. "You have intervened in my kill, fool. For that you will die ssslowly from my poison!"

The snake-man's enraged eyes are deep amber and serpentine; he locks onto the calculating Marine sniper as a large fang comes from the back of each of his hands.

"A Shapen! That's Blackfang, Islander! He's a Shapen assassin!" Shouts Dossman.

Islander spins on the floor, grabbing his bow and comes up with a kick to the side of Blackfang's head. Using the same momentum, he swings around again, creating a ball of N-ionic energy in his hand, then smashes it into the face of the snake-man, causing it to explode. Blackfang flies into the wall as blood churns with the saliva escaping from his mouth.

He whips his tail at Islander, missing his legs. The sniper flips backwards in a hasty roll on the hospital floor while charging up an energy arrow on his bow. Islander lands and fires the arrow, striking the snake-man in his shoulder and sending him back into the wall again.

Blackfang, frustrated, throws poison gas grenades from his lab coat pockets into the group of watching policemen and slithers forward, charging Islander. He strikes the Marine from behind by using his reptilian speed.

Islander flings himself forward, sliding down the hall into the nurse's desk and cracking the bottom of it with his shoulder. Some of the police try to open fire at the snake-man while others collapse from the inhalation of the poison. Blackfang easily slithers through the gunfire and stabs two of the men with the poison claws on his hands.

Flat on his back, Islander pulls back a blue energy arrow and holds it as the hue changes to an intense deep-red hue, then releases. A whisper goes through his mind as a reminder of his order not to kill. This 'super–hero' that so many are watching within this very room has been asked to do something different from what he has been trained for. For Islander, death is as instinctive as breathing; from this he grasps the difference between killing and murder while delivering death to his enemy. With not only his physical change, a cultural change has also been forced upon him, making him more alien to whom he once was. He has been ordered to stand away from the shadows, to be someone other than he what he knows and to stop his enemy without taking his life.

His crimson bolt has no concussive force but pierced straight through the tail of Blackfang, causing him to hiss in excruciating pain. Blood runs along the floor as his tail slaps the tile with small convulsions. The bloodied assassin lives. Islander rises slowly while powering up another red bolt as the snake-man slithers backwards into the wall with both of his hands up. Islander aims directly for Blackfang's skull while taking a single step forward. He is losing patience with his foe. "I will kill you, snake-man! Get rid of tha claws and tha tail and lay on your stomach. I will only ask you one time."

The searing crimson N-ionic energy arrow begins to crackle as though it is hungry for a target. The snake-man retracts his claws and submits as the flesh on his tail splits to display his bloodied legs pierced through the lower thighs. The policemen tackle him with handcuffs.

Dossman rushes out to the poisoned officers and begins to work with the medical staff on saving them. The youth takes command, issuing orders with the single focus of protecting lives.

Islander walks up to Blackfang as he leans against the wall with a smile on his face. "My mission was accomplished, bowman. There's nothing that you can do to me! I am a Child of Pandora. I do not fear you, but know that my task is completed."

Islander looks at the two policemen guarding him. They both turn their heads in the opposite direction as Islander punches Blackfang in the face, knocking him out. He then turns quietly and walks back into the main room with Dossman as more Elite Forces Guardsmen enter the hospital to help. Dossman rests his hand on Islander's shoulder. "Thanks for stopping that guy, sir. We got to the lieutenant colonel just in time; he should be able to pull through. These guys in here will be alright, also. The only lives lost today were those enemy soldiers. The Elite Forces Guardsmen have established a perimeter around the hospital under the command of Worm. Everything should be fine."

Islander turns to survey the scene one last time. He makes a mental note of Dossman's earlier comment, "He's a Shapen," then faces the youth with resolve. "I guess it's time to go home—and don't call me Sir."

CHAPTER 16

MAGISTER

"Stand amongst your people and stand strong."

<u>The Sioux Tribe Reservation, South Dakota</u>
The mines hidden on their land have always been the legacy of their people; not because of spirituality, but because they provide revenue to pay back their debts to the United States government. Today these very same mines became the source of the Sioux's greatest fear. Twelve Native American miners are trapped underground surrounded by darkness, dust, and terror. Their slow suffocation is a looming terror wanting to cause inevitable death.

The mine caved in at noon and the rain started three hours later. Now, in the early evening cold, the local fire department struggles against all odds to save the fathers and sons trapped below. Earlier rescue attempts have failed. At the present, a snapping of ripped metal cables and the grumbling of earth covered tractors fatigued in fuel and effectiveness remind those witnessing that failure has not reared her ugly head. The storm increases in ferocity to complicate the chaos. High hopes shatter. Despair gathers strength. Whispers of mourning fall onto the bitter-chilled air alongside harsh comments of acceptance. Both murmur the topic of death and yet all are careful not to speak too loud. The mud slows the pace of rescue to almost a halt. No one wants to accept it and so rescuers tinker with their machinery while debating new ideas.

In the sky a silhouette can be seen breaking the darkness with his arms held out to his side. Lightning strikes create a divine illumination which blesses the edges of the hovering figure's uniform. The emerald and gold hue piercing the sullen heavens, delivers hope to the weary rescuers below in that the self-proclaimed hero of their people is here. He is Magister.

He levitates down in front of the mine entrance, landing in mud that creeps up his legs, almost to his knees. Twisting his body while opening both of his hands with his fingers separated and tense, he commands the formations of pure emerald energy into a pulsating sphere. Extending both of his arms before him with his palms touching, the sphere spins as arms of power jump from it, displacing the rocks and mud that was closing in the entrance to the mine. The rain from the storm runs down the creases on his aged face. His eyes stab into the darkness as he pulls his arms back into his chest and inhales. Rain water splatters against the force of his shout as he thrusts his hands before him once again, causing the entrance of the mine to crumble open, pulling the wood and boulders backwards through the air.

Magister enters the mine and vanishes into the gloom as the rescuers and families wait outside, watching the last glows of his emerald aura fade away, swallowed by the darkness. Thirteen minutes later, the self-proclaimed hero levitates out of the mine with four barely breathing miners enveloped in his green aura. Medics go to work on the men as soon as he lets them down. Coughing up small drops of blood, Magister turns to re-enter the mine, but then whirls his head around at the sound of a large black jet craft hovering above in the storm.

The jet craft lands and two figures leading a small group of ten Elite Forces Guardsmen rush out into the mud and rain to confront Magister.

"How can we help, Master Sergeant?" Asks one of the leading figures.

Puzzled and stunned, Magister takes charge and speaks in a commanding tone to the Marine wearing a general's uniform. "Sir, do you have a medic with you?" His conversion to military warrior is instinctive and immediate. It is not something he invites; it is something that is embedded within all that have served.

The general points to his partner who is dressed in light armor with a utility backpack. "This is Dossman, and he's one of the best!"

Magister pauses in the rain, and then nods his acknowledgment to the medic.

"Who are these other Marines, General?"

The General opens his hand while pointing it at the Elite Forces Guardsmen, "They are here to help you if you need them, Master Sergeant."

Magister nods once again and redirects his attention to the medic. "I need you with me, Mr. Dossman. General, I need you and your Guardsmen to work with the rescuers up top on securing this area. They will be answering to the elders who are over there with the firemen. It looks like the entire mine is about to collapse underground. I am going to have to go deeper for the other miners!"

The general agrees and rushes with his men through the rain over to the elders. After receiving an earpiece radio communicator from the medic, Magister surrounds Dossman and himself with bright green energy and levitates back into the shaft of the mine.

The two descend to almost half a mile down before they detect any life. Dossman enables the bio-optics in his helmet visor in order to locate the miners by heartbeat and thermals. He directs Magister through the darkness by activating his helmet and belt lights to guide the way.

Magister moves rocks and boulders out of the way by surrounding them with his green aura. The duo churn through the darkness as a worm crawls through the soil. Dossman is locked in awe as much as he is in fear, as blackened rocks dislodge from rest when touched by Magister's powers. The rocks, be they pebbles or boulders, dance within the coursing energy towards the duo and shuffle through the gloom out of the way as they pass though foot-by-foot deeper and yard-by-yard into endless darkness.

Breathing becomes increasingly shallow for the platinum-haired hero seeking to save his people as the dust and strain take a toll on him. Dossman pulls out a sheet of plastic the size of a small hand towel from his backpack and presses it against Magister's face. The plastic molds to his face and becomes transparent as he presses the side of the small pin-sized plastic tank embedded on the cheek.

"This is a filtered re-breather," Dossman says. "It will protect you. I am picking up eight wounded figures behind this wall of rocks; do you have strength enough to move it, sir?"

Magister catches his breath and drops to one knee. He welcomes the voice of the medic amidst the loneliness of this darkened cavern. He imagines the terror being felt by those trapped... and it gives him strength. He balls up both of his hands into fists and rises from the ground, commanding an aura so bright that Dossman has to shut down all of his optics to shield his eyes from the light.

The rocks tremble and jerk as they, once again, begin to dislodge from the cavern walls to create a pathway for the weakened men. On the other side, there are only two men with enough energy to respond to questions asked by Magister through the hole. Dossman pulls out eight plastic re-breathers and holds them up as Magister surrounds them with energy and levitates them through the hole. The two miners begin to place the re-breathers on all of the men, giving them fresh air for their weakened lungs. Dossman calls the general on his radio. "General, we have located the miners and given them re-breathers, but some of them are in serious condition. What is your situation up top?"

The General responds with crackles and static, "The elders are sending a rescue team down with cables that are connected to our jet craft. The schematics show mining carts beyond the cave-in. Force the cable through the holes and connect them to the mining carts."

Dossman acknowledges the transmission and guides the rescue team to the hole. The team feeds the cable through and orders the men to put all of the miners into the carts. Magister orders the rescue team and Dossman to head back to the surface. He takes a radio from Dossman and informs the elders on the surface that he will use his powers to protect them on the way up.

The elder in charge signals the general, who in turns orders his pilot, Myth, to take off slowly, pulling the miners upward through the mines. The entire process seems to be the longest twenty minutes of their lives for everyone witnessing the event.

The carts protected by Magister's emerald aura emerge from the mouth of the mines with all eight miners alive. The cables are disconnected as the medical staff rushes over to give aid to the injured. Each re-breather mask disintegrates when removed from the face of its wearer.

Magister stands with his face to the sky, inviting the rain from the storm to cleanse away the dirt from his stern and chiseled face.

The elder in charge walks over to him, placing his hand onto his right shoulder and thanking him for his help. Magister looks at the elder, then glances at Dossman, the general, and the Elite Forces Guardsmen.

"Teamwork was the hero today," says the fatigued warrior.

Magister then walks over to the general and Dossman as the rain stops. The Guardsmen enter the Sky Ghost alongside Dossman, leaving the general alone to speak with Magister.

Standing in front of the general, the platinum-haired warrior speaks as his eyes take on a slightly jade hue. "The last time you people visited me, they sent some psycho woman with a warning, escorted by one of those damn Ghosthawk assassins. Now you're here? A general? Why are you here?"

General Black reaches into his jacket and pulls out a cigar case. He surveys the area while lighting a cigar. "I think that you know why we are here, Master Sergeant."

Magister does not react to the aroma of the black cherry cigar smoke that is blown from the general's mouth. "Stop calling me by that title, General. I am done with your government. I kept to the warnings and made up for my mistakes! We are a sovereign nation here and I am a citizen and servant."

The general removes his cigar from his mouth while exhaling slowly. He squints one of his eyes as the smoke passes over his face.

"Two divorces, drug rehab, and two serious bouts with alcoholism that leaves you coughing blood on every other night of your life; you came back here to try to piece your life together and to give back by becoming a 'hero' to your people...not a servant. The sad part is that you've been messing up the entire time, son. You put six people in the hospital five years ago and you've amassed thousands of dollars in property damage by using your powers while either high or drunk. They don't all see you as the 'hero' that you want to be, Master Sergeant Runninghawk." The general's tone is more informative than forced, although the latter would normally be expected from one of his rank. Magister recoils from flood of truths that pours into the rising tension between him and the General. The simple fact is that the nonchalant demeanor of the commanding officer was enough to remind him that this was not a debate to be won. General Black continues, "It seems that you're caught between an eternal readjustment from the Marine Corps and finding your place among your peers. I'm here to help you with that, Devil Dog." The general then smirks while saying, "...as for me calling you by your rank and name...'Once a Marine, always a Marine,' Master Sergeant Runninghawk. I can't help you with your people, but I can help you with yourself and your powers."

Magister lowers his head as the silken platinum hair surrounding his bald upper scalp falls across his shoulders and silhouettes the stern structure of his face. He rubs the top of his balding skull while contemplating his wants and needs. He knows not where to focus his resentment. General Black looks beyond the perplexed, glowing man to those gathered in the distance to witness. Wonderment, fear, apprehension, and distrust mark many of their faces while hope, admiration, and inspiration are loosely scattered amongst the same stares like fireflies dotting the scene of a moonless night.

"It seems that you are more stuck on the stereotypes of what you want your people to be rather than accepting what they are. They don't see you as one of their long lost spirits, Master Sergeant. That old way of thinking is gone. They see you as someone that can't be contained; some even fear you. You're going to have to give everything to be the hero that you want to be."

Magister surrounds himself with an aura of verdant swirling energy as the general's comment strikes an emotional nerve within him. He hovers a couple of inches off of the ground. "You bastards should stay out of my life! You are the reason that I wanted to die. You are the reason that I ran away from everything and hid myself. I will never work under your command again, white man! I will handle things here... my way! Thank you for your help today, but get off of my people's land, now!"

Dossman stands in the entrance of the Sky Ghost watching the conversation. The general turns to enter and stops in the doorway. Magister hovers over to the general and stands before him with his chest out in defiance. General Black calmly pulls out a card and offers it to the hovering Marine.

"Master Sergeant Runninghawk, I am not here to recruit you, I am here to warn you. They know who you are now and they are coming. Here is my card with my direct extension on it."

The door of Sky Ghost begins to close as Magister snatches the card and glares back towards the general. "Who is coming?"

General Black flicks ashes from his cigar away. He then turns and walks further up the ramp turning to answer Magister's final question.

"The Third Nation. Oh, and Magister, these bastards know about Nimlok."

Magister's aura dies as the look on his face registers shock at the recognition of that name. His mind floods with memories as the Sky Ghost rises, then rockets off in the stormy sky. The name spoken is one that stirs feelings of confusion and fear within Magister's soul.

CHAPTER 17

KNIGHTMARE PROPHECY

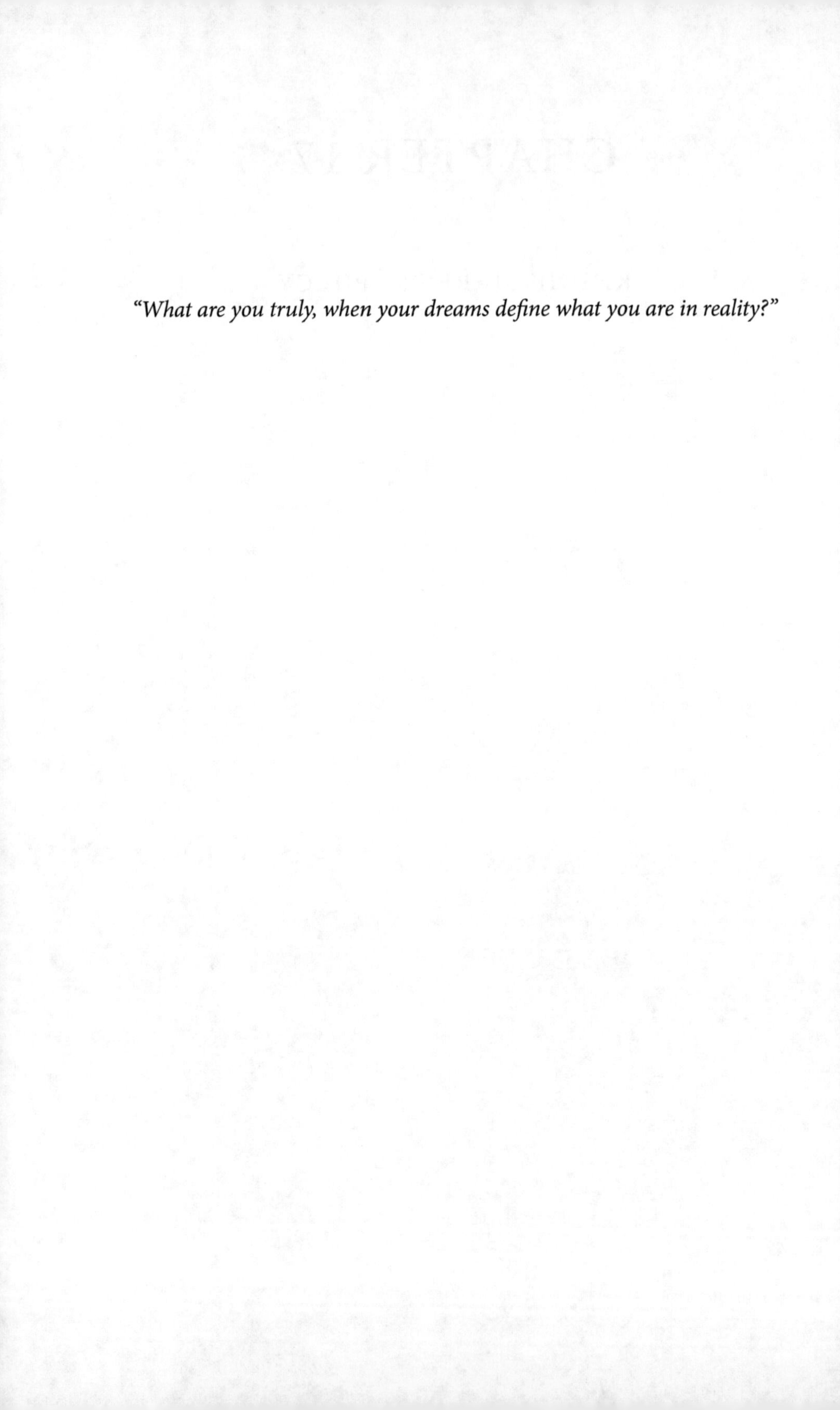

"What are you truly, when your dreams define what you are in reality?"

<u>Operation Dream Catcher</u>
The early morning alarm, along with the tender aroma of scrambled eggs and maple flavored turkey bacon, awakens Staff Sergeant Livingston to a warm and clear Southern morning. The tinkering in the kitchen creates a melody distinct from the washing of glass and silverware by a lovely wife and companion. When he opened his eyes this morning there was a slight feeling of disorientation, but this was instantly, seamlessly replaced by the beauty of his woman and the comfort of walking up behind her and enveloping her in a hug. She pauses to wipe the soap from her hands and looks back with her deep blue eyes to receive a soft kiss on her neck and finally her lips; Staff Sergeant Livingston is home.

~~~

His mask is soaked with sweat while his actions radiate determination. Knight uses all of his heightened agility to evade and subdue a mob of townspeople in their attempts to kill him. Blue and scarlet rips through the night with each of his escapes. With his back against a cashier's counter in the back of a small home improvement store, Knight flips backwards, kicking a shovel out of an attacking man's hands. He lands on the counter, then jumps back to the top of a metal shelf, using his shield to block thrown tools from the mob. Breathing hard and searching desperately for a way out, he notices a skylight on the ceiling above the crowd. He leaps from shelf to shelf, panting for air whenever he pauses to regain his balance from the shelves being pushed over. He knows that he has to save his teammates.

~~~

"Hey, Dad, Catch!!"
A perfectly thrown football lands in the raised hand of Captain Edwards as he pulls a barbecue basting brush from his favorite grilling apron before throwing the ball back to his son. He smiles contentedly at his wife, Alicia, standing beside a rack of ribs and hamburgers galore, grilling to the tasty feel of early summer songs. She compliments him with a pinch on his butt and a rub on his chest, beneath his sports shirt. His chest is normal, there is no Retro N-ionic Amplification Core embedded in it and his family is one. Captain Edwards knows that he is home.

~~~

Crashing through a cramped window, ripping his uniform on the frayed wood, Knight gains a quick chance to catch his breath and think. The townspeople move like zombies. Their eyes are white and glow with an eerie light. Their movements are stubborn and forced. Pulling the bottom of his mask up to wipe his mouth he remembers that was the exact reason they were sent to this sleepy little town. The reports of milk-white eyed zombie-like civilians were as true as the government's attempt to ensure that the public would never know. He never heard of Mount Olivet, Kentucky, before today and he will never forget it if he survives this mission. He pulls glass shards from his back and bites down on a large piece of wood to muffle his anguished grunt. He prays that the doctors were right about his extrability to heal three times faster than a normal person, because God knows that he needs it right now. The thing he has learned about this new ability to heal is that flesh kneading together unnaturally quickly creates just as much pain as the injury that caused it. Leaning forward to peer out of the window, he steals a glimpse of the source of this town's madness, a church.

The paltry church in the center of this small town glows with an unnatural cerulean energy that infects all that it touches. It seems that this very-same energy is crawling within the swamp mist, hovering above the ground, crawling as though it was a thing alive. The town is covered with it, adding to the horror of the entire situation. Knight knows that his friends are in that haven of worship and wonders briefly why he hasn't been affected by the energy. He takes out his crucifix from his belt pouch and kisses it, then pulls his mask down and says a quick prayer to God. The youth focuses. He knows that he has to save his teammates.

~~~

Staff Sergeant Livingston spends the day mostly relaxing on the front porch while reading literary history books and talking about politics with his wife. He enjoys her intellect and adores her sexual nature, demonstrated through her actions and vocabulary. Her chosen words often have more than one meaning, as do her actions. She is everything that he could want in a woman.

Early evening invites the full of the moon and the climax between the couple. The night is theirs and for each, it is spent in the grasp of warm flesh, making love to one another. Her skin has a pleasant tan from the afternoon sun, flavoring his desire with salt from her sweat and satisfaction to be heard in his voice of need. He grips her blond hair with the arrogant pull of manliness and eases into soft caresses of intimacy only after her failing voice of gratification whispers softly. This woman does not hesitate to give all that she is to her husband through the darkness. A single warm glow outside the windows watches over their embrace. Golden hair and golden eyes are clear within the brilliance. It is the flapping of the wings that give definition to the form... it is an angel.

~~~

Engulfed in unholy energy, Knight enters the back of the church and moves through the shadows. From the curtains of the backroom doorway, he gains a clear view of the pulpit area. His body stiffens as his beliefs are challenged, the same as a man meeting the devil. He glimpses an individual dressed in clerical vestments with his hands outstretched in each direction. His skin is dry with a bluish-gray tint and his hair is weathered, thin and wispy with much of his skull showing. He rants in broken languages, Italian, Latin, and Ancient Egyptian, as he bellows in anger to the heavens and to the Earth. Knight moves forward a single step and recognizes his two teammates on the ground between the pews with their eyes rolled back, their bodies jerking periodically. The Dark-Priest would say something over them, then raise his hands above them, causing their bodies to glow and jerk more as energy streams from their mouths and eyes into his palms. Islander looked the worse of the two, his body almost completely tapped, making his uniform hang loosely off his shrunken frame. Both are surrounded by a small group of townspeople, different from those on the outside, their eyes glowing with the same type of cerulean energy coming from the Dark-Priest. They all stand around as part of this darkened ceremony of evil, holding altar candles for their self-proclaimed savior.

Suddenly, one of the possessed farmers walks from the back room through the curtain and bumps into Knight, causing him fall against the altar table. The Dark-Priest stops his chanting, then turns to face the front of the church from the aisle between the pews. Knight knows
~~~

that he has been discovered and stands erect with his shield beside him without a word. He gazes into the face of his enemy.

The Dark-Priest has four eyes, with a pair above his normal ones on his forehead. His top two eyes glow with his signature unholy energy while his bottom eyes are rolled back in his skull, showing only white. The Dark-Priest stares forward with confused apprehension, crosses his arms, and speaks in English.

"Where are you, my little sinner? Come out so that we can see you!" The energy breaks around the Dark-Priest as his beastlike nostrils flare to snatch the young hero's scent. Moving his tongue along his front teeth, the unholy villain licks the air and says, "Malignant." He cannot see the shield-bearing Marine, but he knows that he is there. "You are the malignant one to start it all. You are here! I can feel the taint of your curse!"

Knight becomes confused. He is standing clearly beside the church altar, no less than 10 yards in front of the Dark-Priest, and yet seems to be invisible to his frantic search. Without a word, Knight steps on top of the altar, kicking the fallen candles onto the floor. The Dark-Priest sways his head back and forth, lowered jaw out, sniffing for the Marine.

"I smell your sickness, Malignant-One. I feed on the futures of the living as they envision it and yet you are not here for my holy vision to feed on. You are not 'truly' alive are you? You are a Fallen. A Fallen brethren; a little more than the demon that you must become. You are the source of the infection. You are the one whom the darkness seeks, Malignant One." He then raises his hands, causing the townsfolk with glowing eyes inside to also look around.

"You cannot hide and you will not stop me, sinner! The living must see their visions and I must feed... the same as you will need to. I can see through the eyes of those closest that I control! I will find you!!"

Knight finally realizes that he is invisible to the eyes of the Dark-Priest.

<div align="center">~~~</div>

With everyone fed and the sun beginning to set, Captain Edwards goes over to the park's football field to watch his son play a game with his friends. With his son scoring most of the touchdowns and leading his team, the captain feels a brief sense of pride and accomplishment as a father. It is the last play of the game that makes his rush of feelings quickly change to wariness. The sky becomes yellow, orange, and then a deep blood red while the outer edges of the park change to desert. A piercing cold sets in within seconds, stilling the warm ambience of evening hues and leaving dank swirling gray clouds laced with crawling blue streaks of energy. His son screams out to him as he tries to get across a football field that is changing into the landscape of a battleground strewn with rubble and destroyed military vehicles. His voice begins to drown beneath the sounds of a distant thunder. His words form nervously upon his lips, seeming to deliver warning and not fear. Captain Edwards runs through the debris, passing wounded soldiers grasping for weapons, firemen clinging for life, and civilians begging for help. He desperately yells out to his son as the entire ground starts to shake with a thunderous pound of urgency. His son falls down and turns around on the ground to see the form of a large demon ripping from the ground with skin of ash and cold flame. The darkened storm above serves the monster, as heavenly bolts of lightning begin to strike around him, displaying amber eyes of yesterday's failures, and horns protruding from his shoulders add to the distinct essence of evil about this beast. The demon grabs the captain's son and roars, knocking Captain Edwards back into a pile of rubble. He yells out to the hell spawn that clutches his son. He screams and calls only to realize that his voice is nothing more than a muffled plea. His son dissolves into chunks of soft dust within the grasp of the beast. The failed father's heart contracts in guilt-ridden agony. Poisoned by anguish, he is paralyzed as the demon crosses over him, bringing attention to his panicked wife running towards him with her hands out, shouting for their son. The hellspawn bellows to the storm above while laughing, fire billowing from his mouth. Its body slowly begins to rise amongst the cold winds piercing the surroundings with the icy touch of hell. The massive frame of the beast spins slowly, rotating clearly in the eyesight of the collapsed captain. The yellow line of letters scarred into the side of the demon's thigh grabs his attention: Property of the U.S. Government.

He knows that he has failed his family and himself. This beast cannot be stopped. He has lost control.

~~~

Pharaoh awakens in the church to see Knight battling the Dark-Priest among the burning pews. The Dark-Priest's bottom eyes have rolled back to their normal position, giving him the ability to see
~~~

Knight. The enraged villain's sighted eyes are drawn by the movement of Pharaoh and he comprehends that the large man is recovering and shrinks away from the gleam of his golden eagle.

"You have freed the God-Maker before his time, malignant one! My feeding is not complete! His vision is unanswered! For this you will die!"

The Dark-Priest is stronger than Knight physically, throwing him into different parts of the church's interior. The masked recon Marine uses his extrabilities to roll with the blows directed at him, delivering effective counter-attacks into the mid-section of the Dark-Priest. Through a bloodied mask, Knight tries to get Pharaoh to act: "Pharaoh! Pharaoh! Snap out of it!! I need your help!"

Pharaoh sits up on his knees, detached and oblivious with tears in his eyes, deaf and blind to everything around him. The determined youth continues to battle for the minds of his teammates as the situation devolves further into chaos. The Dark-Priest acts as a nightmare prophet caught between the two worlds of his visions and reality; he becomes desperate to kill the young shield-bearer. "You will bring the famine, Malignant-One! You must die! God knows that you must die!" The frenzied prophet begins to fire bolts of energy from his forehead that destroys entire sections of the inside of the church. As Knights gains more of this nightmare prophet's attention, scared townspeople begin to awaken from his mental grip, panicking. They drop more of their altar candles, causing flames to erupt in all parts of the church. The situation becomes critical as Knight uses his shield to deflect the mental blasts from the psychotic Dark-Priest into the double doors of the church. The doors explode outward, creating an escape route for the people.

~~~

There is a loud bang on the front door of Staff Sergeant Livingston's home, waking him up beside his wife; the angel from earlier is gone. He gets up and notices the sound of horses outside gathering in front of his home. He becomes wary as something in his mind stirs. He feels that something is not right.

When he opens the door, he is greeted by a large man wearing white with a large, cone-shaped hood. He stands face to face with a Klansmen holding a torch, speaking frantically with excitement. Behind him, there are others laughing on horseback with a long rope tied around the arms of a weary black man in tattered clothing. His
~~~

body is soaked in sweat and blood. His head is held low, gasping for the life-giving air that is quickly fading from the grasp of his lungs. He is the living memory of the escaped slave with a large frame and broken spirit.

The cloaked men begin to laugh and celebrate as they pull the black man away behind the horses. Tired and weak, the man falls to the ground only to be welcomed by razor sharp stones, wood, and dirt, digging into his flesh as he is dragged. His face twists and bumps against the ground, his face hidden beneath a mask of blood, soil, and dust. Staff Sergeant Livingston's wife comes to the door, inquiring about the visitors and catching a glimpse of the black man vanishing into the shadows behind the horses. She hugs her husband and kisses him on the cheek with a smile.

"They caught themselves a big one this time, honey," she whispers.

Staff Sergeant Livingston stands totally aghast. His home begins to crumble and vanish around him, opening into a large field with groups of woodpile bonfires. The scene is grotesque. Staff Sergeant Livingston looks around to see black people hanging from the nearby trees while some are burning on the bonfires. Their screams are silent, but the impact is that of a collision between surprise and expectation. His hands hurt as he raises them to see rope marks. He wipes his eyes, then turns slowly in a circle, looking around only to stop at the vision of his beautiful wife joining the jubilation. A torch is passed from his wife to his rope-bloodied hand, which rises to grasp it from her against his will. He stands next to a new bonfire with the black man that they were dragging. The man begs for his life as everyone yells out racial slurs at him; they stone him with rocks. The staff sergeant shakes his head furiously and tries to call out to his wife with unheard words. The light from the burning torch reflects against his milky white flesh to remind him of what he has become, just before his body forces him to light the woodpile beneath the black man creating a new bonfire of pain.

"Where is the angel now?" He cries within his thoughts as the strength of his faith is tested.

The slowly burning man calls out to Staff Sergeant Livingston as the flames engulf his flesh and for the first time he sees the face of the man that he is killing...it is not his own, as he expected. It is his captain; charred, blistered, hurting, and his target. He watches his best friend disintegrate into the nothingness after bone and dust. The uneasy acceptance of who he has become brings the golden-haired angel back in the distant sky above. With forearms of crystal and amber energy jumping between his hands, he hears a lone spoken word that is delivered as a whisper: "Executioner."

Islander awakens screaming at the top of his lungs as blood runs from his nose and ears.

~~~

Grabbing Knight by his throat with both hands, the Dark-Priest holds him down as he fires a mental blast at him from point blank range. "I have no pity for your death, demon! You are cursed! You are the sickness with no cure! For God's sake, die!" The blast has no effect. Knight takes advantage and breaks his grip, flipping him backwards. He then kicks him into an organ in the front of the church, causing a cross hanging above to drop down, crashing into the priest, knocking him out.

Smoke and flames engulf the room as the remaining townsfolk are freed from the mental commands of the Dark-Priest. Through the ash and haze, tears can be seen running from the eyes of the unconscious preacher. Pharaoh finally rises to his feet and uses his super-strength to grab a nearby fallen pillar, previously caught in the mind blast of the Dark-Priest . He throws it through a back wall, creating another exit. The masked youth slaps his hand on his captain's chest and takes charge, ordering the people out with Pharaoh following to help him carry the wounded.

Islander struggles to come to his senses as Pharaoh turns to him through the chaos. "Save the priest!" He commands through coughs and heaves for air. Standing in the heat and flames, Islander stares at his hands and looks around as parts from the roof fall about him. He leans against a burning pew and feels no pain as the char, which is so familiar, burns the gloves around his fingers. His natural immunity to heat and fire has grown exponentially. Stumbling deeper into the inferno as his clothes begin to catch fire, he grabs the unconscious villain and escapes through one of the stained glass windows to the eastern side of the church where everyone is gathered.

Those outside stand in grim reverence as they watch a man walking through the stained glass of Jesus with angels above him, unhurt from the flames of the Lord's house, carrying his enemy to safety. The sounds of helicopters in the distance are a welcoming sign of a successful mission to Knight, who kisses, through his mask, the
~~~

crucifix that he carries. Pharaoh stands away from the crowd, staring into the sky and rubbing his 'Y'-scar through his mask. Islander walks over towards the church to stare into the flames.

The first person out of the landing helicopters is OCD7-Webb, followed by his marketing team, who snap photos and record video as they approach. The team gathers around him as he begins to address them. "I want to congratulate all of you on the apprehension of this EMD. The code name that he goes by is Knightmare Prophecy and, as you can see, he lives up to his name."

Pharaoh rubs his neck as the elite forces corpsman, Dossman, approaches them to attend to Knight's wounds. Knight is still shivering from his adrenaline rush. Pharaoh looks at Knight, then looks into the eyes of Islander, pausing for a moment. He finally faces his commander.

"Sir, did you know what the guy would do to us before this mission? Did you know that he would screw with our minds the way that he did?"

The commander hesitates with his answer, first ordering his marketing team to discontinue the photos and recordings. "We weren't sure. That's why we had to send your team in, Pharaoh. We needed the best to save this town!"

Knight uses his fingers to remove his crucifix from his belt pouch and holds it in his hand as he speaks to Webb

"He called me a demon. H-He said that I was sick or something." Knight gives a quick look back towards Pharaoh, as though seeking permission, then turns back to his superior. "I have a question, sir. Why didn't any of his mental attacks affect me? Did you guys plan on that? The priest said that it didn't affect me 'cause I'm truly not a-alive. What kind of crap is that?"

Looking towards one of his marketers, who is signaling in the background with the mayor, OCD7-Webb answers Knight. "No, we didn't plan on it, Knight. In fact, Dr. Sharpe is going to analyze the data on this mission to see if he can understand what happened. Once we know...you will know, I promise."

Commander Webb waves his hand in acknowledgement to the marketer behind them and turns to leave the team.

"Oh yes, I almost forgot to mention that you have all been medically cleared to leave the base starting today. Oh, and Knight, according to our reports, you are very much alive! Once again, congratulations! I will see you all bright and early Monday morning."

Pharaoh moves slowly through the Marines and clean-up crews towards Knight. His emotional core is almost broken from the visions of this day. He realizes that the loyalty of one soldier was what saved them all today. He rests his hand with a gentle firmness on the shoulder of Knight and attempts to release a "thank you" through a throat swollen with gratitude; the "thank you" that is heard is one that does not come from the deep voice of Pharaoh. It is felt by each one of them as the statement comes from Islander who approaches from the other side of Knight.

"Today you were tha super hero that saved tha day, Knight. You're nothin' like the guys in your comics…you're better. Thanks for saving us, Gonzo."

Standing with a slight wobble and a single nod to Dossman, Knight places his open hand out, palm down, as Islander and Pharaoh place their hands on top of it. Knight turns to Dossman and waits, signaling to him that the team grasp is incomplete without his hand. Dossman places his hand on top and feels something stir within him.

Through his mask the youngest member of the team gleams with greatness as he looks at his band of brothers surrounding him and thanking him.

"Man, if only my momma could see me now. I need a drink."

For on this day, Corporal Gonzalez is really a knight.

~~~

Six hours later, Captain Edwards anxiously pulls into his driveway and pauses a moment before going into his home. Dim amber light peeks through the evening windows of his home. His mind races through the nightmares that he had that morning, only a few hours ago, and everything that transpired. Turning his vehicle off, he quietly says a quick prayer to God for control and ends it with him giving thanks for his family.

The warrior stands outside, relaxed; tactile sensation in this state allows him to enjoy the cool night air. The front door eases open, exposing a slender vertical strip of warm living room light, then widens in less than an eye blink, broken by two silhouettes rushing through the darkness. Love strikes the Marine captain far before a first touch can be felt. His son grabs him, choking out the most powerful word in his vocabulary, "Daddy," and his wife repeats the same in her own special manner, "Jon."

This husband and father does not want to cry; instead, he has to, while gripping the dearest people to him in his life, his wife and son.
~~~

They didn't know when he was coming home. He keeps his experiences to himself for the night and inhales the welcoming aroma of home-cooked dinner as he enters the house with a smile that says, "I'm home."

~~~

Staff Sergeant Livingston moves into his apartment, shuffling unsteadily, and sits on his couch. "An angel," he thinks. His surrounding walls, colors, and smells feel uncomfortable, almost alien. "An executioner," he resolves to himself. Resting his head in his hand, the confused staff sergeant leaves his position of mild discomfort to press the well-worn needle on his 1974 classic record player. Soulful harmony eases his tension as he glides his Caucasian fingers over the record covers. He remembers the char burning his beautiful, brown flesh. His heroes are frozen in time within the images on each cover; they seem to peer at him. They seem to notice his blue eyes...they seem to glare at his stringy blond hair. He drops the stack in his hand and recovers them one by one, announcing each name in his mind: Sam Cooke, Bobby Womack, Bobby Bland, Gladys Knight, Ben E. King.

The walls of the room display his pride, a picture of Malcolm X on one and Dr. Martin Luther King on the other, while also presenting his internal conflict. Malcolm motivated his shrewd desire for knowledge against the white man. Dr. Martin Luther King inspired him to have faith that change would come. It is the final picture of President Obama that represents that the change has arrived; for Staff Sergeant Livingston, the change was far deeper than he could have imagined. The ambient rhythm and smooth vocals of 'Moon River' begin to play. He contemplates the differences of these great leaders and his new form. "I bet they could never imagine a monster such as me," he thinks to himself. His thoughts drift back to the angel and his burning black flesh.

The sniper sits, once again refusing acceptance and embracing disdain.

"White?" He whispers as a question.

"White," he replies.

A portrait taken months ago, showing him hugging his love and special to his heart, sits on his side table; he misses her. He has tried not to think of her.

"Rose," he speaks clearly and brushes his thumb along the shape
~~~

of her body. "She's a proud black woman. She'd hate me like this."

Sickened by love's self-pity, he places the picture face down on the table top. The sniper closes off his emotions to those thoughts and memories. He becomes cold.

Walking over to the corner of his couch, he rubs an African mask, mounted on the wall, that was given to him by his father. He curls his fingers and rubs them slightly against his lips. He angrily begins to remove all of the pictures and statues from his room. Shoving the items into old boxes, he tapes them up and titles each one meticulously with black marker.

It is the final box that bothers him the most. The last object that he places within it, the old Atum-Ra Time magazine with the hero battling Klansmen on the cover, stings his soul. It was the last symbol of his childhood before his father died and left him alone. He used Atum-Ra as his reason for black pride and guidance. It was this magazine that reminded him so much of what he wanted to be...and now a final strip of tape sealed it away; leaving him with an empty room, white skin, and blue eyes.

<div align="center">~~~</div>

Corporal Gonzalez sits in a dimly lit corner of a bar with a bottle of warm liquor, a shot glass, and a small pamphlet labeled Top Secret, written by Dr. William Sharpe. He worries about the 'sickness' and the curse that was spoken about earlier. He instinctively rubs the small crucifix between his fingers as he stares at the title on the pamphlet before flipping it open. "Will it explain what I really am?" he questions before gulping his alcohol. He realizes that he is simply lonely.

A single song in the background seems to define his environment, as the lyrics by a heavy set piano player are offered into the smoke-filled atmosphere as almost a religious calling. He utters Billy Joel's "Piano Man" along with the patrons as they become the large musician's choir, raising bottles of beer and glasses of liquor in the air. The song is desolate and yet inviting to the lonely. It fits the young corporal sitting in the back, confounded. Flipping through the pages, he realizes that he is the harmonica within this song. Different, and yet a critical part in making the song work. He is the 'harmonica' to the song of his team and today he felt as though he belonged.

"Maybe the captain will like me now," he thinks. "Maybe Staff Sergeant Livingston will trust me now? I'm not a demon... Maybe Staff

Sergeant Livingston will trust me."

His hope rises with the thought of the Captain and drops just as quickly at the realization of the sniper's general attitude towards life. "Staff Sergeant Livingston doesn't trust anyone." He grips the bottle of Captain Morgan and drinks it straight from the bottle, ignoring both the shot glass and the burn in his throat.

The women in the bar around him are beautiful. On a normal night such as this, he would be spending his time hunting for his next prey, hoping for a single night of conquered pleasure. Tonight is different. He glides his finger over the bold ink on the top of the pamphlet. The title is "N-ionic Energy: The theory of the evolution of man." This experience was nothing like he expected. He was called a super hero, but his pain was real. The blue skies, happy faces, and great adventures from his Hero Federation comics were tainted by dead people, mind control, and a sick madman with abilities and warnings that were a religious sin. He makes a special, drunken prayer and wonders about the nightmares and prophecies experienced by him and his teammates today. He wonders about his immunities. He wonders if it is an omen in itself to have to no foreseeable future. The youth's hand begins to twitch and his mouth becomes dry as he reads more and more of the pamphlet. He fears what he is to become. He closes the booklet and stares out at the women around him; he stares out at his prey.

CHAPTER 18

EVOLUTION

*"Always wonder who thy father is, young one.
For one controls the traits in thy blood
and the other offers you a Will to decide the traits of thy spirit."*

–Father Solomon

Alaska, six months ago—the fire fight was hell. The frozen winds and dry cold did well to hide an underground lab which produced anthrax packages for distribution to various organizations throughout the world. Members of the FBI, Homeland Security Forces and Marine Recon Tactical Squad 7—The First Factor—were sent in to eliminate all traces of the anthrax and those responsible for its creation.

The terrorists protecting the complex were prepared, as though they knew that they would be raided that day. A small army of well-armed enemy fighters engaged the FBI and Homeland Security Forces in the ice and snow outside of the complex while the lab workers below loaded the anthrax packages into escape vehicles. The First Factor approached from the western flank, infiltrating the complex from the roof. The point-man was Gunnery Sergeant Leander Lewis. Captain Edwards commanded his squad of five men to move through the corridors with haste, acting as the spearhead of the assault. Sergeant Mark "Doll" Daldgerin cleared the way with a barrage of short and accurate bursts from his M249 SAW, the sound like a belch on steroids, followed by the piercing ring of hundreds of spent 5.56mm casings dancing on the floor of the complex. It was role reversal for the others as they used their M4 assault rifles as support tools to his raging weapon. Opponents were neutralized with speed and precision.

The firefight in the loading bay caused multiple explosions and the death of team member Corporal Robert Scott. The last thing that Captain Edwards could remember was the sight of the corporal's body grotesquely opened by gunshots and the pouring of his precious lifeblood onto the floor, ending with Scott going into spasms and convulsions. An explosion beside Captain Edwards brought him instantly into nothingness.

He was awakened by the sting of frost bite on his cheeks and by the warm hands of his point-man, Gunnery Sergeant Lewis, yelling at him to stay awake while Lewis was performing first aid on him. His ears were ringing, he could not see well, and he tasted a mixture of gunpowder and blood in his mouth. Captain Edwards realized where he was when the ground began to quake from multiple explosions within the building behind them. The gunnery sergeant leaned over to protect him from falling debris and ice. Once the explosions were over, Captain Edwards surveyed the area, only to stop at the dead body of his teammate, Corporal Robert Scott, lying beside him in the snow. The fluttering poncho used to cover his body did very little to conceal the gunshot wounds exposing his frozen organs and drying

blood splattered on his cold-hardened uniform.

With his face soaked in blood from the Y-shaped wound on his forehead, the captain asked about the other team members. The gunnery sergeant, trying to save him, pointed towards the burning compound and said that they went back for the guy who killed Corporal Scott. From the ash and smoke of the destroyed complex, the last three members of the First Factor approached the wounded captain. The Young-Old Man threw another body down in the snow. Captain Edwards recognized him instantly as the enemy soldier that had riddled their dead teammate with bullets. Doll spoke first. "Liv got him, Captain," the sergeant said. When Captain Edwards asked why they went back into the complex, he knew that the reason was more than their mission. Both men looked at Staff Sergeant Livingston, who merely reloaded his weapon and said, "Cause we're family."

Captain Edwards said nothing else. On his team, Staff Sergeant Livingston had always been the executioner.

~~~

Camp Sparta (USMC Reserves), Antiquity, New York
Daylight Labs Underground Complex, Department Level-7

The training room that is designed for the First Factor is one of the most advanced in the world. There are over two thousand sensors, measuring almost everything there is to monitor from environmental changes within its walls to the amount of perspiration that comes from the pores of it occupants.

A hydraulic rack lowers from the ceiling and drives downward into the ground, forcing Pharaoh to his knees. The density and moisture sensors attached to his midsection each immediately register increases. The four corners of the rack connect to waiting sockets in the floor and systematically increase the pressure on Pharaoh's arms and back. He struggles to his feet against the tremendous load.

The gauge on the side wall displays "2.75 tons," then jumps to an even three as Pharaoh grits his teeth while pushing against the rack. The gauge increases to 3.25 tons, then creeps up slowly, ultimately surpassing 3.65 total tons of pressure.

Pharaoh's eyes glow and crackle with energy as his body begins to shake from the exertion. Sweat starts running down his entire body in rivers, as even his N-ionic enhancements cannot overcome the laws of physics and are using a tremendous amount of energy, generating
~~~

heat. He pushes upward on the machine, forcing the pressure to readjust to his strength. The computer controlling the rack increases its pressure to an equivalent of 3.8 tons. Pharaoh drops to one knee again, straining so hard that veins show in his neck. N-ionic energy begins to crackle and jump from the glass-like opening on his chest as it surrounds his body.

The pressure gauge jumps up to four tons, then struggles to increase weight as Pharaoh pushes against it with all of his might while regaining his footing. The machine smokes from the overload and cracks, releasing hydraulic fluid from all of its joints. The oily, reddish fluid squirts like blood all over the room as the machine dies a violent death. Pharaoh stands erect and forces the rack above his head. The pressure rack rips apart with the last setting on the gauge displaying "4.25 tons." Everything shuts down.

"This was recorded yesterday, General."

Dr. Sharpe presses the pause button on the remote control in his hand, then turns to face the monitors above the conference table. He speaks to the members of the Omega Cabinet via video, while General Black and OCD7-Webb sit at the sides of the conference table as witnesses.

"The results from this last test yielded great results. We discovered that Pharaoh's anatomical density increased by twenty-five-point-six percent and his height increased over an inch in his powered up state."

The portly scientist grabs a pointer from the table and directs it towards a white poster board with a single, poorly drawn circle in the middle. In the center of the circle there is a small dot, labeled "Heart." "We've discovered a sand grain-sized particle within the center of Pharaoh's RA-Core and found it to be living. It is his heart, compressed and micronized in a fashion beyond anything that our science can explain. The process of the compression has turned it into a living source of endless power with an output comparable to our very own sun… if it was, in fact, the size of a sand grain. We know nothing of the true potential of this pure N-ionic power.

"We know that he can pull from this energy in times of need, but we have no device to test the upper limits of what is being produced in his chest."

"Are you stating that Pharaoh is a potential bomb waiting to explode? A bomb that can rival any of our atomic weapons, Dr. Sharpe?" Asks one of the shrouded figures on screen.

"No, sir. His power shows no sign of building to an explosion. In fact, it shows something much different and personal to Pharaoh. Somehow it is being absorbed into his very being and enriching him. He is extremely resistant to most poisons and diseases. While already bright, his intellect and knowledge retention seem to be increasing; as a-matter-of-fact, his main weaknesses are his emotions and humanity."

Webb stirs in his seat with a cynical smile. "And sooo... his confidence and his willpower dictate his aptitude and strength. He's as strong as his focus, which makes him weak. This is one of the reasons why I should have made the decision on the team and its members."

Dr. Sharpe responds in such a way that he dodges showing bias towards the comment made by Webb. "His body releases excess stored N-ionic energy when needed in order to increase his strength and durability. During the tests, Pharaoh's base strength increased temporarily, then dropped back to normal when he felt he had done his best."

The doctor begins to show other video footage of himself working with Pharaoh to lift everyday items without crushing them. "Pharaoh is all but invulnerable whenever his Retro-N-ionic Amplification Core is active. Because of this, his natural sensations of touch and feel are almost non-existent. We have been working for the past month and a half on controlling his N-ionic output levels."

The video shows Pharaoh placing eggs into a carton and drinking water from various types of glass cups.

"We have learned that when he totally relaxes, his RA-Core subsides and his skin density decreases to levels close to normal, giving him the ability to feel. This is an important accomplishment for this Marine."

The doctor clicks his remote to display training footage and statistical information on Islander and Knight. "What we have noticed is that each of these Marines evolved N-ionically from the first day that they received their extrabilities. Islander's reflexes and vision have increased his accuracy with a bow to a ninety-plus percent hit-miss ratio when standing still with four seconds to aim. It drops to eighty-six percent when moving and less than four seconds to aim. He displays a high resistance to heat and fire... while his racial change seems to be permanent in every regard.

"Knight's body functions have increased again, from two to three times that of a normal human, to somewhere near four to five times. He can hold his breath underwater for over twenty minutes and lift six-hundred pounds; mental assaults and hypnosis seem to have no effect on him, unlike the others. His awareness has also increased to an undetermined level. He can sense the presence of others flawlessly within a twenty foot radius."

The video conference screen changes to a silhouette of a woman, who introduces herself to Dr. Sharpe before expressing her concerns.

"Dr. Sharpe, I am the newest member to The Omega Cabinet and a civilian business owner. I know how the military feels about the creation of their 'special' warriors-of-mass-destruction, but I am wondering what safety mechanisms we have in place to ensure the safety of the nation's population in case one of these soldiers goes rogue. After all, we all remember what happened with the Shapens. "

The focus of the question stings the doctor back to reality as he is faced with a topic for which he has no solid answer prepared.

"Well, uh…that's why we chose these Marines, Ma'am. They believe in honor and…" He is stifled by the woman's visible annoyance with his answer and interrupted by a new military scientist walking into the room. The darkened woman on the video screen turns her head downward as though she is frustrated, then faces the camera again. "Dr. Sharpe, my father has told me nothing but good things about you and your work. I have total faith in your capabilities. As you know, the Elite Forces Division receives major support from corporate sources; hence, you are employees, under the military's command. You need to understand that our job here has nothing to do with faith. It has to do with facts, data, and multiple layers of security."

Dr. Sharpe stares at the tall, pale individual that walked in. He has a thin frame and bushy eyebrows. The mysterious woman speaks again, introducing the scientist. "This is Dr. Sisten. He will begin to work and train underneath you to gain an understanding of the team members and your progress. He is a specialist in genetic science and nanotechnology. He will work with you to ensure that one of our devices is implanted into each and every one of these soldiers to protect us from them."

Dr. Sharpe takes offense to the presence of the new scientist, whom he considers an interloper and a spy, but tries to hide his feelings from the members in the monitors watching.

"Dr. Sisten will begin the development of a special project that we are titling "Sand Dwellers." We will implant remotely activated Nano-bots into the Marines that can be triggered to release an acid capable of killing them on the spot. We expect that you will give him your full cooperation and support. He will update you with the details of his responsibilities to this project. You are dismissed."

The meeting ends sharply as the monitors turn black. Dr. Sharpe stands at the edge of the table pondering what had just happened, as General Black and OCD7-Webb leave quietly. Dr. Sisten waits until the others are completely out of the room before he says anything.

"Things are going to change, Dr. Sharpe."

He then leaves.

~~~

<u>Manhattan, New York</u>

A crowd of over a thousand people gather downtown to watch the announcement of the nation's first government-sponsored team of superheroes, led by Mr. Michael Webb. The press bombards the team with questions, most of which are answered by Mr. Webb. Music blares out into the air along with fireworks and ticker tape of all colors. Brochures are passed around and T-shirts are sold along the sidewalk by marketing team members.

The First Factor enjoys the limelight as children choose their favorite hero and adults marvel at the uniforms. There is a magic and a hope that spreads amongst the people as The First Factor is introduced as a team for the people. For OCD7-Webb, this is the moment that he has always waited for; this is his moment to shine.
~~~

CHAPTER 19

THE ENEMY

"Know thy enemy; know thy self...for this is a critical rule of war."

–Sun Tzu

It has been two weeks of intense training for the First Factor. Hostage rescue, facility take downs, cutting edge battle technology training, advanced command tactics, and organizational strike operations are just some of the areas covered. The Marines are pushed to the edge of their physical and mental limits in order to grow into their newly announced roles of America's premier super-hero team. The excitement of this pressure can be felt by all, but it is most adored the most by the Operation Commander of Department-7, Michael Webb.

The training room on their floor has some of the most technologically advanced equipment ever created. The walls are made of titanium and steel in order to absorb the brutal sessions that are delivered. The strength development area is made up of hydraulic barbells linked to the floor with pressure sensors located on the faceplate of each system. There is an internal track and a twenty-foot deep double Olympic-sized pool for survival rescue training.

Today's workout ends with Pharaoh sitting on his weight bench in his utility uniform with his mask removed. His arms tremble from the last four hours of weight lifting and cardio exercises. Wiping the sweat from the scar along his brow he looks up as the rest of his team completes their workout.

"I really like the blue-and-gray uniforms," he thinks to himself.

Their attention is focused on the small gathering of unfamiliar people assembled on the sidelines. Knight approaches Pharaoh while removing his mask. "Hey Captain, what's with da new faces over there? They look like Elvis, Tupac, and Megadeth in concert…nothing but noise! Who are they?"

Knight tips his head slightly, directing his eyes to the group of 'new faces'. At first to a scientist standing beside Dr. Sharpe and then a woman in a pantsuit, military in appearance, talking to General Black. The warm, yellow tone of her collared shirt peeking out from her three-button tropical-black jacket appears as a warning sign of things to come.

Pharaoh acknowledges that he sees them also as Islander joins them, collapsing his bow and connecting it to hooks on his uniform's back. "They've been studying us for the last few days."

Islander presses a release button on his face plate's earpiece to remove his mask. He then places himself in front of his teammates with his back towards the clustered scientists along the side of the training room. "Tha woman's security tag says OCD4-Grante. She's an Operation Commander just like Webb…you don't think that it's kinda fishy how she's watching us like a damn swamp-bird?"

Pharaoh stands up, tucks his mask into the side of his belt and faces Islander. "I've noticed it, too. C'mon let's find out what's going on."

Just as Pharaoh begins to lead his team over to the group of scientists, General Black approaches, heading him off, and orders them to muster in the lobby of their level in thirty minutes. Everything is cut short as all of the scientists compare notes while leaving the training room.

Thirty minutes later, the team meets with General Black and OCD7-Webb in the lobby. Each Marine has showered and changed into his dress blue uniform except for Islander. The flamboyant nature of the colors pisses him off and Commander Webb has yet to drum up the courage to order him to wear them. Instead, the sniper merely dresses in a clean utility uniform.

Pharaoh speaks directly to the general, ignoring OCD7-Webb, who is standing beside him. "Are we getting briefed for another operation,

General?"

Before the general can reply, OCD7-Webb crosses in between the two, heading towards the elevator and answers Pharaoh, "No, Pharaoh, we're going to the fourth level for a general security briefing...that's all."

The Marine captain straightens his posture and acknowledges Webb only by his glare. With a cynical smile and a stroke of confidence, in an effort to impress the general, Webb adds small talk to their conversation. "By the way, Pharaoh, I think you will be excited to know that I've been approached by Marvelous Comics about selling the creative rights for you and the team for a new series of comic books. Your character, in particular, is going to be the son of a ruler of a secret African nation that gets destroyed by earthquakes. Your father is also the most intelligent scientist of his people. He knew they would be destroyed, so he hid you as an infant in a special made ship and shot you over to America... as he and the kingdom was destroyed. I thought that last part was funny."

Pharaoh attempts to ignore Webb's sarcasm as he watches his small fire-haired commander fix his tie. Rolling his eyes over to the general in a self-indulgent manner, Webb continues, "The rep from their company said that we would draw minority demographics to their readership. I found myself laughing at that thought, General. I told them to make Islander the leader of the team and I would approve a license to them for three years at five million a year." Webb redirects his attention back to Pharaoh. "Needless to say, you're now going to be even more famous amongst your demographic. You'll be a great inspiration, Captain, and we will be famous."

Pressing the button on the elevator, Pharaoh responds with careful respect, "Thank you for the update, Commander Webb." The team enters the elevator with a sense of apprehension. General Black types in the security code for level four and notices the enmity growing between OCD7-Webb and Pharaoh. He chooses to remain silent about it and lights a black cherry cigar while relaxing on the ride. Filtered air-cleansers built into the ceiling of the elevator kick on to pull the smoke from the compartment.

The elevator door opens on the fourth level and the first thing that can be felt is a wave of damp cold. It is a familiar introduction to each department level floor in the Daylight Labs complex. The walls are gray and blue with a general feeling of loneliness and secrecy drifting in the atmosphere. The team is escorted down an empty corridor, passing tinted doors along the way, to a large conference room.

The conference room is a bleak gray with a large stone table in the center. There are three folders on the table top in front of seats designated for the team members. Standing at the head of the table is the woman in the yellow collared shirt from the earlier training session, talking to General Black and two uniformed soldiers standing beside her.

General Black steps to the front of the room, takes a drag from his cigar, exhales a plume of smoke, and introduces the woman all in the same breath. "Gentlemen, I would like for you to meet OCD4-Diantha Grante. She is the Operation Commander of the Intelligence Department for the Elite Forces Division. She commands the warriors standing beside her as well as the EF-Guardsmen and knows more about our enemy than anyone else in this entire compound."

Each of the uniformed soldiers standing beside her has a full-face, carbon-fiber hockey goalie-style mask with a single 'V'-shaped blue optics visor strip. Their uniforms are all identical except for the chevrons that identify their ranks on their deltoids. The battle-wear and small uneven scratches on their uniforms and masks are detected clearly by Islander as he mentally assesses the lethality of the soldiers before them. His first thought is Navy SEALS, and then drifts to Delta Force and CIA finally stopping, with a single low whisper, on "Assassins." Commanding the mysterious soldiers to attention, General Black introduces them. "These warriors are known as Ghosthawks. They specialize in the infiltration and investigation of specified targets or situations. There are five of them in all and they all report to OCD4-Grante. We think of them as our eyes and ears with the First Factor being our heart and fists."

The general raises his right hand, ordering the Ghosthawks to stand at ease, and then hands the meeting over to OCD4-Grante. She stands in an intense fashion, staring at the team before speaking a word. Her hair is sleek and black, with gray near the roots contrasting against her creamy pink skin and her yellow dress shirt struggling for attention beneath her black pants suit. Her face shows a stern beauty laced with years of worry, poorly hidden through a light application of make-up. After standing for a brief moment she presses a button on the wall behind her, causing a large screen to descend from the ceiling and beginning a visual presentation of the subject they were brought here to cover.

The screen shows multiple profile facial pictures, like mug shots, stacked in a hierarchy, with a single large one residing above all the others and lines attaching it to each subordinate image. Knight instantly recognizes one of the pictures as the Apostle General that he fought during the ambush operation on the freeway. He doesn't say anything and waits to see what Commander Grante has to say first. "Good afternoon, Strike Team First Factor. What you are currently looking at is an ongoing roster of our confirmed enemies. These individuals are members of a secret organization known only as The Third Nation."

Pharaoh leans forward, placing his elbows on the table while lacing his fingers together. "What do they do?"

The stern-jawed female commander points at the manila folders on the table labeled as Top Secret. "The Third Nation is a terrorist faction of a larger 'intra-national' community known as Reservation Blankadyne-21, led by a CEO known as Alexander Demonestri." She points at a lone picture, separated from the other known terrorists, to identify the CEO. "We know that he is involved, but there is no evidence to prove it. So we monitor him, for now." She continues with her information on their active opponents. "This faction is designed as an insurgent spearhead for terrorist actions against the United States government and our way of life. Please understand that these people are killers in every definition of the word."

"Intra-National? What is that?" questions the Marine captain somberly.

"Any sovereign nation within the boundaries of the United States that we have a relationship with," answers the Commander.

Islander rears his head away, slightly twisting his body in disbelief. "Blankadyne...hmmm. I remember them, they're tha secret research company that was working unda tha umbrella of General Motors way back in the 80s before the factory shut down in Flint, Michigan. That guy Demonestri was a part of that, too. The guy was found to be racist scum."

The commander stands back, correcting her yellow collar, impressed by the bold comment made from the Marine sniper. His comment strikes into the heart of her report as if it is one of his targets. She offers uneasy respect for his knowledge and allows him to continue.

"When tha word got out about Blankadyne's secret experiments...on blacks and other minorities, they shut down and high-tailed it leaving GM to crumble. GM left Flint to save face and all of tha brothers and sisters up there lost their jobs, dumping tha entire city into poverty. The government didn't touch him then, and I am not amazed that you're not touching him now."

"How do you know all of this, son?" Interjects General Black.

"Some people call it 'Black History', sir, the kind that don't get published and tha kind that don't get attention."

The general stares at the white man before him and contemplates the irony of his situation before offering his usual slight nod of approval. Pharaoh allows himself a small grin and hides it behind his hands by resting his face on his knuckles. They are only getting a taste of what truly makes my teammate so deadly and such a great friend, he thinks to himself.

"Impossible. I ain't never heard of this, Staff Serg...er, uhm... Islander," states Corporal Gonzalez.

OCD7-Webb steps forward to address Islander's comment. "Not impossible, Knight, just improbable...at least we thought it was six years ago. Their organization specializes in science, defense, and finance. It does exist. Under the leadership of Alexander Demonestri, Blankadyne has recruited some of the richest business owners in this nation and abroad. They're all hungry for more power. The company became a beast; although there is no proof of any direct attacks from their organization, we are sure that they have organized them. Our strength against these types of companies will be through general public support. This is why fame and publicity for the team is so important."

OCD4-Grante agrees with him and continues her briefing by directing the team's attention to a timeline displayed on the screen covering the last year, with points indicating attacks and operations. "The Third Nation was more of a controlled threat in the past. We have recently discovered that they are the faction that has been carrying out the attacks against us lately. We previously considered them a distant threat compared to the potential of other known terrorist groups such as the Muslim extremists making up Al-Qaeda or the disfigured race of Shapens calling themselves the Children of Pandora. We listed them, as mere annoyances. Once we took out Osama Bin Laden and Al-Qaeda dumped into disorganized confusion, The Third Nation stepped up their assaults as though they knew it was their time to move."

Islander shifts in his seat, with a sharp glare at the term "Shapens." It was the word that Dossman used to describe the snake-man Blackfang that he fought in the hospital earlier. It was a term that the brass seemed to know very well and yet he and his team were ignorant of it. He quietly commits it to memory for the future.

Sternly, the commander continues. "It has been within the last year that The Third Nation's threat status has been upgraded to number one. We've had a total of seven confirmed attacks in which we've used your team to respond to them."

"You mean when we were under Colonel Bishop's command?" Questions Captain Edwards.

Commander Grante smiles, "That's affirmative, Captain. Your previous commander, Colonel Bishop, was briefed on general operational parameters, while many of the details were classified."

There is a quick pause as tension rises with sudden realization. "You're talking about Alaska and the Udosion Labs missions, right... Commander Grante?" Asks the captain.

She eludes the direct answer tactfully. "We know that they are attempting to acquire a weapon of mass destruction to unleash on American soil." She then points to the picture above the others. It is an older photo of a businessman in an expensive suit, with chalk white skin bordered by thin ice-blue veins. "This is Lord Syphon. We believe

that he is the quiet right-hand man of Alexander Demonestri. It is the most recent photo of him that we could acquire and it is over six years old. He is the epitome of evil. He is N-ionically enhanced and has the extrability to control kinetic energy in more ways than our scientists can figure out. He goes where he wants and does what he wants. He has no qualms about murder and death. He is a business genius and a brilliant strategist. The bastard is a hero among his people. Don't ever underestimate him. He has absolutely no compassion."

Knight raises his hand and speaks out, "Excuse me, Ma'am...but has anyone come out to say that this bastard looks crazy?" The young Marine directs his finger to the blue veins bordering Lord Syphon's face. "I mean lookit' that blue shi...uh...stuff growing on da edge of his face."

Pharaoh looks at Knight causing him to drop his hand and to sit back in his seat. He shrugs both of his shoulders towards Pharaoh with his palms out.

"Uh...sorry, sir, I was just being honest."

Grinning once again, Pharaoh turns towards OCD4-Grante.

"He has a point, Commander. This entire thing sounds pretty crazy. Why don't we just strike their base of operations? Why don't you attack the company as a whole and arrest this Alexander Demonestri and make him talk? He has to know something about Lord Syphon."

"That is because we know very little about this organization, Pharaoh. We know that they have secret alliances with at least two other nations with sufficient power to cause an all-out war if we were to attack them directly. There is no proof that Blankadyne, itself, is responsible for anything; only The Third Nation. Demonestri is the most professional form of analytical businessman. This coupled with absolutely scary charisma. This allows him the ability to strategize and manage the operations run by him and his allies with utmost efficiency."

Islander stares at the satellite photos of Third Nation's base of operations from the folder on the table in front of him. "They're still here in tha United States? This is tha mid-west. Pharaoh, take a look at this. I thought Blankadyne left the US...that was what was reported on tha news."

OCD4-Grante explains, "This is the other reason that we do not want a direct assault on them. They are a sovereign nation on ten thousand acres within the boundaries of our country. The terrorist actions that have been taken against America have been done by members of their society and not by their nation as a whole. This would be a media nightmare for the U.S. government if we were to attack the entire nation of people because of the actions of a few; Demonestri would ensure it. Hence, we have to maintain a stable and politically correct intra-national relationship with them...even if we don't trust them. If we attack one sovereign nation within our borders, what type of message would this send to the others?"

"Uhm, what other 'intra-national' sovereign 'whatevers' are there exactly?" Asks Knight, appropriately air-quoting the terms, confused by the amount of new information that he has just learned.

"Each Native American reservation is considered an intra-national sovereign entity, Knight. If we attack one nation for the wrong reason we will lose whatever trust we have with other sovereign entities," explains Commander Grante.

"Yea, look at what ya did to the Native Americans. We wouldn't want a repeat of that now, would we?" States Islander sarcastically, peering hard across the table with cold blue eyes.

OCD4-Grante rubs her face then places both of her hands behind her back. "This is a new type of terrorism, Marines. Six months ago a senator and his family were found burned alive in their home. The autopsy showed that the daughter was dead before the flames burned her body. We still don't know how she died, but we do know that the senator knew about the meteorite hidden in the Udosion Labs complex."

She then shows a short video of the destruction of the twenty-ninth floor of a building in Manhattan's financial district. "This video shows the remains of one of the offices of the financial company First American Acceptance. They handle most of the finances for our Elite Forces Division as well as for Joint Special Operations Command. Everyone in the office was killed by a mysterious explosion except for the CEO; needless to say, we can't get anything out of him. In the following few months after the incident almost half of the board members died under questionable circumstances."

Pharaoh leans back in his chair and looks around the room in disbelief. "Was all of this done by the Third Nation? Have you considered that the Third Nation might just be a hit squad for Alexander Demonestri?"

OCD4-Grante nods her head slowly. "We believe it is."

General Black stands from his seat to address the team. "Make no mistake, Marines, we have a task before us. I will make this crystal clear...We exist to eliminate the threat of The Third Nation and to terminate Lord Syphon with extreme prejudice. Let the higher-ups deal with the politics and Demonestri."

The general speaks the language that these newborn superheroes relate to more easily. He speaks the language of Marines. Each warrior welcomes the candid nature of their senior officer as he rests his cigar in the ashtray before him.

"We will accomplish this mission while shining in the public's eye as superheroes to this nation. How you shine will be Commander Webb's problem; that's why he's in command. I expect you men to do what you do best...nothing less and always more!"

OCD7-Webb brushes his fiery-red hair to the side with a brief single swipe while scampering to his feet to add to the general's last statement. "This is why it is so important to follow my orders. I will make America adore us and the enemy fear us, all at once. We will have toys, movies, comics, and songs all over this nation praising us as their heroes. We will be famous!"

A small beep is heard at the back of the room as General Black answers a phone call on his cellular earpiece. The general removes his cigar from his mouth and exhales while saying, "My God." He disconnects his earpiece and takes control of the meeting.

"Webb, this meeting is over. We have an emergency. Pharaoh, I need your men in the hangar now! Commander Grante, I need you to activate two platoons of EF-Guardsmen and have them meet us at the hangar."

Pharaoh takes control as his team heads to the hangar. General Black orders OCD7-Webb to report to Dept-CU to prepare for the political backlash from this situation. He then joins the rest of the team in the hangar as they load into the division's custom-built C130 cargo plane, piloted by Myth. The team is greeted by Dossman and the two EF-Guardsmen platoons sent by OCD4-Grante. Dossman delivers the mission update to the entire team, including the general, as everyone finds their seats on the massive aircraft and straps in.

"There appears to have been a massive attack on the Sioux Reservation in South Dakota. There are heavy casualties reported and they are still fighting. The reports are still coming in, but it is believed that the attack is being carried out by the armed forces of The Third Nation. General, I have received intel informing me that Magister is on site battling the enemy."

The general grimaces as he leaves his seat to call headquarters from the back of the craft. Dossman continues with his update to the rest of the teams, answering their questions to the best of his ability as Myth pushes the C130 to its top speed.

CHAPTER 20

A MESSAGE OF SLAUGHTER

"A truthful whisper is nothing more than the future waiting to be heard."

–Dr. Sharon Gray, Clinical Psychologist

<u>The Sioux Reservation, South Dakota</u>

The C130 drops speed and altitude in order to survey the location before landing. The entire town is utterly destroyed. Buildings have been razed to the ground and fires are raging everywhere. Rescue helicopters struggle to remain in the air because of the amount of smoke and ash.

The streets are littered with the dead. Men, women, and children have been slaughtered indiscriminately. All around there are bullet holes and plasma burns; the signs of battle are obvious. Some of the injured tribesmen walk around in a daze while others try to help those in worse condition.

The aircraft lands and Dossman and a platoon of EF-Guardsmen, under the direct command of General Black, immediately go to work offering their aid to the local emergency medical technicians. Pharaoh and his team begin rescue operations with the other platoon of EF-Guardsmen in the burning buildings and other crumbling structures. The general heads to the center of town, following the path of destruction, while searching for Magister.

General Black crawls over a ridge and stands, holding his hand above his brow. He enters a large clearing with rings of debris laid out in a circular pattern. In the center of the circle, the general sees the silhouette of a man on his knees, leaning over with his weight on his hands, crying. The man is surrounded by a weak emerald aura and his uniform is torn to shreds.

The General walks through the smoldering circle of destruction and stands before the man sitting in the center.

"Master Sergeant Runninghawk...Magister...I-I'm sorry."

Magister looks up as the last bit of his jade aura fades away, showing his bloodshot red eyes. He looks around while lifting one of his hands, showing his bloody palm. His face is soiled with ash, sweat, and blood.

"G-General...they're all gone. It happened so fast."

Pharaoh passes over the ridgeline, approaching the general and Magister. The distress on his face is accompanied by a single head shake simply telling his superior officer, "No."

The general pulls Magister's arm across his shoulders and helps him to his feet. Pharaoh positions himself on the other side of the Native American Master Sergeant and holds him up like a pillar. Magister coughs up blood on to the back of his hand and speaks again, "They came like you said. They told me to join them...they wanted my elders to swear allegiance to them. The elders would not do it. General, this is their price. They hate your nation. They hate your people and they want blood."

Dossman comes over the ridge and begins to bandage Magister's wounds. Various shades of blood, wet and dry, are smeared all along the medic's uniform. The young soldier bites into one of his bandage bags, ripping it open, while mumbling to Pharaoh hysterically. He doesn't make eye contact. "I-I've never seen anything like this, sir. There are so many dead; I've never dealt with so many at once, Pharaoh."

"Stay in control, son. Everything's going to be alright," reassures the Marine captain. His words provide a quiet strength to Magister, who looks long and deep into his eyes.

"You are Pharaoh?"

"Yes, sir."

"General Black told me about you."

The Native American hero stands erect. Glowing green energy returns to his eyes as though vitality was transferred through the very touch of the large soldier that held him.

The general is speechless as the evening sky darkens before the sun sets. Magister shakes from exhaustion; his eyes are wide and brimming with tears that don't quite fall.

"My people had nothing that they could ever want or use. Why would they attack us? Why did they have to slaughter so many innocents? I think that they took some of the children, but I can't tell, General. Those weapons burned the bodies into ashes! We can't even tell if our people were taken!"

The general does a last survey of the destruction and faces Magister. "They did this because your people exist as a sovereign nation. They want to build an army to take over America and they needed land and soldiers. Master Sergeant, they came for you and your people. They wanted to hurt us by destroying you. They wanted us to know that we can't defend everywhere at once."

The General uses his foot to kick a small pile of wood ash. "This wasn't only a slaughter, Master Sergeant. This was a message."

Despondently turning away from the general, Magister signals his exit by making a feeble attempt to surround himself with N-ionic energy. He fails. It is the weight of Pharaoh's hand resting on his right shoulder that beckons for his attention a final time.

"Magister...we will hunt down those responsible for this and if it's up to me...I promise you that you will have your time with them. I mean that from one Marine to another."

The presence of the large Marine captain gives the broken hero of his people hope, which sparks the reemergence of strength. He stands and lifts his head towards the senior ranked general as a distant call beckons Pharaoh away.

Once alone, these two war-torn bastards of conflict stare at one another, sharing understanding by merely reading each other's expressions. Magister's voice trembles as he shares the parting message left by his attackers. "General, a storm is coming. They spoke of doom. They cried out prophecy. They praised a deliverer of death to be unleashed on their enemies. They warned of Nimlok."

CHAPTER 21

COLORADO – PART 1

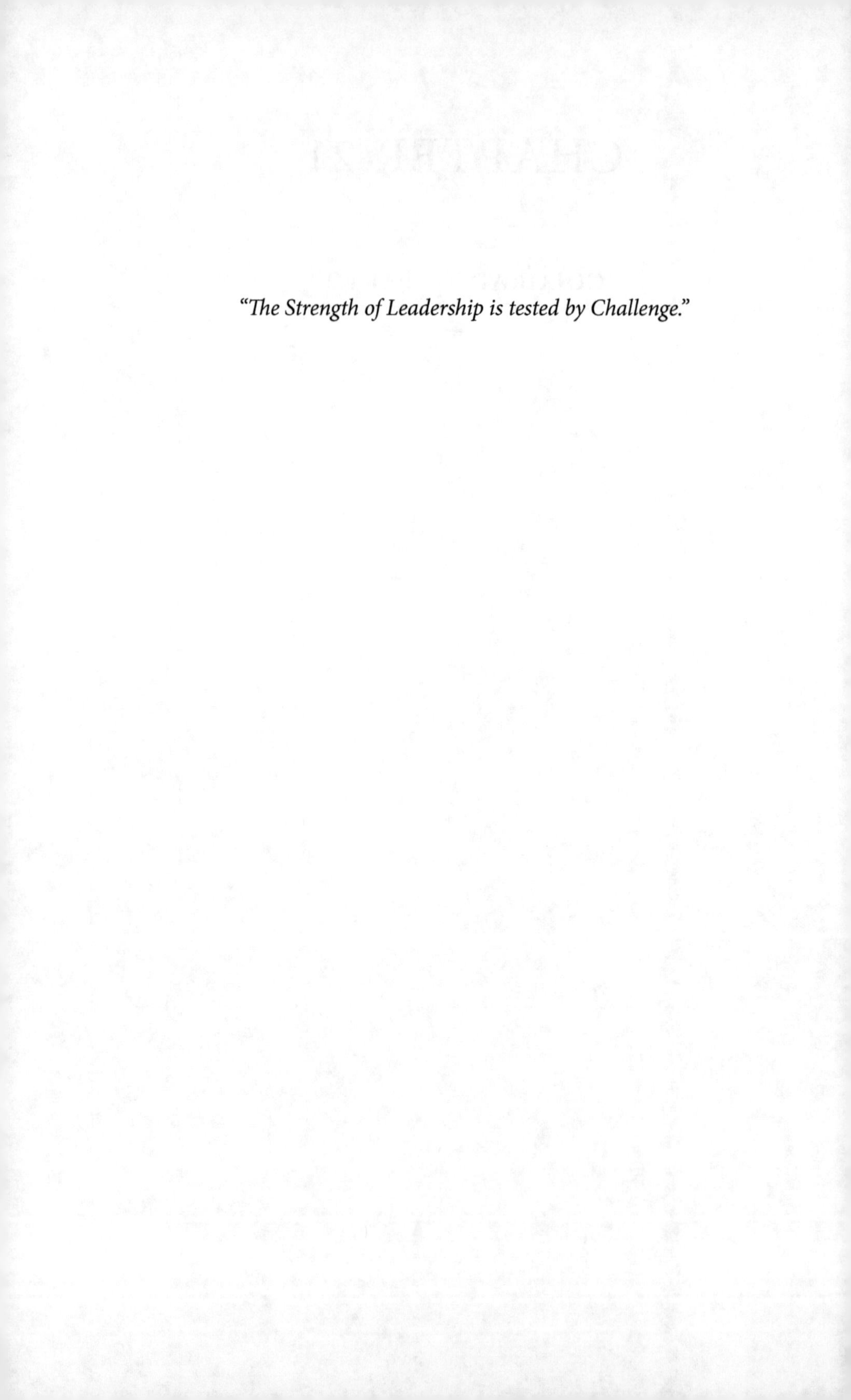

"The Strength of Leadership is tested by Challenge."

The clammy and somewhat frigid night could not be felt immediately by the lone figure darting in and out of the shadows. The figure spent most of the evening collecting intelligence on para-military soldiers. They are located in what appears to be an old, dilapidated mining supply depot built into the mouth of one of the many canyons outside of the small town of Cañon City, Colorado.

The figure uses the early morning darkness to escape to high ground without making a sound. He stops moving near a small group of trees and bushes only after he has covered over a mile of distance from the hidden industrial base.

He waits another twenty-one minutes, ensuring that he hasn't been followed, then speaks quietly to his main base through his faceplate communicator.

"Hawkbird-1 to HQ, come in... Hawkbird-1 to HQ, come in..."

The figure climbs quietly to the higher branches of one of the frozen trees in the dense brush.

"This is HQ; report."

The figure's single pieced V-shaped visor glows a low, deep blue hue as he scans around him, searching for enemies.

"This is Hawkbird calling in with my SitRep. Operation Lost-n-Found is a success. I repeat, Operation Lost-n-Found is a success. The penlights have been located and confirmed. I am prepared for extraction at location Bravo Delta."

There is a slight pause on the communicator, and a stern female voice comes says, "You've done a great job, Hawkbird-1. Extraction is on the way."

The living shadow of a warrior removes himself from the tree and carefully races off to extraction point Bravo Delta. The jut of the snow-covered cliff sticks out like a stage where gods peer down upon the lonely valley below, for it is beautiful. With a double click on his earpiece, the signal confirming his arrival is sent to those seeking him.

Seventeen minutes later, Myth hovers down out of stealth mode with his Sky Ghost to retrieve the lone Ghosthawk.

<u>Camp Sparta, New York, Base Housing-Home of Captain Jonathan Edwards</u>

The past few months have been one of the most difficult times in Captain Edwards's marriage. His wife stands with her arms crossed and her head tilted slightly downwards. Captain Edwards stands behind her, rubbing her shoulders and offering her comfort for the worries of his new role as a super-hero. She is the only civilian given permission to know because of the power core on her husband's chest. She's seen the results of the ambush on the news as well as the results from the operation in the small town in Kentucky. She sleeps less now than she has ever slept before.

She is engulfed with anxiety tonight because she knows what a beep on his cell phone means. There is nothing that Captain Edwards can do but kiss his wife as she grips him with anger, passion, and the fear that only a hero's wife can have. He knows that she is his strength, as he leaves to answer the call. He loves his Alicia as much as she loves the man that is her husband and hero.

<u>The Daylight Labs Level 7 Conference Room</u>

The overwhelmingly sweet aroma of black cherry cigar smoke hovers over the room like the angel of death. The atmosphere is serious and grim, controlled by an uneasy anxiety for this new mission to start. Pharaoh walks into the room dressed in his blue-and-gray utility uniform, hurrying only to find that there are three others already waiting. Webb instantly notices his choice of uniform and becomes angry. His jaw tightens as Pharaoh takes his place beside him.

OCD7-Webb, OCD4-Grante, and Pharaoh stand at ease as General Black paces leisurely in front of them with one hand holding a folder full of data and his other hand in his pocket.

"Operation Commander Grante's team has located the missing plasma rifles. These are also the rifles that were used to slaughter the Native American tribe in South Dakota."

The general stops in front of the three Marines as his facial expression changes to one of disgust. "This report claims that we will be facing a force of over a hundred well-armed enemies."

He then opens the folder and holds up a picture of what appears to be some type of modified, single-riding all-terrain-vehicle with insect-like legs instead of wheels. There are various models of them with different payloads attached to their bodies for the riders to control.

"Pharaoh, meet your new enemy. The damn place is flooded with these simple and effective vehicles. The intel-boys call them beetles. Be prepared to face off with enemy soldiers riding these things into battle."

The general puts his cigar out on the table and stands directly in front of Pharaoh, looking deep into his eyes. "This mission will have members of the FBI's Department-13 and the 10th Special Forces Group from Fort Carson there for assault support. Pharaoh, you can trust these guys not to quit, they're Airborne; 'quit' isn't in their vocabulary. Do not forget that there is a cache of our plasma rifles out there and you can bet that they will use them against us liberally. I have appointed you as the overall tactical leader of this operation. You will lead them. You will not fail me."

N-ionic energy burns in Pharaoh's eyes as the first jolts of anticipation grip his body.

General Black turns sharply and faces OCD7-Webb, who is disturbed that he is not in control of the mission. OCD7-Webb speaks in a commanding tone. "General Black, we will be exposing ourselves to a lot of outside organizations with this operation. When they ask questions about us, don't you think that I should be...."

The general interrupts, "Commander Webb. I have agreed to your strategy to allow the Army and the FBI to be a part of this operation. I personally would have used our Elite Forces Guardsmen instead. The superiors agree with your report on controlled exposure for the group, but you will not be leading these men."

General Black settles down and addresses OCD7-Webb again after viewing the faces of everyone in the room, "You will be in total political command, Commander Webb. You will head into town with members from Dept-CU to inform the mayor and others that we are performing some military bomb testing in the canyon. You will control the media and our exposure."

OCD7-Webb looks at Pharaoh, and then asks to the general, "What about the police and the national guard? Sir, what about the fame that this is going to create? What about...?"

The general turns around and steps towards the table, looking at his crushed cigar. "Son, these people are going into a Top Secret battle today on our nation's soil. There's a serious chance that many of them are going to lose their lives. Four hours ago we located the rifles; the next few hours will be the last for some of these soldiers. Many of them are married and many of them have children. This is not a game. This is not for ratings. Operation Commander Webb, you need to understand this...If they are going to die today, then these heroes are not going to die following an Operation Commander or even a general. These people are Marines and Special Forces soldiers. They expect their commanders to lead from the front." Webb's face pales at the implication. "Son, they are going to die following Pharaoh as they fight to protect what we take for granted. This is why I did not want your team in those gaudy 'dress' uniforms. In this mission there is no public to impress; I wanted them in their utility uniforms. Combat is the dirt that Marines know best."

OCD7-Webb and OCD4-Grante turn to Pharaoh. The general then walks out of the room, vanishing into the shadows of the silence that has taken over the room.

CHAPTER 22

COLORADO – PART 2

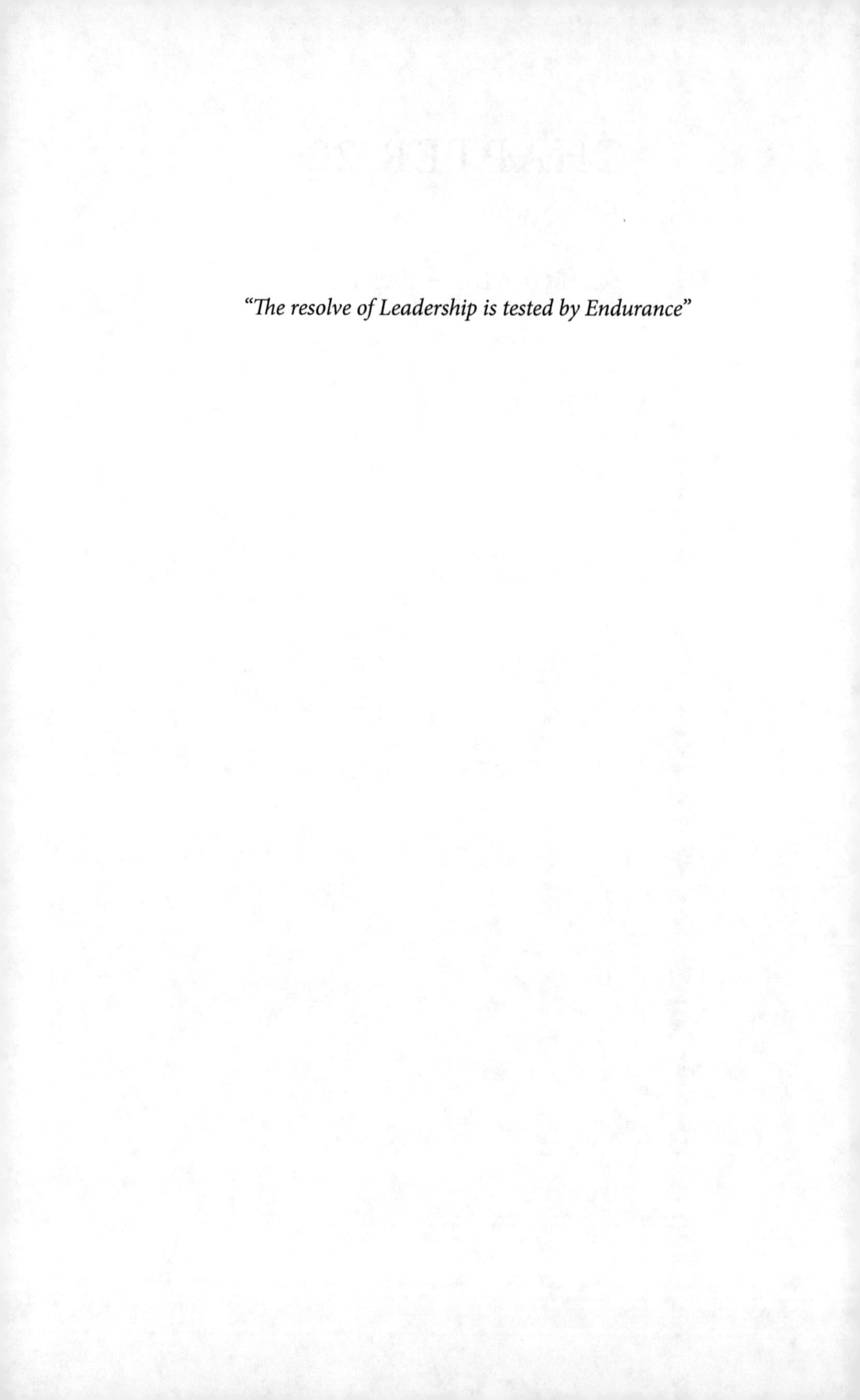

"The resolve of Leadership is tested by Endurance"

<u>Operation Light Catcher</u>
<u>Location: Fort Carson Colorado</u>
<u>Time: Seven hours after Hawkbird-1's SitRep</u>

Inside one of the Army's sealed hangars stands a force made up of seven Tenth Special Forces Group (Airborne) Operatives, fifty-one infantry soldiers from the Seventh Division, twenty soldiers from the Third Armor Cavalry Regiment, twelve members of the Combat Support Hospital, and two FBI agents from Department-13 assigned to this operation by special permission.

The soldiers have been gathered around a makeshift stage within an old hangar at a small local airport. They listen to Pharaoh's strategy for their impending assault on the location that they are now referring to as the "Canyon Base."

Many of the soldiers stand without fear and with added courage, knowing that they are going into battle with actual superheroes. Some are still in disbelief; they thought that superheroes were created by television and that they didn't exist. It was always unclear whether or not cartoon characters such as Atum-Ra and Ultra-Max from the past were actual people or merely propaganda created to motivate each new generation of potential enlistees. Today, both types of soldiers stand together, doubters and believers, for one united mission.

Tactical planning and worry ceases, as action becomes a starving beast, ravenous for the food of success. The soldiers carry out the orders of Pharaoh and split into small groups, scrambling to their respective locations for the assault. A single aircraft rumbles outside the meeting hangar as a squad of soldiers accompanying Knight rush out to embark upon it. They pass General Black, standing in back, witnessing each action taken like a symphony of battle. He holds his black cherry cigar without lighting it as he offers an almost invisible nod to Pharaoh, who receives it as a sign of approval. The mission begins.

The military force is broken into three major groups, each led by a different member of the First Factor. The first team is made up of the Airborne Special Forces soldiers, one FBI agent, and Dossman, all under the command of Knight. Their aircraft reaches its destination before the other forces are even fully organized. Speed is a powerful tool for Special Operations, and for this squad it is a resource that cannot be spared. That team drops slightly over two miles from the Canyon Base's cliffs. The Airborne soldiers welcome the chill of the air slicing into their uniforms as they lead the way by jumping first.

The FBI agent, Ishmael Goodrum, nervously steps to the door of the aircraft, swallowing his fear of heights before leaping from the plane. Dossman and Knight are the last to go. Knight takes a moment to rub his crucifix and gasps a quick thought of admiration for the Airborne soldiers before debarking the aircraft himself, with a gritty yell of, "Marine Corps!"

The team lands in the snow below and organizes their gear before moving. Four of the Airborne soldiers carry demolitions kits in their backpacks for their infiltration mission. All wait patiently as Knight moves to the point position to guide the team in.

Islander is assigned two squads of the infantry soldiers. His group leaves second and splits into smaller fire teams as they are transported half a mile from the Canyon Base by top-secret stealth vans driven by members of the EF-Div's Knightcrawlers, led by the Elite Forces Major called Worm. The groups take up their positions on each side of the canyon walls, creating a flanking design. Islander's leadership is almost non-existent as he moves with the clear message that he would rather be alone. He is a Marine Corps sniper and each of his actions reflects this to the utmost. The soldiers dig in, blending into the environment, fully camouflaged as they wait for the silent signal from their ominous leader.

Pharaoh's group leaves last. He orders complete radio silence among the troops while waiting on the word from Webb as the maternal roar of his vehicle column pushes to give birth to war. His group is made up of four tanks and two armored personnel carriers for the remaining infantry soldiers. Their twenty-two mile journey to the Canyon Base is done slowly and conspicuously. As enemy forces quickly become aware of the Army's presence, Pharaoh notes the increased activity in the canyon on his monitors.

The tanks arrive at the edge of the canyon forty minutes after their departure with anxiety as their companion. Each driver maneuvers his tank next to the one in front of him, creating a horizontal skirmish line approximately three thousand yards from the entrance to the canyon base. Pharaoh sucks in a single breath of icy air and thinks to himself, control, before grabbing the radio transmitter and speaking into it on the open frequency military band. He stands on the top of the lead tank while speaking. "This message is for the leaders of the unauthorized army occupying the supply depot at the base of the southern canyon. You are hereby ordered to surrender yourselves and your illegal army to the government of the United States of America for terrorist actions and conspiracy."

The radios go silent as Pharaoh clicks over to the EF-Div's secret communication channel, waiting for word from General Black.

Enemy soldiers flood out of the supply depot entrance armed with fully loaded automatic weapons. Concealed bay doors in the side wall of the canyon then open up as more enemy soldiers exit, riding mechanical ATV beetles towards the tanks at full speed.

Pharaoh's radio comes to life, and General Black's voice comes across the channel. "The mayor has been informed of our 'military bombing' tests. You are given permission to proceed."

Pharaoh cracks a small smile and raises his hand, balling it into a fist to order his men to hold. Incoming rocket-propelled grenades rip through the air, launched by the enemy soldiers but falling short of his tank army as the enemy forces hurry to close the distance between themselves and Pharaoh's army.

The Force Recon Marine Captain drops his fist, ordering a full forward attack on the enemy ranks. The tank barrels rage in sequence, and their explosive rounds tear through the enemy soldiers like birds scattering from a firecracker. Pharaoh presses the tanks forward and redirects their attacks to the side of the canyon wall above the supply depot entrance.

The infantry soldiers in the APCs exit and engage the oncoming enemy forces that have been softened by the initial tank assault. The side of the canyon buckles and crumbles, exposing a large steel wall hidden beneath the rocky cover. Two of the tanks remain in place, providing artillery cover as the other two close in to under fifteen hundred yards and launch direct hits into the bays of the base, creating chain explosions inside the enemy fortress.

Suddenly, two large, mechanical cannon turrets emerge from the ground on the edge of the canyon cliff. The cannons target the tanks and fire, destroying the tank beside Pharaoh in one shot. The concussion of the blast ejects Pharaoh from his own tank into a canyon wall, and subsequently causing the tank to collapse on top of him.

Larger, two-person mechanical beetles create a second wave of assault as they charge out of the burning bay. They are ridden by an elite squad, armed with the stolen plasma rifles. These heavy-weapon beetles flood the entire canyon and head towards the tanks and the assaulting infantry, firing plasma bolts and rockets as they approach.

Pharaoh forces his way out of the rubble, wiping blood from his ears and nose, and orders his infantry to pull back. He then notices

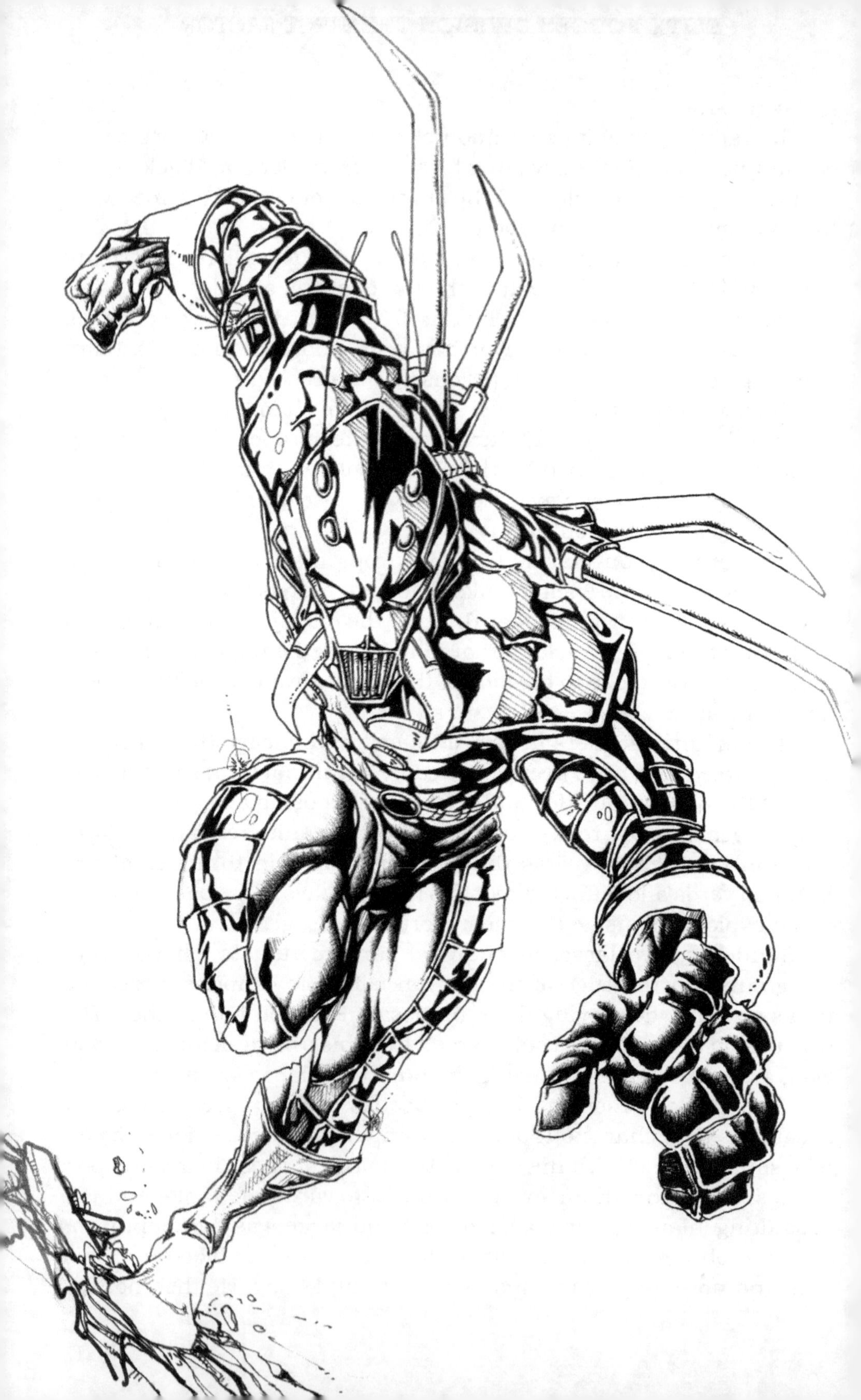

the two figures leading the attack on his men; one stands like a holy man, holding his divine tool of worship, and the other is someone that he does not recognize. The holy man jumps into the ranks of soldiers, scattering them with his weapon, blow by blow. He pauses only when he recognizes Pharaoh, and the recognition is returned…it is Shrine. The second figure wears armor that resembles a heavily armored insect. He is the maker and controller of the technology being used against the soldiers. The insect man raises his hands, causing large insect wings to emerge from his armored backpack. He then presses a button on his belt, causing the wings to vibrate rapidly and lift him into the air.

"I am the Apostle Warbug! On this day you will feel the wrath of my creations. You will feel the power of my children! The Lord of technology and darkness will not fail me today!"

"What the hell? Why do these idiots introduce themselves in battle?" Cries Pharaoh while turning to his men. "Sergeants, rally your troops!"

The wall of the canyon base opens up, exposing another hangar bay from which dozens of flying mosquito-like mechanical insects rush to join the counter attack by the Apostle Warbug.

Shrine jumps into the air and slams his mace into the front of one of the tanks, pulverizing it. The downward impact is so powerful the back of the tank actually lifts off of the ground, and the surrounding shockwaves knock the infantry soldiers backwards and off of their feet.

Pharaoh turns to see the second open bay and calls out on his radio while watching the flying bugs head towards the front of the battle.

"Knight, move your team now. We need those cannons neutralized for our final approach. Islander, they took the bait and launched an air attack. We are going to need your people! By the way, that damn bug-man introduced himself like one of Knight's comic book! You take him down first!"

Pharaoh grabs a large boulder and throws it into Shrine, knocking him into the far side of the canyon. The Apostle Warbug turns in mid-flight and begins to fire blasts from one of the stolen plasma rifles at Pharaoh. The enemy elite soldiers join the full assault, firing their plasma rifles into the infantry ranks, causing them to drop for cover and scatter for safety.

On the edge of the canyon above the skirmish below, Islander and his men jump up, knocking away their camouflage covering and opening fire to create a flanking assault. Islander's men drive the Apostle Warbug's attack wave into complete disarray, causing some to turn in circles before being shot down. Islander fires a powerful blue bolt of energy directly into the chest of the Apostle, sending him flying across the canyon into a burning ATV beetle on the ground. He then takes meticulous aim with his bow at each elite enemy soldier holding a plasma rifle and fires blue energy bolts, striking each target.

Knight, Dossman, and the Airborne Special Forces team rappel down the side of the canyon wall into the base. The group encounters light resistance before breaking into three teams: Alpha, Bravo, and Charlie. Each team heads to destroy a different cannon. Knight and Dossman head deeper into the base, searching for the data control center.

Team Alpha attacks the eastern cannon with small arms fire and grenades. The cannon is lightly guarded and malfunctioning due to the tank attacks. Team Alpha mostly engages engineers and repair men who surrender a few minutes into the gunfight. The team proceeds to plant their explosives and escort the captured enemies towards the top hangar bay through which they had entered.

Team Bravo, made up of three Airborne soldiers and the FBI agent, meets heavy resistance and two of its members are killed instantly by gunfire. The final two members of the team are pinned down beside a large computer mainframe. The leader of the squad, an Airborne sergeant, calls for support, identifying seven enemy combatants against him and the FBI agent. The sergeant throws two grenades towards the superior enemy force, compelling them to scramble for cover. The grenade injures two of them as the gunfire increases in intensity on the return.

The FBI agent fires through a small opening on the bottom corner of the computer, taking out two enemy combatants. Suddenly, an elite enemy soldier comes up the ladder and opens fire with his plasma rifle. The beams from the plasma rifle penetrate through the computer mainframe, the midsection of the sergeant, and the wall behind him. The Airborne sergeant drops to his knees with a blank expression on his face as life leaves his body. The FBI agent freezes in fear as he waits for the next plasma blast aimed at his side of the mainframe. He thinks about his parents and wonders if there will be pain.

A loud zap echoes off the walls as a blue bolt of energy strikes the elite enemy soldier from behind and drives him into the mainframe computer. The continuous sounds of gunfire sting the ears of the FBI agent, reminding him he is still alive. Frozen with fear, the agent is approached by a shadowy figure with a bow; all that can be seen is a pair of blue eyes piercing the smoke and darkness. The figure grabs the explosives from the body of the dead sergeant lying on the ground beside him and drops them in his lap. "Finish your mission," says the bowman before vanishing in the shadows; he moves like a whisper of wind.

Team Charlie, made up of Knight and Dossman, enters a large control room filled with computers and radios. Dossman goes to work attempting to access the computer's data banks. Knight looks through what appears to be a small lab window and is shocked by what he sees — a lab that is almost identical to the one used to give the First Factor their powers. He quickly turns at the sound of the chamber door opening.

Through the chamber door enters the Apostle General that he fought during the ambush operation, escorted by two elite soldiers armed with plasma rifles. The Apostle smiles as his cybernetic eyes glow bright red – they glare in the dim light.

"You will be a present for my employer, boy. He will enjoy prying information from you."

An enemy soldier fires a plasma blast into the computer equipment, causing an electrical surge to rip through it and knocking Dossman into the opposite wall, unconscious. The Apostle General steps forward towards Knight, clenching his fist.

"Shall we dance, blasphemer?"

CHAPTER 23

COLORADO – PART 3

*"Hold strong, have faith, yield none!
Heroes aren't made during good times!!"*

–Sergeant Major Gregory Carter

The entire area is littered with dead bodies and destroyed mechanical beetles. The enemy combatants have superior firepower and numbers, but the friendly forces have the high ground and strategic planning on their side.

Currently, three of the four tanks that began the battle have been completely destroyed, and the last one has been incapacitated. Army forces have kept losses to a minimum by following Pharaoh's plan to merely hold the enemy in their locations. The soldiers form a forward skirmish line, pinning the enemy into the gulley at the edge of the base. The Army soldiers gain confidence as the battle continues and as return fire from the enemy infantry decreases. Pharaoh engages Shrine behind friendly lines in a powerful test of might; the two warriors rip the battlefield asunder with each blow. The Apostle Warbug struggles to repair the damage to his armor from the attack by Islander. He prays to his lord of technology and darkness for speed to mend his damage and the power to destroy the masked bowman that has delivered a continual stream of destruction against his forces.

The battle between the Apostle General and Knight is fierce. The apostle fires laser blasts from his cybernetic eyes that are deflected by Knight's shield into one of the apostle's elite soldiers. The soldier is cut cleanly in two, the plasma rifle hitting the floor with a rattling sound just before the top half of the soon-to-be dead body also strikes the floor. Knight flips forward, causing the Apostle General to sway back in order to defend against his inevitable attack. Knight uses his landing stance to spring off of Apostle General into the air, flipping once again and coming down with a hammer kick to an enemy soldier who was trying to aim his rifle. The soldier drops to the ground.

The Apostle General twists around with his teeth clenched and swings at Knight with a backhand. Knight blocks upward with his shield and punches the apostle in his side with his free hand. He then twirls his shield hand around, grabbing the Apostle Generals' wrist and yanks downward, pulling his foe's face forward into the computer control panel in front of him. The panel explodes into a shower of electrical sparks and glass, which becomes embedded in the Apostle General's face, destroying his right eye.

Ripping the console out of the wall with his super strength, the Apostle General raises it above his head as he tries to crush his shield-carrying enemy. Knight dodges to the side, avoiding the crashing equipment by inches and countering with a shield punch to the right side of the shadow-armored soldier's face. The metal ribbons on the

Apostle General's uniform buckle from the force of the blow.

The room shudders, as the explosives set by the paratroopers to destroy the cannons begin to detonate. The room lights dim and flicker as the fire sprinklers begin to spray water into the room. The Apostle General takes advantage of the situation and uses his cybernetic arm as a battering ram, slamming it into the chest of Knight. Knight tries to block with his shield but flies back from the impact, crashing into a row of metal filing cabinets.

Outside, the battle is just as tumultuous. The infantry soldiers struggle to keep the enemy pinned down in the center of the canyon as ammunition supplies begin to run low. Strangely enough, the enemy becomes more patient and waits while returning fire. It is only a matter of time before the infantry soldiers run out of ammunition, and the enemy knows that will when the true slaughter begins.

Pharaoh is locked into a brutal battle with Shrine beside one of the destroyed tanks. Flames bleed from the destroyed vehicle, creating an arena of death for the two gladiators. Shrine shows wear from the devastating strikes of Pharaoh as the facial swelling and bruising to his body shows through his torn uniform. His left arm appears to possibly be broken. Pharaoh stands with energy crackling from his eyes and blood running freely from his nose. His right eye beneath his 'Y' scar is swollen shut, hampering his vision. His fists are saturated with blood, both his enemy's and his own. This battle is approaching its end. Shrine raises his mace above his head with his good arm and swings it diagonally at Pharaoh, barely missing him. Pharaoh leans back and grabs the weapon when it passes above him. The two are locked in a struggle for the weapon.

Shrine bends his damaged arm, opening his palm as his fingers eject snaky, tentacle-like cables that snake around Pharaoh's throat, choking him. Pharaoh drops to one knee, grabbing at his throat while holding on to the mace with his other hand. Shrine wrenches the war mace from his quivering hand and tightens his cables on Pharaoh's throat. Pharaoh grasps at the cables with both hands, digging into his own throat in order to wrestle his fingers around them. Shrine stands above Pharaoh, who is now on both of his knees gasping for air, and swings his mace arm as far back as he can. He then releases the cable from his fingertips at the same time as he strikes down at the chest of Pharaoh, implanting him into the earth beneath him. Blood mixes with dirt.

Pharaoh coughs blood as Shrine pulls back and swings down,

striking him again and causing blood, rock, and energy to leap from the crater that is quickly becoming a grave for him. The leader thrashes about, fighting to remain conscious as his body begins to swell and glow. Shrine pulls back again for another swing.

Pharaoh releases energy crackling from his eyes and mouth. The sand grain in his chest that comprises his heart pulses vigorously with an N-ionic power that cannot possibly be measured. His flesh, hardened to more than armor; his soul, converted from a thing spiritual to an entity cosmic, and his will, driven by his determination, makes him something greater than human. He pushes forward as his shredded uniform sways like a thousand little flags waving for victory. He tackles Shrine in full swing and slams him backward, pounding him in the face with both of his hands intertwined. He pounds him over and over while screaming incoherently.

Many of the soldiers, friend and enemy, stop at the magnitude of this battle. Pharaoh stands with Shrine above his head and throws him into the canyon with the other enemy troops. He then grabs his earpiece radio and calls out, "It's time for this to end, now!"

The wind dies. The air becomes stagnant. A hollowness in time can be felt as a wave of energy crosses over the entire area. It moves like a heartbeat from the Earth itself. The sky begins to crackle as small bits of rubble everywhere jump around from the tremors. A black and green cloud covers the canyon; fatigue becomes fear, as fear becomes terror.

Hesitantly, everyone looks up into the sky as if God himself was speaking in a voice other than words and yet understood. The heavens, chained together by blackened clouds like clenched fists, fight to retain their clasp as piercing rays of emerald spears drive them apart. They reluctantly clear.

A mountain of boulders, trees, and dirt crashes through the darkness in the sky, hovering above the tiny human forms below, frozen in horror. They cannot move. The enemy is caught between breaths as the source of this phenomenon makes itself known. It is a lone, struggling figure; it is Magister.

His hair whips and his nostrils flair as the stubborn winds above the canyons fight to bring him down, knowing that anyone who carries a mountain through the sky cannot be natural. The sullen warrior resists the wind. He resists the sky. He resists the Earth. He resists gravity. Never has power on this level been witnessed by those below; once again, they are caught between breaths.

It is realized that he is not a god, for a god would not be racked

with so much pain while holding a mountain of earth in the heavens above. A god would not bleed from his nose and ears as he exercised his divine might. A god would not cry in the face of the mortals that he is above.

Instead, the enemy in the canyon below realizes all at once that they are actually dealing with a man. They are caught in between breaths only to realize that this is the man that they punished for not yielding to them. This is a man that has become vengeance incarnate.

Only at that time does the enemy exhale as one.

The hovering warrior strains, clenching his jaw, as sweat and veins cover his face. He bellows out as loud as he can, "This is for my people!"

He releases the mountain into the canyon.

There are no words to describe the loud silence felt as the heavens themselves crash down upon the mortals below. There is no hope given to those in the path of such a cataclysm. The witnesses gaze as their minds attempt to fathom the events before them. To those that can claim an alliance with this man, he is a god made mortal. To those that this man opposes, He is a vengeful mortal given a god's power. Either way, with a show of power of this magnitude, the very foundations of science and religion have been torn asunder in the hearts and minds of all who watch.

As the mountain of debris, boulders, and uprooted trees falls, Magister guides portions of it towards the enemy forces; chasing them down with boulders ranging in size from a small car to a school bus. There is no escape from this mortal god's wrath. The crawling ATV beetles are crushed and the mosquito-like bugs are caught by falling trees and debris guided by Magister. Entire squads of the enemy forces are eradicated while once heavily defended positions are covered over in hills of gravel, dirt, and raining rocks.

As the very earth itself continues to tremble from the act of one man, those that witness, believer or not, cannot help but feel as if God himself has taken a part in the events of this day outside of the small town of Cañon City, Colorado.

The earth begins to control itself again as shock subsides and it regains its composure. The clouds that had dispersed to make way for Magister's vengeance began to form across the sky once more. This battle had been halted abruptly in a way no one could have foretold. Though it was a battle won this day.

Magister floats down from the heavens, the sun shining from behind him as those who see him shield their eyes on his approach. The green aura around his body is weak and blood falls from his nose and ears. His eyes red, and mouth dry, it can be seen why gods do not give their powers to mortals so easily.

He comes to land beside Pharaoh, trembling from his feat of power. His eyes hold no tears this time; they have dried. He tries to speak, but his voice shudders and his body shakes. He had never exerted his powers to this limit and he knew not if he could. After a few minutes, while being looked at and praised in silence by every soldier around him, he regained his senses and looked to the captain standing before him.

"You have kept your word, Pharaoh."

The Marine captain takes a step towards Magister, but pauses as Magister steps back and raises both of his hands.

"Although I wish there was another way, Pharaoh...I know that this has freed the warrior spirits of my tribesmen, and my people are now avenged. Please find our missing tribesmen whether dead or alive, for we will never give up hope."

Magister then surrounds himself with energy and begins to fly away.

"You are a great leader, Pharaoh. I owe you and my people owe you."

The soldiers under Pharaoh's command, after reorganizing and regaining their composure, move in to detain the surviving enemy combatants that have surrendered. Islander comes out of the entrance of the canyon base with Dossman leaning on his shoulder. Medics run over to help Dossman as Islander approaches Pharaoh.

"Pharaoh...they took Knight."

Pharaoh glances at Islander, then turns to face the massive amount of devastation behind him. Control, a lost concept in the mind of this Marine Captain, evades him and causes him to become lost in confusion. This, added on to the stress and sheer destructive trauma of his fight with Shrine, proves too much, even for this towering idol among his fellow fighting men and women. He stumbles to the side and collapses. In his fading vision, he sees Islander shouting for a medic as the sun sets over the high priced victory of this day.

ELITE FORCES DIVISION
continues in

ELITE FORCES DIVISION
THE SECOND ACT
BOOK II

Continue to the next pages for

GHOSTHAWK CASE FILES
POWER OF CHARISMA
TAINTED BLOOD

A troubled history, coupled with shortness of breath and very little time to reflect, blossoms into a comedian's blundered joke, along with a show soon to fail. How can one find amusement, with the body of a best friend lying in a puddle of blood, the blood running free from a single sniper's bullet hole tunneled from his left ear to the base of the front of his neck? Three hostages sit crouched in back, whimpering in fear like abandoned puppies. Their mouths are poorly gagged. The cords binding their arms are pulled tight, numbing their hands. The look in their eyes reveals the same feeling, as this challenge to reality acts as the cords binding their thoughts.

"Cal! Cal! The goddamn cops are comin' around the back of the house, man! We gonna fucking die! We gonna die, man!" Cries a frantic voice bouncing from the kitchen walls, its source kneeling in the corner, hugging his half-empty hunting rifle.

Rufio is Cal's best friend. Dale was also, but now he lies motionless in his own blood, dead in the living room, guilty of glancing out a window with his father's shotgun held tight in his hand. The shotgun is lying beside his corpse.

"I got it, Rufio! Calm down, I – I'm gonna fix this!" Promises Cal, snaking across the living room floor towards the three hostages.

He ignores the blare of the police horns and pulls himself to a sitting position beside the father of his ex-girlfriend. She is bound next to her mother, soaked in sweat and confusion. Shaking like a leaf from the excitement and distress, Cal raises his hand towards the father after untying him and offers him his fully loaded revolver. The father turns his head to glance at his wife and daughter, then back to the skinny teenager's offering, stopping only to look into his eyes.

Cal cracks a small smile and, instantly, a shimmer of bright green energy illuminates his face and disappears with the speed of a single eye-blink. The father clutches the revolver, stands up, and moves cautiously towards the back of the house, passing the staircase for safety.

Cal uses the opportunity to address his ex-girlfriend. "Dale's dead, Barbara, and i-it's your fault! You heard me! It's your fault!" He pushes past her mother and gently removes the gag to lean his face against her cheek. "He was one-a-my best friends, you whore! Now, he's dead for fucking around with you."

A barrage of gunfire can be heard from the back of the house, and the stutter of automatic weapons fire responds in kind. Something heavy hits the floor with a deep thud as the gunfire ceases and

assumptions are made.

"Daddy!" Screams Barbara, as her mother likewise shrieks, muffled by her gag. Cal looks into the eyes of both Barbara and her mother, smiling as he releases the familiar shimmer of green energy that has made the teenager a controlling bully for the last few years of his young life. The duo slide back into a false state of relaxation and become eerily calm.

"Shit! Cal, these fuckers are moving up! They're gonna try to bust in on us! Cal, we gotta do somethin'!" shouts Rufio from the kitchen, before cracking off two rounds from his hunting rifle.

Amazingly, no gunfire is returned.

A single deep cough from a weapon, fired across the hood of a police car, delivers a hissing canister of tear gas into the kitchen window next to Rufio. Falling back onto a trashcan, he scrambles around the tiled floor and tosses his denim jacket onto the spinning canister while puking on a dining room chair.

Cal glimpses the commotion and calls out to his friend, "Rufio! What's happening?" His reply is a feeble dash from Rufio into the living room, resulting in a hasty escape through the front door and into the arms of a waiting SWAT team.

Cal pulls a shirt across his face, abandons his hostages, and runs deeper into the house, up the staircase. He stops short of the top floor as the darkness before him emits an uncanny feeling. He moves nothing save his head, which slowly turns just enough to see that no policemen have barged through the doors of the living room. It beckons the question of why, unless this entire action was planned. The plumes of tear gas that spread along the walls and floors engulfed all of the ground floor and then dissipated. It was weaker than normal... that is, unless this entire action was planned. The hostages begin to calm down as the police lights outside flicker intensely through the windows. For this young comedian, the amusement from his haphazard actions was dying quickly. There was no applause forthcoming; no standing ovation or calls for an encore. His conscience urges him not to go back down the stairs, as what became an act of gratification through revenge turned into something beyond sinister. For Cal, losing control was his nightmare, and he could never go back the way he came. It is the cold, deep fear within him that recognizes the presence within the gloom ahead, which is the only true path that he can choose.

A shift in the shadows preludes the dark silhouette stepping towards the arrogant teenaged kidnapper. The few paces heard are less than sound and more than warning. Cal squints his eyes at the

figure, hoping for clarity through the obscurity, only to find someone or something that he has never seen before. A warrior stands facing him. The warrior peers into the youth's soul with eyes that can't be seen - he becomes the answer to the question of fear. His mask, a V-shaped visor of non-reflecting, indigo glass, obscures his eyes but not the intensity of his stare. His body is chiseled and tight. He is the predator, anxious before the capture of his prey. His intent is focused through his shaded uniform, defined by the symbol of a hawk on his chest. He holds no weapons and he makes no move.

Stunned, Cal seeks to take control by removing the shirt from his face and staring into the visor of the warrior who blocks his escape. Cal smiles slowly, locking in the final component that activates his extrability to mentally control others. The warrior's indigo visor shifts to black almost instantly, reacting to Cal's attempt. The warrior reaches out his hand and clutches the throat of his target. The teenager grasps the forearm of his assailant, hoping to pry it loose. He lifts Cal from the ground while drawing his free hand back into a mighty, battle-hardened fist.

He slams his fist into Cal's cheekbone, shattering it and breaking his jaw. The impact yanks the youth's body sideways and forward in an attempt to pass the shock through it. His thighs tighten and his fingers dig into the uniform of the dark warrior. The hawk-wearer reels back again as tears from Cal find way over collapsed flesh to gather around the hand clutching his neck.

Blood seeps from his ear as his voice trembles through a shattered jaw to beg for the selfish life that he holds so dear. "P-Puh-weeze... Puhweeze, d-don't kw-kwill me..."

The warrior shifts his grip ever-so-slightly and slams his fist directly into the front of Cal's face. His nose collapses under the impact, and the bridge of it cracks, knocking out multiple teeth and dripping blood. The youth's hands drop from the warrior's wrists and dangle at his side as his thighs release tension and both of his legs follow suit. With a motion very similar to that of a person discarding trash, the warrior flings the kidnapper down the stairs, ensuring that his body receives treatment much like that of his face.

The police enter the living room, led by a single FBI agent who walks over to inspect the teenager before the medics begin their process to stabilize him. The agent moves to the top of the stairs to address the warrior.

"Good job, Ghosthawk. He needed eye contact and a smile in order to use his powers. We're categorizing it as 'Charisma.'" He looks over his shoulder back towards the youth, "That disfigurement you gave him looks like it's going to be permanent. Heh, problem solved huh?"

The Ghosthawk steps back into the embrace of the shadows.

"By the way, thanks for saving the girl's father earlier by tackling him to the ground. Tonight we only lost one life. It could have been much worse. "

The Ghosthawk leaves after an elusive nod and heads off to his next mission.

GHOSTHAWK CASE FILE #1990
TAINTED BLOOD (REGENEX)

1975. Three UH-1 Huey combat helicopters raged into Point32-Oscar, somewhere on the ill-defined border between Cambodia and Vietnam. Although the border was well defined on the maps, the blood-soaked mud of the jungle floor carried no such markings. The end of the war was calling, and this Special Forces fire base was little more than the Army's secret and a general's whisper away from being known.

There were originally one hundred twenty GI's, both Airborne and Infantry troopers, in this location. They had been fighting for seventy-eight hours straight and the battle had taken its toll. By the morning of the third day, sixteen men were killed in action and sixty-three wounded, with over forty of those considered critical. It was the fourth day. Ammunition was low and rain had drizzled from the clouds, but the showers were too weak to wash away the blood.

When three static-filled, broken situation reports transmitted by two dying officers, punctuated by barrages of gunfire and the screams of GIs, were finally pieced together by command headquarters, they translated into "undying gooks." This was enough for the senior officers in charge to activate the entire covert Elite Forces Division Ghosthawk Company.

The three Hueys carried a total of twenty-nine Ghosthawks and supplies for the desperate troops seeking anything that would give them a final thread of hope.

The scene was nothing less than hell on Earth. The helicopters had to pass and circle three times while taking small arms fire from AK-47s before they could find a nominally safe to put down. There were dead soldiers everywhere; fear was mixed with blood and sweat and fatigue.

Two of the helicopters landed successfully, offloading nineteen Ghosthawks, while the final one crashed into the side of the berm ahead of the front of the base, killing ten Ghosthawks, two pilots, and a Navy Corpsman.

Each Ghosthawk wore a specially made helmet with a single non-reflecting crimson visor built into it, giving him various types of combat vision, including night and thermal. Each side of the helmet had ear covers that carried small voice communicators within them, acting as microphones and speakers. A single small wire embedded into the neck of their uniforms connected a small socket on the helmet with the compact radio power controller worn on the back hip of each warrior's utility belt beside their first aid kits.

The first group of Ghosthawks that landed carrying customized M16A1 assault rifles joined the front line infantry between the M60 machinegun posts. They separated to cover both flanks and to add support to the front. The second group of Ghosthawks instantly began to supply much-needed ammunition to each of the key positions held by the exhausted troops. When a soldier fell, a Ghosthawk would move into his position and engage the enemy while other worked to save the wounded soldier's life.

The broken reports on the enemy were horrifyingly accurate, in that death had difficulty in taking the enemy. Each Viet Cong that had charged up the hill and to the wire had required multiple shots to take down. Headshots and heart shots had very little effect; they continued to charge. Some were headless and continued to crawl through the mud with life until a grenade totally disassembled their bodies; they were following the last commands issued by their now-vaporized brains.

The only advantage that the soldiers and warriors had was that the VC came in waves separated by minutes. This gave the medics time to aid the wounded and gave the fighting soldiers precious time to reload and pull injured comrades back to the makeshift hospital bunker filled with blood-churned mud and rats. The very smell of the place was overpowered with musk, gun-powder, decay, vomit, and death. These accursed aromas were never meant to be a stench for man to inhale and yet in war it was common.

The Ghosthawks took up positions in each corner of the base, providing relief for the worn-out soldiers already there. They communicated with each other with handheld radios attached to their utility belts and earpieces. Their leader was Allegiance; young, hearty, and determined. He refused to allow the fear creeping through him to find a home and relied on his training to take control of the situation and act; even as the dead around him gazed on and his fellow warriors' corpses burned out by the berm in the smoldering heap from the earlier helicopter crash. He had seen death before. He had seen death as much or more than any of these men battling for life this day. For Allegiance, death was as constant as the shadows that followed him; it was a friend that promised no love.

Relaying combat orders through his radio, Allegiance fought to regain control of the battle even as he watched an increasing number of his Ghosthawks fall in battle. He knew that no quarter could be given and none would be received – they were warriors.

The highest ranking soldier that could be found was a wounded Sergeant First Class, manning one of the M60 machine guns on the southern corner of the base. The bottom of his abdomen was ripped open by shrapnel from an explosion and his left earlobe was missing, torn off by a gunshot that just missed his head. He leaned against the machine gun, one hand squeezing the trigger and his other hand holding in his exposed intestines. He was running on his last bit of adrenaline. The corporal beside him loaded a new belt of the 7.62 mm ammunition into the M60 each time it rang empty. The corporal occupied his time not spent reloading by firing his M16A1 full-burst into the tree line. Mud was his constant enemy.

Allegiance asked, "Are there any soldiers out there?" His voice could barely be heard through the gunfire and explosions. "Sergeant, I'm going to call in air support! I need to know if there's anyone out beyond the line!!"

The sergeant mustered up an answer of, "No, they're all dead!" Through a stream of saliva and blood. He shifted from the pain of his wounds, only to expose the feces collected below his body mixing with his bodily fluids. Shock began to set in on the exhausted soldier.

"Medic!" Allegiance cried out as he scrambled to apply bandages to the sergeant's smaller wounds while keeping him awake. The metal from the pylon bordering the machine gun post ranged and jumped as AK47 enemy rounds focused in on their position. Fumbling through the muddy trenches, a beleaguered corpsman arrived with a broken finger and a gash along his chin. He shoved his hands into the mud below the sergeant to grab his intestines then pushed them into his body as best he could. His medical supplies were nearly as depleted as his ability to think coherently.

"S-sir, I got'em! I got'em! Go! Do what you gotta do! I'll take care of the sergeant!" He said in an absolutely fatigued gasp.

No matter how much training one has, the amazement of the human spirit always causes one to pause; Allegiance paused. An explosion near the M60 jarred the Ghosthawk leader back to action as the enemy closed in. Stone and sand slashed across his cheeks, drawing blood, as he gripped his helmet and assault rifle before falling to the ground. He snatched the radio to call in air support on the entire tree line and ordered everyone to get down.

Two helicopters strafed the tree lines first, followed precisely two minutes later by the roar of the General Electric J-79 engines powering Marine F-4 Phantom fighters, loud enough to drown out all other sounds. The jets passed over the base, dropping their payload into the jungle outside. The napalm-filled canisters tumbled from the belly of the fighters and rotated end-over-end on their descent to the earth. Upon hitting the ground, they split open and ignited, spreading their liquid hellfire for hundreds of yards. The explosions were an odd mixture of bright orange flames breaking through a cover of thick black smoke. The deadly payload produced so much heat that the temperature of the air felt like a thousand degrees as it instantly washed over the American soldiers and Ghosthawk warriors. The targets of the bombs fared much worse. The earth shook from the power of the explosions and the smell of the napalm stung the nostrils of each soldier, reminding them that they were alive. When it was over, there was no movement in the trees for fifteen long minutes.

The first ones up were the medics, who rushed out to help the wounded once again. The soldiers rushed back to their posts, waiting for the next wave. It never came. Allegiance stood in the ash and soil and ordered one staff sergeant to call in a medevac for the injured sergeant in the machine gun nest and the other wounded. The Ghosthawk leader knew the medevac would need the area secured before it could land, and it would be up to him to secure it.

He heaved for air, wiped blood and ash from his face, and commanded one of his fellow Ghosthawks, "Grey, muster the Ghosthawks and meet me at the front gate." He scanned the base quickly through the settling smoke, only to see the need for his warriors to stay in their positions. "This post can't fall," he thought. Pondering for a minute, he spoke to Grey again. "Grab one Ghosthawk from each corner. Get me a squad... we'll make do. We've been in worse!" Grey nodded with confidence and vanished into the smoke as Allegiance checked in with the medics before heading to the front gate.

Nine warriors and a small group of soldiers gathered at the gate within minutes. The Ghosthawks stood at the ready with bandaged cuts and shrapnel wounds. Their fortitude was only second to their motivation; their intent... dark.

"Here's the team, Allegiance. They're reloaded, resupplied, and ready to go! Name the mission," said Grey. Allegiance would have expected nothing less from these warriors. From the side of Grey, one of the senior soldiers approached the Ghosthawk Leader. He was a burly staff sergeant. He took a drag from his wet cigarette and saw how small the Ghosthawk squad was.

"I heard about you guys back in '67. I thought you were made up." He took a couple of tokes from his cigarette before continuing, "We wanna help, sir. This here is our fight, too." Nervously, four of his men, weary and tired, also stepped forward to volunteer.

The group was interrupted by the medic, "What? Staff Sergeant, wh-what are you doing? Are you crazy? Why..?"

There was only one answer to be given by the fatigued Army soldier. "Because we're Airborne."

Allegiance looked at the staff sergeant while removing his helmet to wipe his sweat. "Gather your men, Staff Sergeant."

What the squad of Ghosthawks saw when they walked out of the security of their base was too much for words but commonplace for them. There were more body parts than tree limbs on the ground. There was blood-soaked ash in pockets around many of the corpses and smoke everywhere. Limbs still moved as many of them continued to burn from the napalm. Members of the Airborne squad began to vomit and one of the soldiers began to cry as he moved a large stone only to discover that it was the partial head of a young Viet Cong boy. He had a teenaged son at home; this represented the true ugliness of war. A Ghosthawk's stare from his side reminded him that this was combat as his tears stopped to give way to this reality.

The squad traveled the perimeter of the woods for about thirty minutes before Allegiance declared it secure and had the medevac helicopters fly in. He wanted to follow a trail that they discovered. It cut into the darkness of the jungle ahead. Before exploring the trail, he spoke to the senior Army soldier, "Staff Sergeant, get your men back to base, your job here is done. I need you in charge of the evacuation of the wounded." The young Ghosthawk's voice was deep, decisive, raspy, and did not invite debate. "A counter-attack will be coming soon; I need your men to hold the base. Get them resupplied, recharged, and re-motivated!"

"Yes, sir," replied the staff sergeant.

Allegiance approached the staff sergeant and smiled, "Don't call me 'sir', I work for a living." The smile was returned by the weary Airborne soldier before he returned to the base under a gray sky. Allegiance was left with only his fellow Ghosthawks. This portion of the mission was for them alone; after all, it was the true reason they were there.

The trail led to a small clearing on the far side of the woods almost a mile away. There, the Ghosthawks watched from the defilade of a natural ditch covered over by tree branches. The Viet Cong were regrouping and staging for another assault. Their numbers were severely reduced because of the last attack and they only had between an estimated fifty to a hundred men. This was still enough to overrun the base in its present condition. Grim and driven, the shroud of heat and darkness would not allow the soldiers anymore peace than necessary. Allegiance and his team were built to be the answer to this need. The Ghosthawk leader's vision became as sharp as his attitude was shrewd; he decided that it would be better to hit them now before they could fully prepare. He would decapitate their force before they could organize into a venomous serpent destined to attack the exhausted soldiers back at the base.

"Quarterman, relay the coordinates of this camp to HQ for a strike. We need to..." whispered Allegiance before seeing an object of interest from the corner of his visor. Crawling even lower into the mud between a pair of large surface roots, he inched to the edge of their protective position to gain a better view of the camp.

On the edge of the Viet Cong's staging area was a small red-rusted pickup truck with two men and a woman on the back. One man was administering injections to each one of the soldiers as they went up to the truck, while the other was an older man holding the woman's hand while he sat alongside her and cried. The older man had bruises on his face and dried blood on his dingy shirt, which was nothing more than rags. The love he felt for the elderly Vietnamese woman being used was unmistaken.

"Belay that order, Quarterman" said Allegiance. "Grey, take Solace and Etch and get me some eyes on that truck. I need confirmation!"

"On it," responded Grey before slapping two of their comrades on the shoulder to meld into the jungle to the right of their position.

Grey and his two Ghosthawks took up a flanking position to the east of the pickup truck on the edge of the woods. Grey and Etch held back as their sniper in the middle, Solace, inched forward against the tree line holding his M40A5 sniper rifle low. Without raising the barrel tip or uncovering the scope, he lifted his head from the mud just enough behind a small moist pile of banana tree leaves to peer at his target. He held in a small button on the side of his helmet visor which increased its magnification of its view.

The woman on the back of the truck was well above seventy years of age and drained to the point that the veins protruding along her muscles had changed to a varicose, purplish hue. Increasing his helmet's sound amplification, Solace could distinguish the Vietnamese words of 'wife' and 'love' from the beaten old man holding her weakened hand.

The Ghosthawk used his radio to deliver the ghastly report to Allegiance. "We have our target, Allegiance. Her vitality is low and I see plasma being fed to her left arm." Solace paused, then continued after a few seconds, "She's got foam on the side of her mouth... she's dehydrated. We've got to move fast."

"Affirmative, Solace." Responded Allegiance. "Confirmation on her 'extrabilities', Solace?"

"Affirmative. They're extracting her blood and injecting it into the other soldiers. Allegiance... I'm watching gunshot wounds heal on some these guys from the injection."

"Message received, Ghosthawk, we've got to secure that target ASAP, otherwise the base is going to get hit with another wave of these self-healing bastards!"

Scratching the early morning crud from his face mask, the leader of the Ghosthawks knew that his time for a fully thought-out plan was limited. Sweating with anxious confidence, Allegiance grabbed four of his men and stepped back ten yards behind the base of a small tree to draw attack plans in the dirt.

Tapping the side of his helmet lightly and rapidly, Allegiance struggled to contact the main base to inform them of the inevitable attack to no avail. Radio chatter instantly squealed through his receiver as soon as he connected to the base camp's band, making it impossible to deliver his intelligence. Pressure for action increased as he used the palm of his hand to rub out his previous plan in the dirt, only to hastily draw up another; failure was not an option. Removing his right glove to draw in the dirt allowed the perspiration escaping from his pores to collect along his hand, stopping only at the dirty fingernail pointed at their goal. At this point, words were no longer used. Each of his fellow warriors nodded in agreement and moved into action as though any fear or doubt that they had no longer existed.

"We are death," he whispered to his men.

"We will kill them all," they responded.

Allegiance pointed at each of the three Ghosthawks accompanying him, directing them to their predetermined position to wait. Each moved as though they had been trained for actions such as this for a thousand years. To the right of Allegiance, the fireteam's M60 gunner, Steam, took his position. His weapon was much different than the normal machine gun used by standard soldiers in that his was shorter, compressed, and of lighter weight. The stock had been designed with dual-spring shock absorbers. The base of the barrel was weighted for increased stability. For Steam, his weapon was nothing more than an extension of his intent. On the other side of Allegiance, Quarterman was closest with his command radio and shotgun loaded with low-explosive anti-personnel rounds. The rounds were designed to not only extend the common effective range of the weapon, but to enhance damage to light armor worn by the enemy with its searing burst blasts. Goodman and Disciple positioned themselves to the right of Steam as they took aim with their scoped M16A1s. Goodman clicked to single-shot mode, acting as the fireteam's sniper, while Disciple brought up the corner assault by preparing for full-automatic bursts and the use of grenades. In less than a minute, their loose skirmish line was set along the front edge of the tree line. The team, anxious and devoid of fear, now waited for their signal to action as they watched their enemies eat their final meals before battle preparations.

On the east flanking tree-line, the Ghosthawk sniper, Solace, eased backwards at a half-crawl. Once returned to his center position, he pointed to Grey on his left side with two fingers and then balled his hand into a fist. Grey watched intently as Solace pointed downward with two fingers, then back to his eyes while splitting his two fingers to point at each one. His final hand command was a chopping motion towards the enemy with all of his fingers together and his thumb pulled in. These gestures commanded his teammate to hold his position while preparing to fire into the enemy group only after he saw Solace move into action. The sniper then turned to his right teammate, Etch, to deliver similar hand commands which differed by ordering him to hijack the truck once the action started.

The remaining two members from the team of ten Ghosthawks, River and TK, were ordered by Allegiance to return to the base. They traversed the thick brush and headed towards the main base as fast as they could to inform them of the attack. The two soldiers ran at top speed the entire way, knowing how critical the information was that they were carrying to the lives of their comrades as well as to the remaining fatigued and wounded soldiers in the base. Halfway through the return, River peeled away from the other Ghosthawk and headed in another direction, into the trees, leaving his teammate alone to complete the journey.

The remaining Ghosthawk stopped to catch his breath at the edge of the remaining forest, decimated by the napalm strike. The bright-white ash on the ground had collected around trees and charred corpses, creating an image strikingly similar to a snowy Christmas morning. The remaining heat and piercing odor from spent napalm singed TK's lungs, which caused him to gasp with each breath. It reminded him that his reality was here in Cambodia. Stepping over the burned and broken corpses of the Viet Cong, the Ghosthawk put his arm between the sling and the body of his M16A1 assault rifle and placed it over his right shoulder; he waved his hands above his head while approaching the main entrance to the base. Weary GIs rushed out to escort him in, guarding his rear as he moved expeditiously to the highest ranking person in charge, the Airborne staff sergeant from earlier. The wounded sergeant first class from the earlier attack had already been medically evacuated from the base, leaving a mere shell-shocked, chain-smoking staff sergeant in charge of the smoldering leftovers.

"Staff Sergeant, I need you with me!" TK ordered. The puzzled staff sergeant followed. "Where are your other boys? You the only one that made it?" Asked the anxious soldier.

TK stammered through the slosh in the trenches and leaned against a bullet-shredded sandbag while summoning the Radio Telephone Operator. "My men are good, Staff Sergeant, but we've got trouble!"

A patch-worked private, barely eighteen years of age, emerged from a corner sandbag nest carrying a radio. He was without pants and had blood-covered wraps on each of his thighs. The young soldier had a constant twitch accompanying each of his movements that made others who spoke to him repeat themselves to ensure that he understood. The radio transmitter was cracked in three locations, wet, and held together by duct tape. Handing it to the Ghosthawk, the private sat down in the mud, mumbling to himself while rocking slightly back and forth.

TK's information was spoken through a series of ash-infused coughs loud enough for the staff sergeant and his men to hear... as well as the colonel that was receiving the message on the other end. "Hawkbird-3 calling HQ, Hawkbird-3 calling HQ, over."

"HQ here...go ahead Hawkbird, you are loud and clear, over."

"A unit of fifty to a hundred 'enhanced' enemies preparing for counter attack of our base within fifteen minutes. I say again...A unit of fifty to a hundred 'enhanced' enemies preparing for counter attack in fifteen minutes, over!"

"Understood, Hawkbird-3...What is the SitRep on the missing 'toy'? Has it been found, over?"

"That's an affirmative, HQ, missing toy has been found and recovery in process. We are going to need heavenly tears on signal, over."

"Heavenly tears will be available on your signal, Hawkbird-3. Let us know when you need them, over."

"Thank you, Sir. Hawkbird-3 over and out."

Placing the radio transmitter in the private's lap, the Ghosthawk stood up to face the staff sergeant without speaking a word. With everyone in shock, the staff sergeant threw down the wet cigarette in his mouth and began to bellow attack preparation commands to his bedraggled men. Scavenged belts of ammunition were carefully stacked at each machine gun nest. Waiting near the center of the encampment were the remaining medical supplies and two tired medics. They were staged near the center to better respond in any needed direction. Knowledge of an impending attack drove many of the frontline soldiers into a state of paranoid hopelessness. Amidst the clacking of weapons, splashing of mud, and hustling of equipment...the prayers whispered by each soldier was the one sound that stood above the rest.

TK moved hastily to an ammo stack near the center of the base and grabbed an equipment pack from the clutches of a weighted ammo can resting on top of it. He loaded it with Claymore mines and fragmentation grenades before moving back towards the gate to speak a final time with the staff sergeant. "I'm going back out there, Staff Sergeant. My teammates will hold the enemy as long as possible, giving your men more time to prepare. Keep your eyes open for us when we pull back. Make sure that your men don't fire on us. Each one of us will break the battle line with one of our hands in the air as a signal. Hooyah?"

The staff sergeant stared into the deep crimson visor of the Ghosthawk, hoping for only a moment that he could see into the eyes of someone going to his death with fearlessness such as this. He made a promise at that time to himself to never forget what a Ghosthawk was if he made it out of this. He then responded in his native Airborne tongue, "Hooyah!"

Lifting the pack of explosives out of the mud, TK left the base at top speed. Standing on the edge of the smoldering forest, the Ghosthawk briefly dropped to one knee and clicked his shortwave radio transmitter button twice to send a breaking signal to Allegiance. After receiving the return clicks, he lifted himself to his feet and vanished into the thickness of the brush, bringing the eerie silence of anticipation for each waiting GI. Along the way to his comrades, he surveyed the terrain and hurriedly placed Claymore mines along his anticipated line of retreat. Some of the explosives were individually placed while others were clustered together in group formations.

Back at the Viet Cong camp, the men finished their meals and organized themselves for the assault. Allegiance received the signal from his teammate on his radio and instantly raised his left hand with two fingers up to make sure that his men saw him. He then grabbed a grenade from his side pouch, pulled the pin and released the safety-lever, counting to three before throwing it into the center of a gathered group of enemies. Startled for a moment, the enemy only had enough time to watch the grenade bounce then roll between them before it exploded, sending shrapnel in all directions. The other Ghosthawks instantly opened fire into the VC soldiers, causing many of them to drop in their tracks during the confusion. Quarterman and Disciple threw grenades toward the side positions of the enemy forces, forcing them to bunch in the center in a befuddled attempt to return fire. Steam rained hell into the enemy group as his M60 chopped into them and kicked back with an echo of anger from his trigger pull. The targets of highest value, those carrying RPGs and explosives, were systematically eliminated one at a time by the lethal touch of Goodman, acting as the calm sniper amidst the chaos.

"Let's move!" Chirped Allegiance in a sharp voice while slamming another magazine into his rifle. Quarterman and Disciple delivered two more grenades to the confused VC as Steam and Goodman fell back further into the brush while reloading their weapons.

The Viet Cong finally began to regain control in order to push forward as their commander screamed at the group from the back of the truck. AK47 gunfire preceded by RPGs rained hot lead and explosives on the Ghosthawks while the VC smashed into the tree line. Allegiance, Quarterman, and Disciple withdrew into the brush and reformed ten yards behind Steam and Goodman, who by then were fully reloaded. The first enemy breaking the tree-line carried an RPG, but never experienced the feeling of pulling a trigger before it owner's skull was blown apart by Goodman's sniper shot.

The brush caught fire, adding smoke and char to the humid air. This made perfect cover as the Ghosthawks continued their leap-frog tactics to fire, reload, and draw the enemy further away from their camp.

Once the larger portion of the enemy forces were committed to pursuit of the Ghosthawk squad, Allegiance and his men stopped firing and broke into a full sprint towards the base. The Viet Cong's confidence increased as their shouts became more of a cheer. That was until the first portion of the group crossed a low padded point between two trees and pulled the preset tripwire lain out by River, the Ghosthawk that was returning to the base with TK. The C-4 explosive in the Claymore rigged-traps detonated, causing the segmented steel in the front of the mine to fragment. Almost all of the VC within the fifty meter kill radius were struck by the jagged steel fragments. Dozens of the enemy fired in multiple directions, thinking they were being ambushed by a greater-sized force. Quarterman and Disciple threw grenades to the outer edges of the groups, creating explosions to force them back together. More concentrated gunfire from the enemy forced the Ghosthawks to leap-frog further back into the brush to reload for another attack.

Meanwhile, Ghosthawks Grey, Solace, and Etch, on the east side of the truck, waited until the main force was in the woods before they began to act. There remained a small residual force guarding the N-ionically enhanced human on the truck. Solace aimed his sniper rifle at the VC commander and squeezed off a single shot, causing his skull to snap hard against the muscles in his neck, ejecting blood and brain matter across a wide area. The commander's body shuddered as it hit the side of the truck before limply falling to the ground. Grey and Etch opened fire on the few combatants that were turning towards them, riveting them with bullets.

Solace then rose to his feet and pushed the attack forward with his teammates on his right side. Etch ran forward and stopped at half the distance between the truck and the tree-line. He dropped to one knee and delivered accurate gunfire at the enemy soldiers that attempted to move to cover. Solace ran straight to the back of the truck and jumped into the bed, speaking Vietnamese to the battered old man who was crouched against the truck bed dodging gunfire. "We are here to help! We are Americans! We are here to help, do you understand?"

The man nodded his head with a stiff jerk and muttered the word "wife" to the Ghosthawk while pointing toward the older woman. Grey moved forward and dropped to one knee beside Etch, who reloaded and raced to the front seat of the truck.

Entering the cab of the truck, Etch worked feverishly, fingers to wires, to hot-wire the truck. He worked as quickly as he could to avoid coming under fire during their escape. The Ghosthawks alternated returning fire on the enemy and reloading, ensuring a steady stream of lethal lead was poured on the remaining defensive force.

The roar of the truck engine signaled to Grey to move to the back of the truck. Etch slung his head to the side to look out of his window and saw the unliving fear that came across the radio the night before. The dead began to rise.

There was an unreal moment of silence between the Ghosthawks and the enemy as both groups watched shattered and misshapen corpses stand up, wobbly, and move with bemusement to complete the last command that their mind had sent to their bodies. When the commander stood with his open skull and grabbed on to the side of the truck, screams from some of the enemy combatants in the woods could be heard as they threw down their rifles and ran.

The undead commander grabbed repeatedly for the woman without understanding why, as Solace struggled to fight him off. The few enemy forces that didn't run began to fire into the back of the truck, hitting him in the top of his head, the back of his throat, and twice in the shoulder, causing him to fall forward onto the commander.

"Solace is down! We've gotta move, Etch! We've gotta move now!" Yelled Grey. Etch grabbed his rifle and started firing out of his window while pressing the gas. Grey threw grenades into the enemy forces and pulled his dead teammate onto the back of the truck. Breathing profusely with adrenaline pushing him, Grey struggled to get his footing against the blood collecting in the bottom of the truck that forced him to slide around. He scrambled to keep his balance as he instinctively checked Solace's pulse.

Etch slammed into two Viet Cong who were firing into the front windshield in a futile attempt to stop them. A shot to his cheek shattered the lower portion of his helmet mask while ripping through to the windows behind him as a second shot punched him in the right side of his chest. Breath was instantly lost as the vehicle wavered side-to-side while his mind battled with unconsciousness. Training prevailed as a mouthful of blood released through the teeth of a smiling Ghosthawk celebrated the cheating of instant death. The mission was everything. Barely breathing, he continued to drive.

Allegiance and his other three Ghosthawks were about a hundred yards from the location of the earlier napalm strike and low on ammunition. Disciple had been hit with a grazing shot to the calf and they were broken into two groups, with two men banded together in each. Allegiance, Quarterman, and Disciple attracted half of the enemy forces towards them while Steam and Goodman did the same with the other Viet Cong. This stretched the enemy group into a long skirmish line pushing forward towards the base.

Just as the enemy passed into the napalm strike zone, its members began to hit a second set of tripwires set up in all of the flanking directions, previously positioned by River and TK. Explosion after explosion rang out, causing the exhausted enemy to gather with their last efforts, creating a weary force that had no option but to go forward. Behind the enemies hidden in the woods, a new barrage of assault rifle fire rained down with grenades from the two well-rested Ghosthawks. River and TK poured all that they had into the weakened mass of Viet Cong in order to rob them of any semblance of organization.

"They're broken!" Cried out Allegiance. "Return to base!"

The Ghosthawks retreated to the base as planned, using the outer flanks as Allegiance called in to HQ for "heavenly tears" to fall. As gruesome as it may have been, each soul watching from the American base on the small dust covered hill cheered as a copious amount of death was delivered to their enemies on that day. Artillery rained on the enemy position as a curse beyond the descriptions of the sane.

The Ghosthawks rushed towards the base camp, each with one arm in the air and less than half a magazine of ammunition remaining in his rifle. Aerial bombardments continued for hours after their return and deep into the afternoon. When the air strikes and artillery ceased, there was a welcomed uneasiness amongst the men that let them know that death was done with the day.

In the distance, a pickup truck drove haphazardly towards the south entrance of the compound and stopped at its base with smoke rising from the engine. Allegiance and his men ran down to the vehicle to help those within it. Medics rushed down to help as Allegiance pulled the driver, Etch, onto the ground to administer first aid. Grey stood between his dead teammate, Solace, and the bullet riddled body of the older Vietnamese man who was also killed in their escape. He dropped his rifle, removed his helmet, and held his hand to his face while agonizing quietly with anger and gritted teeth. An instinctive glance to his commander, Allegiance, was enough for the grim leader to respond by ordering the radio man to call in a final bombing run.

No enemies will be left behind, he reaffirms in his thoughts as the deep forest ignites from the viciousness of hell delivered from the heavens. Allegiance stands before his fellow Ghosthawk. "We are death," he said.

"We've killed them all," responded Grey.

A small personnel helicopter landed approximately four and a half minutes after the truck engine had stopped and a small group of black clad people rushed out to collect the Vietnamese woman, the body of her husband and the dead Ghosthawks. Another helicopter landed beside it as the first one began to leave. The Ghosthawks then boarded the helicopter, with Allegiance being the last one to enter it.

"We have another mission, Ghosthawks! Clean up and resupply!" He commands as the helicopter pulls into the tainted sky. The team extracted from the location, leaving behind the soldiers that would never forget that they were there; for they were death.

"HEROES AREN'T MADE DURING GOOD TIMES!"